Silent Dreams

Devora Weiner

TARGUM/FELDHEIM

First published 2002

ISBN 1-56871-267-7

Published by:
Targum Press, Inc.
22700 W. Eleven Mile Rd.
Southfield, MI 48034
E-mail: targum@netvision.net.il
Fax: 888-298-9992
www.targum.com

Distributed by:
Feldheim Publishers
202 Airport Executive Park
Nanuet, NY 10954

Printed in Israel

Dedication

To my parents,
Rabbi and Mrs. Baruch Zimmerman,
who have given me all.

And to my parents-in-law,
Rabbi and Mrs. Aharon Weiner,
who have always treated me like a daughter.

1

Chavi checked herself in the mirror one last time. She was satisfied with what she saw. Not thrilled, but satisfied. She wore a stylish, yet comfortable, outfit which gave a dressy-casual impression, and her makeup was meticulously applied yet understated. As for her hair, well, there was nothing more she could do with it. The One Above had decided that it was right for her, so who was she to argue?

The doorbell rang and she sighed, trying to ignore the butterflies in her stomach. Once again, another first date. It was so hard to let her excitement and nervousness take over as she braced herself, once again, for disappointment. She had gone through this routine so many times before, but here she was, twenty-five and still single. Most of her experiences were rather short lived. Either she knew right away that the boy wasn't for her, he knew she wasn't for him, or the feeling was mutual.

Chavi did her best to give every young man who crossed the portals of her home a fair chance, but something inside her wouldn't let her compromise. As each budding relationship developed, she would notice the boy's posture, his style of dressing, or some other small thing that annoyed her, to the point where she couldn't continue seeing him. Occasionally she hated herself for her pettiness, but she didn't have the time or the strength to spare for a personality overhaul.

She envied her happily married friends watching over their growing broods with their unsophisticated husbands at their sides. She was jealous of her engaged friends who were so proud of their plain-looking fiancés, whispering to her, "Isn't he good looking?" Chavi knew herself to be a woman of conviction who would pursue with unending passion her main goals of building a Torah home and having a husband who would be a *talmid chacham*. The problem, she had to admit, was that there were so many side issues that were ultimately unimportant but had a place in her heart nonetheless.

She would hear so many wonderful things about a young man — about his learning, his *middos*, his potential. But then she would meet him and be turned off by his immature laugh, or his worn raincoat, or his stubbly beard. Most often it was his family background that made her so unenthusiastic at the prospect of the relationship developing. She longed to marry into a respectable, normal family, so she could feel respectable and normal and accepted. It was a tall order, though, with the family she came from.

She would be angry at herself, knowing that it didn't matter and she was being given a chance to begin a life with a man who would seriously contribute to the world of Torah. Yet, invariably, she would call the *shadchan* back and explain that he was a wonderful boy, but not for her. As invariably, she would hear the *shadchan* sigh on the other end of the line. Sometimes the covert rebuke would end there and sometimes a few more direct and probably deserved words of *mussar* would be sent to pierce her heart.

Chavi reminded herself that this was no time for self-analysis or self-pity — there was a young suitor at the door and it was time to try once again. She had to hurry to the door to make sure that she was there when her mother answered. Of course, her mother would answer the door. That was the way it was done, and Chavi was desperate to do things the way they were done. But she had to be there, too, to make sure that no uncomfortable situations arose.

She heard her mother's greeting as she rushed down the hall, her heels clicking on the hard floor. "Hello. Come right in. You must be Shmuel Rosenberg. Chavi will be here in a moment. Come in. Take off your coat and have something to eat while you're waiting."

Mrs. Baumel's voice was just a bit louder than normal. Chavi could picture her mother, working hard to be a gracious hostess, with an exaggerated smile on her overly painted lips.

By the time she reached the living room, Shmuel was already inside, standing nervously near a table laid with a silver tea set, china, and two elaborate, freshly baked cakes. Chavi immediately recognized his hesitation: she'd seen it so many times before. He was unsure of what was expected of him. He knew he should probably sit down and eat, but what he most wanted was to be on his way. He heard his mother's voice in his mind chastising him to be mannerly and taste something of the repast that had obviously been painstakingly prepared in his honor.

"Please have something," Mrs. Baumel cajoled. "I always say a *yeshivah bachur* never has enough to eat."

"It looks delicious," answered Shmuel, just as Chavi entered the room.

"Hello, I'm Chavi. I see you've met my mother already." As soon as he replied, "Hello," she announced to her mother, "Ima, we're going to be on our way. We'll see you later."

Saved, thought Shmuel, breathing a sigh of relief. *I like her already.* He was honestly still a bit uncomfortable around adults, even though at twenty-five, one could argue that he was an adult himself. "It was nice to meet you," he said to Mrs. Baumel as he moved toward the open door Chavi was holding.

"Have a nice time and don't keep her out too late!" Mrs. Baumel called with a smile.

Chavi cringed inside. *Don't keep her out too late.* It sounded so babyish and overbearing. Why couldn't she have just said good-bye like any normal person would have? At least now they were off.

She had a chance to look Shmuel over as she walked, a couple of steps behind him, to the waiting taxi. He was nice looking enough, resembling the stereotypical clean-shaven *yeshivah bachur.* His suit was neat and clean, not the latest in style, but not outdated either. She liked the gentlemanly way he opened the door for her and his consideration in going around to the other side to get in and not watching her trying to scoot over the leather seat of the cab elegantly.

We'll see what the next couple of hours bring, she thought, and then cleared her mind to focus on being good company

ꟹ ꟹ

I had a nice time, Chavi thought as they rode back home through the crowded streets of Jerusalem. *It was different than usual. But I'm not sure why.* Pushing her thoughts away to be considered later, she focused on the scenery and enjoyed the breeze lightly blowing her hair. They chatted about her adjustment to her new home and his impressions of life in Israel, as each family had moved there only recently.

Eight months before, Mrs. Baumel had suddenly decided to leave her friends, family, and familiar life behind and move to the Holy Land. She claimed she was making aliyah because she wanted to spend her life in Yerushalayim, in God's holy country and the Jews' homeland. Chavi knew better. She had grown up with years of disagreements between her parents about going to Israel.

Mrs. Baumel was very comfortable in her native Cleveland, where she had been born and raised. Both of her siblings had settled there. All three of her closest childhood friends still lived in the same neighborhood. She knew the shops, had her set place in shul, and knew almost everyone in the community.

Mr. Baumel, though, had been an ardent Zionist who felt that it was wrong to stay in America when the Jews had their own state. There wasn't much to keep him in Cleveland anyway. He made ends meet, but that was all he could manage. Although he had been a hard-working and honest man, his small grocery couldn't compete with the large kosher supermarket that had opened only a few blocks away.

He had his regulars — once you shopped at Baumel's Grocery, you always came back, because it was a place where each customer was greeted with a friendly smile and a kind word. But the younger crowd preferred to go to the modern-looking, fully stocked supermarket. Even the old-timers would buy the basics at Baumel's and go to the supermarket for their larger selection and specialty items afterwards. So *parnassah* wasn't what it had once been. His older son and daughter had married and moved to Lakewood and he only saw them once or twice a year anyhow. He found Cleveland to be comfortable, but longed for the opportunity to settle in Israel.

Mrs. Baumel did not. And so the arguments continued. Every so often soft-spoken but persistent Mr. Baumel would bring up the topic again and Mrs. Baumel would adamantly and vociferously refuse. Sobbing, she would call her friends to share her woes and then mope and mutter around the house for the rest of the afternoon.

There hadn't been any other areas of disagreement between her parents that Chavi could remember. As a rule, Mrs. Baumel listened to whatever Mr. Baumel suggested and they lived in harmony.

When Mrs. Baumel suddenly announced that she and Chavi were moving to the Land of Israel where her heart was, Chavi wondered what her real motivation was. Perhaps it was an attempt to escape from the loneliness and the memories that haunted her after Mr. Baumel's unexpected heart attack and death. Maybe it was the feeling of guilt that she had robbed her husband of his dream. Mrs. Baumel had always worked so hard to please, to avoid friction, in her relationships and in her marriage in particular. Maybe it was an attempt to please him even though it was too late. An apology of sorts. Chavi didn't know. The news of her mother's aliyah shocked her only a little less than the announcement that she expected Chavi to make the move with her.

The plan elicited many emotions. On the one hand, the fact that her mother hadn't consulted her at all made her very resentful. The Baumels' Cleveland home, now up for sale, was also Chavi's home. If she refused to go, where would she live? Maybe she could move in with friends, but there was almost no one her age left in Cleveland. That would leave big old New York, her nightmare. It was so enormous and she knew so few people there, she was sure she'd feel lost. It seemed to her that everyone was lost in New York. How did anyone live in a city where he didn't know his neighbors and where he couldn't make eye contact with a stranger on the street for fear of his life?

And what about finding a job? She loved her teaching job and she knew those were hard to come by in New York. She also needed her afternoon computer programming job to save up money for her wedding and all the expenses involved in getting married and keeping her future husband in *kollel.* She could probably find that sort of job in New York, but in Cleveland she worked with *frum* people, the hours were good, and, most importantly, she already knew the ropes and felt comfortable.

Her other option was to move with her mother. She had loved Eretz Yisrael when she was there in seminary, but that had been a very long time before, and there was a difference between being a seminary student and actually becoming Israeli. Another consideration was the fact that *shidduchim* were all but at a standstill in Cleveland. Although she dated more than many of her friends, the dates were few and far between and her prospects became fewer with each passing month. Maybe the move would bring a change of *mazal,* she thought. Maybe there would be a different crop of boys across the ocean.

But the real deciding factor was the fact that she couldn't dream of letting her bereaved mother move alone. Although her mother was to blame for the move, Chavi was still her daughter, the only one left at home. The move would involve many changes and her mother would need support and someone to share the experience with. There was no way she could do it alone. As much as Chavi had mixed emotions, when she realized that her mother was serious about making the move she knew there was no choice.

The Rosenbergs, for their part, had lived in Israel for three years. They had come with their three younger children, leaving behind Shmuel in a yeshivah in New York and two married daughters in Boro Park. The father's orthodontic practice transferred well, and the family's villa in Shaarei Chesed was actually bigger than their home in Boro Park had been. Both of the senior Rosenbergs were happy in Israel. They were familiar with life in Yerushalayim, as they had frequently gone back and forth over the years while their children were in yeshivah and seminary. Now, they still flew often, but in the other direction, for the birth of grandchildren and other family *simchahs*. Yerushalayim was their home.

Shmuel was visiting his parents for the summer *bein hazemanim*. The conversation between him and Chavi flowed freely and pleasantly all the way back to her apartment.

When they reached Chavi's home and she said good-bye, she hoped she would see him again. She wasn't sure what made the date so different from other dates, but she'd hash it out with her mother. She knew her mother would press her for every detail anyway, and it would give her a good opportunity to talk things out.

ꟿ ꟿ

Chavi's mother was, of course, waiting up for her. At her age, she preferred to be in bed by ten, but there was no way she could fall asleep until Chavi was home. Chavi was the focus of her life, and her dream now was to see her settled with a nice young man.

Chavi looked happy when she walked in. "Come sit down and take a drink," her mother urged. Waiting for Chavi to start a synopsis of the date, she commented, "It sure didn't cool off today."

Chavi kicked off her shoes and sprawled on the couch. She took a few sips of lemonade and began, "I had a nice time, Ima. He was very easy to talk to and had a good sense of humor. We went to the Ramada Renaissance Hotel for half an hour and then decided to go for a walk, which lasted for about two hours."

"Did he offer you a drink along the way?" interjected Mrs. Baumel. "Two hours is a long time to keep someone walking. I hope he let you sit down...."

"Oh, Ima, he kept asking if I wanted to rest, but we were both enjoying the walk, so we continued. On the way, he bought me a bottle of mineral water from a street vendor, even though I refused it when he offered. I thought that was so considerate." Mrs. Baumel nodded in agreement.

"Anyway, we talked for two and a half hours. The conversation was sort of serious for the first date. Usually you just chat, but we discussed more *hashkafah* types of things. I got on my soapbox as usual, and I'm afraid that I was annoying, but he really seemed to be listening to what I was saying. The odd thing was that he didn't have an opinion on many of the topics. Even when I'd ask him what he thought about what I just said, he'd say, 'I don't know. I never thought about it.' "

"You told me that you heard he was quite intelligent. That wasn't your impression when you met him?" Mrs. Baumel asked.

"It's not a question of intelligence. He had plenty to say sometimes, but he also seemed — I don't know how to put it — just not interested in certain things that were burning issues for me. He seemed attentive to what I was saying, but it's hard for me to fathom that he never thought about certain things. For example, the hotel was selling replicas of archeological artifacts as souvenirs for tourists. Next to each piece, there was a card explaining its origins and supposed age, some up to ten thousand years old. I told him that one of my students last year was having a hard time with the fact that scientists feel that the world is so old while the Torah dates the world as less than six thousand years old. I asked him what he thought I should have said. All he said was, 'What did you say?'

"He impressed me as bright, but maybe not so thought out. It was strange because I've only really met two kinds of boys — those who are more superficial or at least more comfortable with superficial conversation and those who like to analyze every situation and share their impressions. I usually follow whatever the boy initiates. Here, though, he was listening and asking what I thought...and not adding that much."

A worried crease appeared on Mrs. Baumel's forehead. Chavi warded her off. "I didn't feel it was a one-way conversation. I can't pinpoint why.... Maybe he said more than I think. I have to go through the conversation again. I'm sure he's not going to be interested in meeting me again. He was probably just being polite by hearing me out, because it was pretty clear that that type of discussion wasn't that interesting to him."

Mrs. Baumel put her hand on her daughter's arm. "There's no doubt in my mind that he'll want to go out again. It sounds like you made a very nice impression. I'm sure he's interested or he wouldn't have kept you out that long."

"I'm not sure," Chavi answered, in the slightly irritated voice she used only with her mother. "You don't have to always try to make me feel better. If he says no, he says no." Yet Chavi knew that this time she would be very sorry if he rejected her. She just wasn't sure why.

ഒ ഒ

At the Rosenbergs', a similar scene was taking place. Dr. and Mrs. Rosenberg were in the kitchen having a cup of coffee when they heard the front door open. "Shmuli, is that you?" called Mrs. Rosenberg.

"Yeah, Ma. I'm home," he answered from the hall and headed toward his room.

"*Nu*, we were waiting for you. Can't you at least tell us how it went?" pressed his father.

Shmuel headed back toward the kitchen. "Fine," he said.

"Do you want to see her again?" asked Dr. Rosenberg.

"I don't know," his son answered. "I want to think about it until the morning." He reached for a glass and turned to the refrigerator to take out some soda.

As usual, his answer upset his mother, but she said nothing. Was Shmuel ever going to be excited after a date? Was he ever going to get married? The other children went so fast, while he barely ever agreed to a second date. He'd met the best girls, pretty girls, girls from the nicest families, girls whose fathers would take care of him well during his beginning *kollel* years and when he needed a business to enter.

At first, Mrs. Rosenberg had excused him as just being immature, not ready to get married. But now, at twenty-five, that excuse no longer worked. He had been dating for four years already. What number was this girl? Eight-five? He was always willing to try whatever she set up for him, sometimes reluctantly, but never giving her any trouble. Yet the dates went nowhere.

She was sure he was starting to get depressed. All of her friends' sons who were his age were married with children already. And if he wasn't getting depressed, she was. It was embarrassing that her favorite was still single. There was nothing wrong with the boy. He was so caring and easy to talk to. But people talked. And at twenty-five everyone wanted to know what his problem was.

She and her husband had let him meet this Chavi in the hopes that maybe some new kind of girl would work. Mrs. Rosenberg squirmed a bit in her chair as she wondered if she really wanted this particular one to work out. At least she lived in Yerushalayim and they would be able to have Shmuli close by again. They had heard lovely things about her...but would the different cultures be a problem? Would she fit into their family? Even her grandparents were American; it was a different mentality. And they were from Cincinnati (or was it Cleveland?). Would she follow their chassidish *minhagim*? Worst of all, she had no father.

I guess she can learn, Mrs. Rosenberg concluded with a mental sigh. *As long as we get Shmuli settled down.*

"Uh, Shmuli," Dr. Rosenberg said hesitantly, "what are you thinking about? Did something bother you? Was there something you liked?"

Shmuel sat down at the table and paused for a moment to pour his drink. He was pouring painfully slowly, thought his mother. He seemed pensive, not his usual easygoing self.

"I don't know. She was very nice and funny and easy to be with, but she is awfully, um, intellectual. I never met anyone like her, except maybe some bookworms in yeshivah. I never pictured myself with someone like that. But, on the other hand, she was so alive. Excited. I don't know how to describe it exactly, but she was excited about things that never even crossed my mind."

Shmuel was almost thinking aloud. That vivaciousness made him want to see her again. She was so animated when she spoke. She had a fiery passion to understand the world, to express herself. It was a new experience. She barely asked him about his family, didn't bring up yeshivish politics, didn't even ask him who his friends were. But she did ask his opinion about *hashkafah*. It seemed almost as if she was thirsting to hear what he had to say, that she respected his opinion.

Truthfully, he was flattered. No one really cared much about what he had to say. Not that he had much to say about anything anyway. The conversation made him feel uncomfortable, almost disappointed in himself. Why hadn't he ever thought about the problems she brought up? She seemed surprised, too. But he wasn't uncomfortable admitting his ignorance to her.

How did all this fit together? Did he want to subject himself to coping with this new territory? That was the question. On the other hand, this was a much more enjoyable date than any he could remember. Certainly more than any first date.

2

Chavi hung up the phone, and then immediately picked it up again to call Gitty. Mrs. Gafni, the *shadchan,* had just called. Chavi was so relieved to hear that there would be a second date that she had to share the news with someone. Her two closest friends were in America, so she turned to Gitty, who had been a friend in seminary. Gitty had gotten married two years earlier and moved to Yerushalayim. Chavi had rekindled their relationship when she moved to Israel.

As Chavi told her friend about Shmuel, Gitty listened and said all the right things, but she seemed distant, removed from the conversation. "Should I call you back later?" Chavi finally asked her. "It seems like I got you at a bad time."

"Why would you say that? No, now is fine. It's quiet here. Shaya left to yeshivah early so he could do some shopping before *seder.*"

Despite Gitty's attempts to reassure her, Chavi sensed something was wrong. They weren't close enough for her to press the issue, so she let it drop, but when she got off the phone, she couldn't take her mind off her friend.

Although they had become friends right away, there had always been a distance between Chavi and Gitty. As hard as Chavi tried, she never felt she measured up to sophisticated, attractive Gitty. Gitty always dressed perfectly, had perfect skin and perfect hair, and came from a perfect family. In seminary, she had been the head of choir. Always calm and cool, she knew everyone that it was "right" to know. She had married the perfect man from the perfect family who had learned in the best yeshivos. When they got engaged, Chavi had been very happy, but, buried deep where no one would suspect, there was also a bit of jealousy. Her perfect friend was engaged to the type of person who would never have even agreed to meet her.

What could be bothering Gitty? Maybe it was the fact that she didn't have children yet. That was probably hard for her. Whatever it was, Chavi had noticed that Gitty wasn't herself for a couple of months already. She seemed less patient, more aloof. As insecure as always, it crossed Chavi's mind that perhaps Gitty just wasn't interested in a relationship with her. Perhaps it was best to give Gitty her space now. With her forthright personality, Chavi wanted to come right out and ask Gitty what was wrong, but she knew that it wasn't appropriate. And with Gitty, you had to be appropriate.

She felt that familiar pit in her stomach that often materialized after she spoke to Gitty, ever since they had met: a physical reminder of her certainty that she didn't meet Gitty's standards. Although she felt like running away from the relationship sometimes, she really did like Gitty. And anyway, she was the type of person that was good to count among your friends.

Chavi finally let the subject drift away so that she could focus on more pleasant things. She anxiously awaited the following night and seeing Shmuel again.

ഇ ഇ

As far as both parties were concerned, things were progressing nicely. After the second date, both Shmuel and Chavi realized that their marriage was intended to be. It was a feeling more than a thought. They were very different, yet their differences complemented each other. Chavi's animated spirit kindled a new life in Shmuel, while Shmuel's unruffled calmness tempered Chavi's brashness. They both enjoyed the same activities. Conversation came easily.

Although Chavi knew in a general sense that they shared the same goals, she wanted to make sure that Shmuel was committed to the same ideals as she was. In the back of her mind lay the understanding that no matter what Shmuel's answers would be, she was going to marry him. But if his responses satisfied her, she would enter the relationship with a full heart, knowing that she was not compromising in any way.

It was late afternoon when they arrived at the zoo, one of Chavi's favorite places. The Biblical Zoo's pastoral grounds always had a calming effect on her, and the beauty and exquisite detail with which God had designed each animal filled her with awe. The ugly animals were so ugly, the elegant animals so elegant. The zoo was walking distance from her Bayit Vegan apartment, and it was her spot of choice whenever she wanted time to just be.

Her favorite spot was the children's zoo, where she could pet and feed the animals. It gave her a certain satisfaction to watch the zoo animals eat and see their thankful eyes beseeching her for more. She was always tempted to bring food to the other animals, too, but it was against the zoo regulations, and so she had to overcome her selfish desire to give. In the children's zoo, though, they sold a handful of seeds for a shekel. She always came with a pocketful of coins to put in the dispenser, so she would have something to share with her animal acquaintances.

She'd had mixed emotions when she heard Shmuel wanted to meet at the zoo. Silly as it sounded, she felt that it was her private domain and going there with anyone she knew was giving up a special, private experience. It was an invasion of turf of sorts. On the other hand, it made her feel closer to Shmuel. It was as if he was asking to share her privacy with him and that their bond was strengthening.

Shmuel, of course, was oblivious to Chavi's emotions. He had picked the zoo as a pleasant alternative to another evening in a lounge. Mrs. Gafni had insisted that a more recreational setting was in order to foster the continued growth of their relationship. It was the zoo, a museum, or a longer trip out of Yerushalayim. The choices were about equal to him, and he had picked the zoo at random.

The weather was still stifling, but a breeze was beginning to blow. Chavi was wearing a ponytail which made her look cute and sporty. Shmuel laughed inside when he thought of what his mother would say. "She wore *what* on a date? What did she think, she was going to camp?"

How many hundreds of times had he heard his mother sending his sisters to change before they went anywhere? "I don't care if you're only going to the supermarket. You never know who will see you. Go put on a little makeup." "Take that outfit off now and put it in the bag in the front closet for the *gemach*. You are too old to be dressing in those *shmattes*."

It took a few postseminary months for their mother's lessons to penetrate, but since then the Rosenberg girls had internalized their mother's philosophies, and there was no doubt in Shmuel's mind that the lessons would be carefully passed down to the next generation when the time came. His mother tried pressing him, too, but to little avail. He dressed all right, but he didn't have the energy for constantly checking himself over and shopping and shining and pressing.

Both his parents tried nagging a bit, as Shmuel viewed it, and encouraging positive behavior. "You look sharp. Like a million bucks," his father remarked every time he wore something new. His mother would get a proud look in her eyes and kiss his cheek. He did feel good when he looked nice, but every human being was born with a limited supply of energy, which he did his best to conserve.

A small smile sprang to Chavi's lips when she saw him approaching the zoo entrance. She was proud to be seen as his date for the day. He always looked so put together, in contrast to her brother and brother-in-law. They dressed respectably, but their polyester blend suits and faded hats couldn't match the elegance that Shmuel seemed to give off naturally. She moved off the ledge she was resting on and went to meet him.

Shmuel told her to wait in the shade while he went to pay. Something about financial transactions broke the quixotic atmosphere that a date was supposed to take place in. But Chavi followed him and called over his shoulder to the cashier that she had a membership, so her date should only be charged for one entrance ticket.

Shmuel felt uncomfortable, though he knew it was illogical. True, there was no need to spend ten dollars on an entrance ticket when she was allowed to go in for free, but the chivalrous impression he wanted to present had been blemished. He was annoyed by her independence and her involvement in money matters, even though she couldn't know about the fantasy courtship taking place in his mind.

They entered the zoo and walked a few yards to the grassy area in front of the monkey island, where monkeys frolicked in their shady playing area.

"Is there anything you want to see?" Shmuel asked.

"Nothing in particular," she replied. "All the exhibits interest me. I would enjoy anything in your company anyway."

Shmuel blushed at her open display of emotion. He got a kick out of her being comfortable enough to say what she was really thinking — it was something he wasn't accustomed to. Hoping to mask his reddened cheeks, he diligently began to read the map that the cashier had handed to him after he paid. "Let's go to the small reptile house. It's right nearby, and it should be shady there."

The reptile house was cool and dark and offered a pleasant respite from the beating sun. Chavi went right up to the glass windows and peered intently inside. When she noticed Shmuel looking on from a few steps away, she called him closer so they could share the excitement of viewing the odd and scary creatures together.

"Look at this lizard! What does the sign say he's called? He's so ugly he looks fake, like a monster from a cheap movie that tramples the whole city and causes mayhem and destruction! Look at his skin. It looks so hard. Like plastic...."

She was aflame again. Over some lizard. But, as Shmuel

looked closer to please her, he did notice the reptile's skin. It sure did look hard. Almost impenetrable. "Look how sharp his teeth are," he said. "Tiny, but they look like they could slice through anything."

"You're right. He's a nasty creature, isn't he?"

"Is this your first time at the zoo?" he asked curiously.

"No," she answered, realizing that maybe she was being too enthusiastic. What if he thought she was immature? She cooled off a bit and waited for Shmuel to progress to the next animal. But Shmuel paused to look at the lizard for another moment. It was kind of fascinating, you had to admit.

They spent the next hour walking from one exhibit to the next and chatting comfortably and contentedly. When they passed by a stand selling drinks and Popsicles, Shmuel offered Chavi her choice. She was quite warm and parched and would have gladly taken a Popsicle, but, not wanting to reinforce her immature impression, she opted for a Coke. Shmuel chose the same.

They sat down to drink on a shaded bench in front of the flamingoes, whose bright coral color contrasted with and complemented the deep green grass and the sunshine reflecting off their pond. The atmosphere was calm and serene.

They were silent for a moment. Then Chavi cleared her throat. Shmuel turned to her, and she hoped he would ask her what she was thinking about, but he just waited patiently for her to begin.

"Ummm.... There was something I wanted to ask you about. Something very important to me, part of my deepest convictions. I want to know how you feel about it."

Shmuel wondered where this was leading, but he didn't say anything; his intuition told him this was going to be one of those conversations he abhorred. When the silence wore on just a bit too much and he realized that she was waiting for him to speak, he asked, "What are you referring to?"

"I know when we asked about you, we heard that you wanted to learn for as long as you could after you were married. I just want to hear if that's really your plan." Chavi paused, then continued in a rush, her words tumbling out one after another. "More than anything, I want a husband who's going to be a real *talmid chacham*. I feel kind of funny saying it like that — maybe it sounds a little corny. But I want to share my feelings with you, so I'm going to say it anyway. My yearning for a Torah home will give me the strength, God willing, to do whatever I need to to keep my husband in *kollel* and learning. I know it will be hard at times, but the hard work entailed would be a labor of love for me. I can't imagine any greater satisfaction than working or taking care of our children, I mean my children, so you, um, my husband could learn. It would make me so proud. So happy.

"I've saved up some money and wouldn't need much to live on if I knew my husband was growing in Torah. I can't even imagine having a husband who works. I think it would kill me.... I would wither from the pain of a broken dream."

She stopped as abruptly as she had begun and she seemed to Shmuel a bit embarrassed by her revelation. He knew he had to respond, but what should he say? Of course he was going to learn after he was married. You went to high school, you went to yeshivah for a couple of years in Israel or America, you got married, and then you learned for a couple of years. Then you went to work and life went on. He did say he wanted to learn for as long as possible, but he never really pictured that as practically ending up for more than three years. How many of his long-term learning friends had made it past five years?

But buried deep where no one could see and ridicule him for it lay a dormant dream of actually learning, well, forever. To be a *talmid chacham.* Maybe even to be a *maggid shiur.* He knew how to learn well, of that he was confident. But he never viewed himself as one to go against the tide. His parents would tell him to abandon his foolish dreams if he shared these thoughts with them. His married friends would tell him that he just didn't know what real life was like. He knew that people would blame Chavi's idealism on seminary indoctrination whose effects would fade with time. He had pushed his own dreams away, squashing them before he allowed anyone else to.

Yet here was Chavi, twenty-five and not a wet-behind-the-ears seminary graduate. She believed in the dream that he had almost forgotten he had. It felt empowering to see her trust in his abilities and to feel her confidence that she could depend on his promises. But he was scared, too. Maybe he couldn't do it. What if he promised and then the world was right that it wasn't possible to stay in yeshivah past three or four years? He learned well, but it was hard for him. He wasted more time than he even dared to admit to himself, lest he give up in hopelessness. But he tried. And he wanted to try. And he would continue to try. He didn't want to lose her by sharing his weakness. And he didn't want to lose himself by giving up before he even tried.

"Don't you have anything to say?" she said, a little impatiently.

He hated having to be so open about his feelings. He hated talking about himself. It seemed so boastful. Who was he to say he wanted to be one of those few who merit to spend their years in the comforting protection of the yeshivah? But he had to say something.

He turned away a bit and softly spoke of his secret dream. He told her it would be hard for him to direct his energy, it would be hard to stick to his plan when society would tell him that he was being the fool for ignoring the "real" world. But more than anything he wanted to try, and he would try his best.

When he finished, he looked up to see her staring at him with a look of respect and admiration that he had not seen on her before. Shmuel, the nice guy with the brilliant mind that was supposed to make him rich one day, was not used to respect and admiration. It felt very nice.

3

Chavi was thrilled when, a few weeks later, Shmuel invited her to meet his parents. She knew this meant that their courtship was nearing a happy ending. She also looked forward to seeing Shmuel in his native environment. You could understand people so much better when you knew their parents. *You get a feel for people's standards from seeing their home*, she thought. A *kallah* would know more of what was expected from her knowing what her *chassan*'s standards were.

Kallah. That word had a lovely ring to it. She had begun to doubt whether it would ever be connected to her name, but, *baruch Hashem*, it looked like it soon would be. She remembered her father constantly reminding her to temper her optimistic tendencies with the old adage, "Don't count your chickens before they hatch." She would have to be on her best behavior at this meeting.

She spent nearly an hour and a half getting dressed. Each of her outfits was scrutinized and discarded as inappropriate one by one. One made her look too modern, another didn't flatter her, a third had seen better days, and the fourth made her look too sophisticated, older than she was, and she certainly didn't want anyone focusing on her age that night. She decided on a light pink suit with pearl buttons which was the closest thing she owned to an outfit from Boro Park. She had picked up hints from Shmuel that that sort of outfit would be a good choice.

She found her hands shaking as she tried to fasten the clasp of her necklace. Was it anticipation or nerves?

Shmuel came to pick her up right on time. He took one look at her and said, "Don't worry. Just be yourself, and everything will work out okay."

Chavi felt her emotions were too transparent for comfort, especially now when she wanted to look cool and in control, but she enjoyed being understood without words and appreciated his sensitivity. She was quiet during most of the ride to the Rosenbergs' home, spending the time alternating between trying to make her skirt remain wrinkle-free and praying silently that all would go well. She hated how every new situation made her so nervous and worked hard to keep that facet of her personality concealed from the world.

The taxi entered Shaarei Chesed, by far her favorite neighborhood. She loved the mix of decrepit hovels that housed Yerushalmi families who had been there for generations and spectacular modern villas that had been redone by American businessmen. The neighborhood reminded her a bit of herself. Her heart related to the simple dwellings whose walls had absorbed so many thousands of hours of Gemara study, whose very simplicity gave testimony to ideals of a pious and enchanting world. At the same time, she enjoyed the luxuries of life which gave a certain expansiveness of spirit, a lifting of the troubles and limitations brought about by mundane struggles.

The taxi stopped and Shmuel paid the driver while Chavi looked at the villa they were going to. Bespeaking grandeur, it was modern and large, yet tastefully simple. The gold and buffed wood of the door and mailbox accented the white Jerusalem stone, and the bay window was lit up with spotlights that reflected off rich, thick drapes. She felt lucky that it was her destination.

"Ready?" Shmuel interrupted her thoughts.

"Ready as I'll ever be," she answered with a brave smile. And in they went.

Dr. and Mrs. Rosenberg were sitting on two armchairs in the living room that was to the left of the entrance hall. Chavi smiled as she and Shmuel entered the room, very conscious of the noise her steps were making on the marble floor. She was relieved to find the living room carpeted.

Mrs. Rosenberg smiled and introduced herself as she motioned for the couple to have a seat on the couch across from herself and her husband. Between them was a coffee table that held an ice bucket and tumblers, individual-sized bottles of soda, and a silver tray bearing a store-bought cherry pie.

Chavi and Shmuel sat down, and an awkward silence ensued. Dr. Rosenberg, leaning back in his chair with his legs comfortably crossed and his hands resting together at the fingers, didn't say anything. Mrs. Rosenberg mentioned how nice it was to meet Chavi and seemed to Chavi to be trying to snatch as many glimpses of her as possible without staring. Shmuel cleared his throat.

Mrs. Rosenberg offered everyone some pie. Both Dr. Rosenberg and his son declined, but Chavi took up the offer and was given a small slice. Shmuel poured himself and Chavi some Coke. There was some more silence. Shmuel cleared his throat again.

Chavi wasn't sure if they wanted the silence or if they felt as uncomfortable as she did. She decided to risk their disapproval and alleviate her discomfort. "I really love this neighborhood. It's so charming, such a mix of old and new. Dr. Rosenberg, what made you choose to live in Shaarei Chesed?"

Dr. Rosenberg seemed startled by the direct inquiry and needed a split second to recover. "Uh, well, a number of our friends had purchased here. The real estate value was good and the lots of land are big enough to allow for a nice-sized cottage."

Chavi commented, "When I was in seminary, I dreamed of living here. It is so...surreal."

Shmuel looked down, a bit embarrassed. What was his mother thinking? They would never understand her. He hoped they didn't consider her direct comments to his father too audacious.

Chavi's voice interrupted his thoughts. "Mrs. Rosenberg, you really did a terrific job decorating. Your house is so homey and elegant at the same time."

Mrs. Rosenberg smiled at the unexpected compliment.

"You must be very creative. Shmuel told me you built this house, so you didn't even have anything to work with. I can't imagine having to make all those decisions. How did you pick the color scheme?"

Although Mrs. Rosenberg had worked hard decorating the house, she didn't want to admit that the interior decorator had chosen the color scheme. She answered, "I was looking for something subdued. The problem with subdued colors, though, is that they sometimes seem drab." She remembered the decorator saying that.

"Interesting point. Were you ever involved in art?"

"Actually, I used to like painting, but I gave it up when the children were born."

"Really?" interjected Shmuel. "I didn't know that."

"Oh, yes," said Dr. Rosenberg. "Your mother is quite an artist. When we were first married, she made a showing of her work as a fund-raiser for *tzedakah*."

Chavi was genuinely excited. "Do you have anything I could see?"

"It would take me a bit of time to find," Mrs. Rosenberg replied. "I'm sure you wouldn't want to wait."

"No, I'd be glad to," Chavi insisted.

Mrs. Rosenberg was flattered by her interest. "Well, maybe I will be able to find something. I'll be back in a jiffy," she said, feeling a thrill at seeing her creations again.

As Mrs. Rosenberg got up, Chavi asked, "Do you mind if I take another slice of pie?"

An almost imperceptible hush fell over the room. Almost imperceptible, but noticeable enough to all four people in the room.

"Were you saving it for something?" Chavi asked, realizing that maybe she was getting comfortable just a bit too fast.

Dr. and Mrs. Rosenberg answered at the same time, "Oh, no. Of course not." "Please help yourself."

Shmuel chuckled to himself. Chavi certainly wasn't what his family was used to.

Chavi scolded herself, but actually enjoyed seeing how ruffled they were. She had to remember her manners. After all, they weren't family yet. Even then, she mused, chances were that she would have to behave herself.

Mrs. Rosenberg left the room and returned less than five minutes later with a desk-sized portfolio that she dusted off as she came up the stairs from the basement. For the next hour, the little group admired Mrs. Rosenberg's work. The time passed pleasantly, and at about 10:15, Shmuel said, "It's getting late. We had better get going."

"Oh! I didn't realize that it was so late," Mrs. Rosenberg exclaimed, with a look at the clock. "I'm so sorry for keeping you so long."

Chavi assured her that she had really enjoyed seeing Mrs. Rosenberg's work and getting to know them. After a few moments of good-byes, the young couple was gone and Dr. and Mrs. Rosenberg were left alone. It struck them that they had gotten so absorbed in the artwork that they had forgotten to pay attention to analyzing Chavi. *"Nu, nu,"* Mrs. Rosenberg said out loud, as if to push away thoughts of her missed opportunity, "it was a nice evening. Shmuel knows what he is doing, I suppose."

Out on the street, Chavi and Shmuel stood under a streetlight. "Was I okay?" Chavi asked, hoping for his approval.

Shmuel replied, "I'm sure I'll find out later. The meeting was different than what I expected. My parents were much more relaxed than usual. We usually have a pretty formal home, especially when my mother is entertaining, but they seemed to enjoy themselves tonight."

His answer wasn't very reassuring to Chavi, but the deed was done and there was no going back. Before she could say anything else, Shmuel said, "I thought maybe we could go to your house now. To visit your mother."

Taken aback, Chavi stammered, "But you already met my mother a few times when you picked me up, and anyway it's kind of late for her now."

"You told me she always waits up for you. I think she'd probably appreciate a visit. She'd feel more included."

Chavi cringed at the thought of popping in on her mother, who was no doubt lying on the couch reading a paper, dressed in a worn housecoat and *tichel*. The contrast would be too severe, and although her mother never meant any harm, Chavi thought it best to keep Shmuel and Mrs. Baumel separate for as long as possible. "But she's not expecting us. Maybe she'd feel uncomfortable that she wasn't prepared."

"We could call her right now. And tell her that I insist that she doesn't prepare anything."

Shmuel walked to a pay phone a few feet away, inserted a phone token, and dialed, passing Chavi the phone when it rang. "Hello, Ima. Yes. I'm in Shaarei Chesed. Yes, it went okay. Anyway, Shmuel is standing right next to me and he wants to know if we could stop by.... You're sure it's not too late? I know you like to go to sleep early. Okay, okay. Yes, it would be nice. Okay, we'll be there in about fifteen minutes."

When they arrived, Mrs. Baumel, as expected, answered the door in her housecoat and *tichel*. They all sat down in the living room. Mrs. Baumel passed around plates of cut fruit and home-baked cookies, ignoring their protests that they weren't hungry.

"Shmuel, Chavi really thinks highly of you. I'm so glad you came by. I've heard so much about you, but we've never really spent much time together. It means a lot to me not to be left out of the picture."

Shmuel smiled at Chavi in a way that said, "I knew your mother would appreciate it. I don't see why you made such a fuss." Chavi blushed a bit at her mother's compliment to Shmuel.

"So, how did the visit to your parents go? I'm sure they are lovely people, if they have a son that my Chavi looks up to so much. Sometimes you have to worry about meeting with upper-class folks. They can look down on people and make them uncomfortable, you know. They're not all like that, though; Chavi said the meeting was fine. I didn't mean to offend you. Oh, dear me, did I offend you? I really wasn't saying anything about your family...."

"Ima."

"Oh, okay. Anyway, Shmuel, please do try the cookies. It's a recipe that my grandmother entered in a *Good Housekeeping* cooking contest. Have you ever heard of *Good Housekeeping*? It's a ladies' magazine. Not Jewish or anything, but my grandmother, may she rest in peace, liked to read it. She won the contest, you know. She was probably the first *frum* woman to win a *Good Housekeeping* contest. My husband, of blessed memory, used to love when I baked these cookies for him. But he's no longer around to be able to share them with us tonight. I'm sure he's watching us from Heaven, though."

Chavi wished her mother would at least pause for breath. Why did she have to mention a goyish magazine? And why did her late husband have to be mentioned in every conversation?

Shmuel helped himself to a cookie. He saw that Chavi was getting agitated, but he wasn't sure why. "These cookies are super. What kind are they?"

"Mocha chocolate macadamia nut," Mrs. Baumel answered.

The conversation went on for another twenty minutes, with Mrs. Baumel doing most of the talking. Shmuel saw where Chavi's talkative side came from. But the atmosphere was relaxed and Shmuel was comfortable, oblivious to all the glaring faux pas that Chavi was keeping track of. When he saw Chavi yawn three times in a row, he took the hint and excused himself for visiting for so long at such a late hour.

Mrs. Baumel would not hear of his apology and thanked him again profusely for the visit. "It's not easy seeing your daughter get engaged without really knowing the boy. I've done it before, but it's still a little scary."

We're not engaged yet, Chavi fumed inwardly at her mother's forthrightness — assuming that he wanted to marry her. But Shmuel didn't seem to mind at all. That was especially encouraging. She turned away so Shmuel wouldn't see her smile.

Chavi walked Shmuel out. "I'm glad I came," he remarked. "Your mother is a very warm woman."

That was it? A warm woman? Good, another hurdle passed!

4

"*Mazal Tov*, Chavi!" read the sign Chavi's neighbors had hung on her door, a reminder of the warmth that had enveloped the Baumels ever since they had moved in. One family in their apartment building had brought them dinner on their first night in Israel. The tuna sandwiches, sliced vegetables, and cold drink were very appreciated to the new arrivals, who had no close relatives nearby. Another neighbor brought over cake, milk, and coffee in the morning and invited them for Shabbos. A third woman came by to say hello and left a list of the neighborhood services and all the English-speaking families who lived there, with her name highlighted. The welcoming gestures mitigated their yearning for their old home quite a bit.

Chavi's *mazal tov* sign, a tangible reminder that she was really and truly engaged, thrilled her every time she saw it. Thank God, the financial discussions that had led up to this momentous occasion had gone smoothly. Mrs. Gafni, the *shadchan,* had foreseen that the families' different perspectives might lead to differences of opinion on this sticky matter and insisted that the conversation go through her so she could mediate.

The Rosenbergs, though financially very comfortable, believed that the girl's family was responsible to support the couple as long as the boy was interested in learning. It wasn't a matter of means, but a matter of principle. Mrs. Baumel, on the other hand, although delighted that her daughter wanted a husband who would learn in *kollel,* had no means of supporting a young couple and felt that they had to manage on their own as best as they could. Chavi was aware of this situation, and even if her mother had been interested in trying to help them with their economic obligations, Chavi would not hear of making her life any more difficult. She knew Mrs. Baumel had lived frugally all her life and did so even more after her husband's passing. Mrs. Baumel had even begun to take in sewing after their move to Israel, although she had never worked before.

The problem was that Chavi knew the Rosenbergs would never understand that Mrs. Baumel expected the couple to make it on their own. They knew that people had financial difficulties, but they expected them to somehow find the resources to support their children. Mrs. Baumel's position was unheard of. As a result, Chavi begged her mother to offer Chavi's savings as if they were coming from Mrs. Baumel herself.

Mrs. Baumel was both hurt and irate. "How dare they imply that I don't have the right to admit that I can't support a very capable young couple with minimal financial obligations! Just because God blessed them with so much money, that doesn't give them the right to put me down — or my precious daughter. Do they understand what a gem they are getting? Is this a business deal or a marriage? Do you know that your father worked himself to the bone to make an honest living his whole life? If these hotsy-totsy people think we're not good enough for them the way we are, then they can take their business contract elsewhere!"

Mrs. Baumel was red in the face when she finished. Chavi had never seen her so agitated, but she had known that her suggestion would touch on a sensitive spot. Her mother often felt herself inferior to people who were wealthier than she was. She had always had what she needed and sometimes more, but she felt it a personal flaw that she wasn't from amongst the high society. She saw again and again that those who had money were honored and treated as important, and by now it was ingrained in her psyche that having money was a quality that showed a person's worth.

Although Chavi, for her part, always had a soft spot for fancy things, it came more from her aesthetic sense than from seeing anything prestigious about wealth. Yet she realized the futility in starting a philosophical debate on the issue at this point, especially when there was so much at stake. Time was of the essence, as Mrs. Gafni was calling to hear Mrs. Baumel's reaction to the Rosenbergs' proposal later that evening.

"Please calm down, Ima. I totally understand your position, and I know how honest and dedicated you are, and Abba was, in supporting our family comfortably."

Mrs. Baumel nodded, slightly mollified. Chavi continued, "Don't forget, I'm marrying Shmuel and not his parents, so it doesn't matter much what they think right now. And, anyway, we're not really doing anything different than what we were planning on doing anyway. We just have to package the facts a bit differently. If it's my personal savings or yours, what difference does it make?"

Mrs. Baumel eventually agreed to do whatever Chavi asked, though she still didn't think it was right.

The negotiations began. Mrs. Baumel explained to Mrs. Gafni that, of course, she would help the couple after they were married. She told Mrs. Gafni how much she was able to offer and said that rather than giving the money to the couple to do with as they pleased, she preferred to put it toward the purchase of an apartment.

When the Rosenbergs heard what Mrs. Baumel had offered, they felt the sum was respectable enough and also agreed to put it toward an apartment. When Mrs. Gafni cleverly pointed out that the sum would only go far enough for an apartment out of Yerushalayim, the Rosenbergs offered to add a significant amount in order to keep Shmuel local.

With all involved parties pleased, the engagement became official.

It was time to plan the *vort*. Hosting social occasions always made Chavi uneasy. She loved planning parties; she loved baking; she loved decorating. But, until the party was over, she was always worried that it would be a flop and she would be embarrassed. To make sure that the inevitable failure of her parties wouldn't be her fault, she would plan meticulously down to the last detail as early as possible. But the aspect that was beyond her ability to control was who would come. She always worried that no one would show up, and everyone would realize how unpopular she really was. Oh, how uncomfortable that would be! It was so important that it didn't happen at her *vort*.

The *vort* was to be held in the Baumels' house. Mother and daughter worked hard to make everything elegant and tasteful, from the paper goods to the refreshments to the decorations. Chavi called everyone she knew, both to share her happiness with as many people as possible and to make sure that at least a handful of people showed up.

Throughout the preparations, Mrs. Baumel made sure to keep a detailed list of her expenses in the affair, so that if the need arose for any sort of settling of accounts with the Rosenbergs, she would be prepared with the facts.

ℬ ℬ

The day finally arrived. Mrs. Baumel had been beaming from the time she had woken up in the morning in anticipation of her daughter's happy event. Her happiness was marred by only one thing: her husband's absence. It was an internal loneliness that no one could understand, except for someone who had also gone through the loss of a spouse.

Although she could share her joyous feelings with Chavi, it wasn't the same as sharing with her soul mate. So many heavy emotions accompanied marrying off one's baby — a sense of completion, an emptiness and a feeling of uselessness, a sense of hitting a milestone that screamed that one's youth was undoubtedly over. She could discuss these feelings with her friends or with Chavi, but there was no one who would understand without her needing to say anything. That was something only a husband of four decades could do. In the early afternoon, before they began to set up for the *vort*, she sat down to say a few chapters of *Tehillim* for her husband's merit.

Afterwards, she sent Chavi to rest and began to arrange

the living room and dining room according to Chavi's specifications. Knowing Chavi would have a number of criticisms, she tried to anticipate, and thus perhaps eliminate, as many as possible as she went along.

As she was putting the finishing touches on the tables, Chavi came into the room, looking refreshed and graceful in the shimmering, silver-gray tea-length gown she had bought for the occasion. She twirled in front of her mother, proudly making it clear that she would gladly accept any compliments her mother had to offer.

"You look radiant, my dear. Just radiant."

Chavi started to look around the room, examining every table. "Thank you, Ima. You did a wonderful job of setting up. Everything is exquisite," she said, planting a kiss on her surprised mother's cheek.

Will wonders never cease! It seems engagement has done Chavi well, reflected Mrs. Baumel as she went to check on the food in the oven.

Just then, the bell rang. It was a delivery boy carrying a large white box addressed to Chavi. She thanked him and handed him a very generous tip. As soon as the door closed behind him, she sat down to open the box.

Inside were three dozen white roses and a short card, whose every word she savored. Lingering for a moment to enjoy the feel and smell of the flowers, her eyes misted over as she thought of the commitment their beauty represented. She arranged the flowers in a large vase, fussing over them as if they were children needing attention and encouragement.

Soon enough it was time for the guests to arrive. Shmuel and the Rosenbergs arrived twenty minutes after the appointed time, knowing that no one would arrive on time. After Chavi thanked her *chassan* for the lovely flowers, he and Dr. Rosenberg disappeared to the other side of the *mechitzah*. Mrs. Baumel was warming up some hors d'oeuvres in the kitchen, so Chavi and Mrs. Rosenberg were left alone.

Mrs. Rosenberg looked around. And looked around again. Chavi's eyes followed her future mother-in-law's with the innocence of a puppy looking for attention from its master. "May I get you something?" she asked.

"Oh, no," Mrs. Rosenberg said. "I was...well, I had expected a sit-down affair. I was surprised when I heard the *vort* was going to be in your house, since I knew you wouldn't be able to seat everyone for a meal. But I didn't want to say anything. I don't like to mix in. It's all right. This is fine."

Chavi's face fell. But before they could dwell on the issue any longer, her married sisters-in-law, Ruchie and Freidel, came in. Mrs. Rosenberg introduced them to Chavi.

"Wow, you flew in for the *vort*," she said in surprise, though she vaguely recalled Shmuel saying something about her meeting his sisters.

"Of course," said Ruchie, the older one. "We wouldn't miss this for the world."

"Your sister and brother won't be here?" Mrs. Rosenberg asked, surprised.

"No," said Chavi quietly, as if trying to hide the answer.

"Oh, your poor mother. It must be hard for her to go through this alone, your father being gone and all. It's a shame they weren't able to make it to be here with her."

The first well-wishers entered the room then, interrupting the conversation. People poured in as the night progressed, crowding the little apartment, but bringing much happiness to both families. Chavi was surprised at how many people had come to share this day with her. As she was looking around the room during a break between speeches, Gitty came in.

"*Mazal tov,*" she said, giving Chavi a quick peck on the cheek. "You look lovely. I'm so happy for you."

"Thank you. Please come take something to eat. And I want to introduce you to my future mother-in-law." Smiling, Chavi locked arms with Gitty, her closest friend in Israel at that point.

After a quick exchange of *mazal tov*s with Mrs. Rosenberg, Gitty said, "Uh, Chavi, I'm feeling a little under the weather. I really want to stay, but I'm afraid I have to leave now."

Disappointed, Chavi walked her friend to the door and then was swept up in conversation with other guests before she had a chance to give the matter any more thought.

The party came to its conclusion late into the evening, but long before Chavi wanted it to end. She had had a glorious time. As she lay in bed that night, happy memories washed over her. Suddenly she recalled Shmuel's mother's first comments. The recollection stung and she didn't want to dwell on it. Maybe she was being oversensitive — she and Mrs. Rosenberg probably just had different styles of expression.

She was worried about Gitty and made a mental note to call the next day and check how she was feeling.

5

"Hello?"

"Hello, Gitty. It's Chavi."

"Hi. How are you?"

"*Baruch Hashem*, I'm tired, but happy. I was calling to see if you're feeling any better."

"Yes, thank you for asking. The *vort* was beautiful."

"Thank you. I was surprised you didn't stay longer."

Silence.

"Gitty, I was actually a little disappointed. You're a good friend of mine."

"Oh, sorry."

Silence.

"Um, Gitty? Is everything okay?"

Again there was nothing from the other end. Then Chavi heard a sigh.

"Chavi, Shaya moved back to America last night."

"Oh, no," Chavi said, not grasping the implication. "Is he feeling all right?"

"Chavi, we're getting a...divorce." Gitty let the last word

slowly roll off her tongue as if she wanted to have no part in its creation.

Neither one said anything for a full minute. Chavi was shocked. Her thoughts zoomed in and out faster than she could process them. *We're getting a divorce.* Divorce. It was such a horribly ugly word. Especially to someone who had just become engaged. Marriage held such promise and dreams. It was the glorious start of what was supposed to be life lived happily ever after. Gitty had certainly also felt that way when she became engaged, and now she was getting divorced.

Divorced. So many questions popped up in Chavi's mind, partly out of caring and partly out of curiosity. She had heard of many people getting divorced; it wasn't scandalous as it had once been. But she had never personally known anyone who had gotten divorced, except for one of her mother's friends, who had been middle-aged. How did it happen? Who initiated it? How long had Gitty known about it? Did she see the problems starting while they were engaged?

She didn't dare ask Gitty anything. She knew how hurtful it could be, and most certainly Gitty was very sensitive about things now. Such questions would also probably entail *lashon hara.* Chavi controlled her natural curiosity and said only, "Oh, Gitty, I'm so, so sorry."

Gitty let out a small sigh, but said nothing. More silence followed, and a sudden thought occurred to Chavi.

"Gitty, are you at home alone now?"

"Yes," answered Gitty, sounding terribly alone.

"I'm coming over to pick you up. You'll sleep at my house, okay? I'll be there in fifteen minutes."

"Thank you, Chavi," was all Gitty said. That was enough

for Chavi, who knew how hard it was for her friend to show her emotions and to appear vulnerable.

As Chavi waited for a taxi outside her building, she wondered if she had made a mistake. What if she didn't know what to say to Gitty? What if her mother got involved and said the wrong thing? Well, it was too late now.

When the taxi pulled up to Gitty's apartment building, Gitty was waiting outside, holding a small overnight bag. Her *sheitel* was a bit crooked, and she looked pale and uncharacteristically helpless, like a wounded child. The entire ride back to the Baumels', neither said anything. In addition to the natural discomfort that the situation brought with it, it felt strange to Chavi to see Gitty this way. She had always seen Gitty as the strong, perfect, confident one, while she, Chavi, was the weak, flawed, jealous character trying to keep her nature hidden. Now, here was Gitty in the needier position. The role reversal was jarring.

When they arrived at the Baumel home, Mrs. Baumel took one look at Gitty and told her to sit down while she made her "a nice cup of hot tea." The two young women sat down at the dining room table and waited for Mrs. Baumel, who soon brought out a tray laden with three mugs of steaming tea, sugar, and cream.

They each prepared their drinks, the clanking and clattering resounding noticeably in the silence. Chavi took her first sip. Over the rim of her mug, she saw a tear trickling down Gitty's cheek.

Mrs. Baumel stood up and put her hand on Gitty's shoulder. "There, there, my dear. It's okay. Let it all out. I know how you feel. You see, my husband, may he rest in peace, died less than a year ago. I know it's not the same thing, and I don't mean exactly to compare. But maybe I can understand some of your feelings...."

Chavi squirmed in her chair. Did her mother really think she was helping with those comments about her husband? What was the comparison? She excused herself to bring out some cookies — anything to escape the discomfort for a few moments. When she returned, she was surprised to find her mother's arm around Gitty and Gitty's head resting on her mother's shoulder, with Gitty weeping unabashedly.

ꙮ ꙮ

The next day, Chavi tiptoed around her room preparing for work. Gitty was still sound asleep, having stayed up until two in the morning talking to Mrs. Baumel. But Chavi had to get up early — her new job was starting that day. For five months she had been tutoring the neighborhood children in English while she looked for suitable employment. Luckily, she had landed an appropriate job right before her engagement and didn't have to start until two days after the *vort*. Although she knew it would be hard to get back on schedule, she was relieved that she had found a lucrative job at just the right time. With her savings being locked into an apartment, it was imperative that she had a way to support her family. The programming job she accepted wasn't ideal, but it certainly met her needs and came just as she was about to give up hope of finding something.

She hated to leave without saying good-bye to Gitty, but there was no choice. She left her friend a note saying that she had to go to work and would be home at about five-thirty, and she hoped to see Gitty then.

Chavi's first day on the job went pretty well. The work assignment she was given was challenging yet bearable. Her coworkers seemed friendly, although she hated the feeling of being the new one on the block. Her business suit was terribly out of place and she was glad that she would be able to dress more casually and comfortably — even her casual clothes would look quite businesslike in comparison to the average style of dress in the company. The office was air conditioned and carpeted, two comforts that she had sorely missed since her aliyah.

There was only one other religious woman there, a secretary in her early forties. Chavi knew immediately that her religious practices were going to be noted — one of the first five questions that each coworker asked her when they were introduced was whether she was religious. She had never worked in a secular environment before and wondered about the effect her job would have on her perspectives on the world at large. There were certainly going to be issues to deal with, and she was glad that she was getting married and would have someone to discuss them with.

When Chavi arrived home that evening, supper for three was on the table. She was exhausted and hungry and glad to be cared for. Over dinner, she described her new work environment, and the conversation flowed from topic to topic.

At one point, Mrs. Baumel asked Gitty if she was going to remain in Yerushalayim or return to New York.

"I haven't given it much thought," Gitty replied, "but I think I'll stay at least until the school year is over. I don't think it's responsible to leave my job in the middle of the year." Both Chavi and her mother nodded in agreement, though they both knew that Gitty's night-time tutoring job could hardly be the only reason she had decided to remain.

Gitty, for her part, was not yet ready to face her parents and childhood community. She knew the terrible pain and shame that her parents were dealing with and she didn't want to exacerbate it by forcing them to face their emotions every time they saw her. She also wanted to avoid the pitying glances and clucking tongues of her neighbors and the insolent and assuming words of rebuke that some well-meaning souls would find as their moral obligation to share. Keeping all these thoughts private, she said, "I can't afford my apartment's rent anymore. I'm going to have to find something less expensive."

Mrs. Baumel was quiet for a few minutes as Chavi and Gitty discussed rent in various Jerusalem neighborhoods. After five minutes, she left the table and called Chavi to the kitchen after another minute had passed on the pretense of needing her help to get something down from a high shelf.

After a quick conference, Mrs. Baumel and Chavi returned to the dining room and sat down again. Mrs. Baumel said, "Gitty, would you like to move in with us? Chavi will be leaving soon anyway, and it will be hard for me to live alone. It's nice and quiet here, and you could have the extra bedroom."

Gitty was amazed by the gracious offer from a woman she was not related to, whom she only met in person a couple of nights before.

Chavi added, "We'd love if you came here. I can also help you pack up your apartment whenever you need to."

Although this type of decision usually took some time to consider, Gitty accepted immediately. One of her biggest worries had been where to go — she couldn't afford the high rent in Yerushalayim, New York was out, so what did that leave her? Now the perfect solution had been offered to her.

Although it would be hard to live with someone she barely knew, Mrs. Baumel was one of the most giving people she had ever met and she hoped everything would work out.

Later that evening, she called her landlord to apprise him of the situation. He assured her that she could leave whenever she wanted to, even though the rental contract was not yet up, and he would have no problem finding another tenant. She knew she was being granted another gracious kindness, and she thanked him and said she would be leaving at the end of the week.

ೱ ೱ

The next evening, Gitty and Chavi went to pack up Gitty's belongings and move them to the Baumels'. Chavi had been to Gitty's apartment a number of times, and she could picture it in her mind as they rode toward it. It was a two-bedroom apartment with a small kitchen and living room. Typical of an apartment that had been rented out for many years, it had a worn and tired look. The white plaster on the walls had a yellowish-gray tinge at night from the dim lightbulbs, and blue and white Formica covered the kitchen counters and cabinets. The furniture, which belonged to the landlord, was Israeli furniture typical of the seventies.

Although the apartment lacked aesthetic beauty, it still radiated a cozy warmth. Maybe because the furniture was so used and worn, the apartment felt inviting. Most of the apartments that the young *kollel* couples rented were of a similar nature, and everyone accepted the conditions as they were in order to live near their friends. No one had to be embarrassed of their standard of living.

Chavi saw Gitty pause before putting the key in the door.

This was going to be a difficult emotional ordeal for her. Each item in her house would undoubtedly remind her of past events, some agonizing, some delightful. Perhaps the delightful ones would be the most painful, as they represented lost dreams.

Gitty opened the door and the two of them stepped inside the living room. The dark wood table, the tall bookcase, and the brown couch all looked as Chavi remembered them. Irrationally, she had expected the apartment to look different as a result of what had transpired since she had last been there. But everything looked just the same.

"Where should we begin?" Gitty said with a sigh.

"How about right here?" Chavi suggested.

Gitty dragged out a few large suitcases from a storage area hidden over the front door and Chavi assembled some boxes she had brought with them. The *sefarim* belonged to the owner of the apartment, so that whole section of the room did not need packing. Gitty opened the bottom section of one of the bookcases and began removing her tablecloths, placing them in one of the boxes. When she was finished, she took her candlesticks from one of the shelves, wrapped each one in kitchen towels, and added them to the box.

Following her cue, Chavi removed the pictures from the walls, wrapped each carefully in newspaper, and packed it in a different box. When she took down an olive-wood plaque bearing Gitty's wedding invitation, she hesitated before wrapping it. Seeing her pause, Gitty said, "Throw it out." Quickly, Chavi placed it in the garbage bag.

The living room only took about twenty minutes to pack. The guest room was empty except for some linens and towels, which were easily taken care of. Then, in order to give

Gitty a little privacy, Chavi said, "I'll take care of the bathrooms while you do your bedroom."

Gitty nodded in resignation.

It didn't take Chavi long to pack the toiletries and trinkets in the two small bathrooms. Hearing nothing from the bedroom, she knocked on the open door and went in to check on Gitty's progress.

She found Gitty sitting on the bed, tears silently escaping her eyes and slipping down her cheeks. She did not seem to notice Chavi when she entered and just stared straight ahead. After Chavi sat down next to her and took her hand, she began to speak, as if to herself. "What have I done? I'm ruined. I've ruined my life and destroyed my future. I should have seen it coming, but I didn't. I was selfish, but I didn't mean to be. I fought for what I wanted, because I felt that if I didn't I would lose out. I got upset and moody or angry when things didn't go my way. I just assumed that marriage was forever and I could do what I wanted. But Shaya got sick of my moods and my tantrums, and now he's gone.

"He told me so many times that he was hurt by my attitude. He was angry that I seemed to view our relationship as a competition. I was warned, but I didn't believe it could really end. We went to *rabbanim*. We went to counseling. I just couldn't back down. I wanted him to appreciate everything I did, and, when I felt he didn't, I protested. I wanted him to chase after me and apologize, but he just turned off and then I couldn't back down. I didn't realize marriage needed so much work to last. We shared so many wonderful times. I thought they would counterbalance the fights. But they didn't.

"I'm not saying that the problems were all my fault, but I wish I could turn the clock back and try again. Oh, what have

I done! I'm so ashamed. Ashamed of my failure. Ashamed because I'll be looked at as a failure. The loneliness is like a deep, black ocean engulfing me. I feel like I'm drowning. If only I could have another chance now that I know what it's like when it's too late. Oh, what have I done...."

Chavi squeezed her hand tighter, not knowing what to say. She wished she could console her friend, but what could she say? That it was *bashert*? Gitty blamed herself and maybe she was right — how could Chavi know? Could she promise her a better marriage in the future? Could she tell her the loneliness would lessen with time? She had nothing to say. She sat quietly, hoping her presence would offer Gitty comfort in her time of need.

Suddenly, Gitty said, almost as if her emotional display hadn't taken place, "We should finish up. It's getting late." Following her lead, Chavi rose and rolled the suitcase Gitty had packed to the entranceway.

Only the kitchen was left, and they worked silently side by side. Gitty emptied the cabinets, and Chavi removed everything from the refrigerator. As she carried some open food packages to the table, she froze in her place. On the kitchen table rested a vase identical to the one she had bought for herself only the day before after admiring it in the window of a shop next to her office. In the vase were three wilted white roses.

White roses in her vase. White roses at her engagement party had symbolized all her dreams and aspirations for the future. What would marriage bring her? Would it be as blissful and beautiful as the roses she had received from Shmuel only days before? She had assumed that it would be. But maybe things wouldn't be as simple as she imagined. Only time would tell.

6

Chavi and her mother considered returning to America for the wedding, since Chavi felt uncomfortable getting married in a city that had only recently become her home. However, since both families now lived in Jerusalem, and none of the Rosenbergs' family and friends were in Cleveland and most of the Baumels' family wasn't there either, they decided to make the wedding in Jerusalem. The Rosenbergs left the wedding location up to them, saying that it was the bride's prerogative to choose where to get married.

The hall they found was very nice by Israeli standards, but certainly not high class. Chavi cried when she first saw it. The *chuppah* would take place in a parking lot with the large neon sign of the neighboring supermarket illuminating the background. The hall was a simple white-walled room with a mirrored ceiling, presumably to set an elegant ambiance. The floors were standard Israeli tile, while the *yichud* room doubled as a storage area for extra chairs. The fairy-tale wedding so meticulously planned in her daydreams was just not meant to be.

Yet the cost of the wedding was significantly less than it would have been in the States, even after factoring in the money spent on flying in family members. She reminded herself to focus on essentials and not to worry about the rest.

Chavi's wedding day started with *shacharis* at the Kosel. There she poured her heart out in thanks for the tremendous blessings she had received and in supplication that she should merit to build a home truly devoted to Torah ideals. From there she went to have her hair and makeup done, and before long she was at the hall posing for one picture after another. Her brother and sister and their children, who had come from America, greeted her at the hall and added to her joy on this wonderful day.

The wedding was attended by many people that the Rosenbergs and the Baumels had met at various points in their lives. Chavi was introduced to a number of the Rosenbergs' relatives and friends who had flown in for the wedding, and she enjoyed the dancing even though the usual crowd of single dancers on the bride's side was replaced to a large degree by older married women, many in maternity clothing. That was her luck for getting married at twenty-five and in Jerusalem. The lack of energy in her friends' steps, though, was more than made up for by their genuine joy at participating in the wedding.

Chavi delighted in dancing with each of her guests and sharing her appreciation for their attendance at her *simchah*. As she pulled her sister-in-law Freidel closer to her during a dance step in the center of the circle, Freidel whispered to her, "You're a real sport for putting up with this hall. Such a *tzadeikes*. You're certainly handling it better than my mother. I can't even tell it's bothering you."

Chavi thought of her mother-in-law's comment during the photo session: "Now I understand why you told me that I could wear any color dress, that there was no color scheme. Don't worry, I understand things have to be like this in a situation like yours." Chavi tried to ignore the comments and her own personal disappointments and to focus on the wonderful happiness and love that filled the air.

ꙮ ꙮ

Sheva berachos passed quickly. The new Rosenberg couple, more exhausted than they had expected to be, spent their afternoons napping. Each evening, *sheva berachos* was hosted by a different group whose style ran from a potluck dinner sponsored by the neighbors in someone's living room to dinner in a party room at a posh hotel. Chavi listened to the speeches carefully, hoping not to be embarrassed by someone saying the wrong things about her or not saying the right things. She also listened carefully to what the speakers said about her husband. They said many things that she knew to be true, but she noticed that there was barely any mention of his learning. How she thirsted to hear the speakers extolling the depth and devotion of her husband's Torah study. *Oh, well,* she shrugged, after a particularly long-winded speech finally came to a close, *these speeches don't mean anything.*

She enjoyed the week of *sheva berachos*. She loved relaxing with Shmuel, having nothing to do but get dressed for the evening and show up more or less on time. She loved spending time with her friends and family night after night. And she loved being fawned over, at long last the *kallah*.

One small issue came to her as a surprise, though. After

twenty-five years of being served day in and day out or at most only being responsible for herself, she was now in charge of serving meals. Although before her marriage she would have undoubtedly agreed that it was both her responsibility and no big deal, it was still difficult to adjust to. Because it was *sheva berachos* week, the main cooking was not her job, but even putting out cereal bowls and making coffee in the morning seemed like a bother.

She couldn't believe that such a small thing had become a large issue in her mind. She had always assumed that her love for her family would make household chores pretty effortless. But, tired after a late night, she didn't feel like setting the table or washing the dishes or thinking of what they were going to eat.

Silly as it seemed to need her *kallah* teacher's *mussar* so early in the game, she reminded herself that marriage was about giving and that her turn to be *chesed*-oriented had come. She visualized how pleasant it had been in the past to have her bed made and her meals prepared, especially when she was tired, and realized that it wasn't just a chore but a gift she was giving her husband.

She was sure that had Shmuel heard the dialogue taking place all too frequently in his wife's mind he wouldn't have taken too kindly to it. Setting up a simple breakfast or lunch should not take Herculean effort or a motivational *mussar* speech — they were just normal jobs that wives did for their husbands. Chavi kept her thoughts to herself and prayed that such expected giving would soon become second nature.

ဢ ဢ

It wasn't long before Chavi got into the rhythm of

things. She worked hard at setting up their house and making it a welcoming place. The apartment was located conveniently on the second floor of a building in a neighborhood full of young American couples, though their particular building was completely Israeli. It was bright and airy, with brand-new furniture and appliances. Mrs. Rosenberg's mother had given the new couple a bedroom set, and they picked out the rest of the furniture together, using money they had gotten as wedding presents. The house had been freshly painted before they moved in, and the faint lingering smell from the paint job gave it a new, fresh impression.

Their meals didn't require too much preparation on her part. For breakfast, they had either cold cereal and milk or sweet rolls and coffee. Shmuel ate lunch in yeshivah, since Chavi was at work during the day. Chavi would alternate between packaged sandwiches and yogurts which she bought from the corner store next to her office. When she came home from work, she would nap for about an hour and then put together a light supper. Because Shmuel ate a heavy meal for lunch, he was satisfied with an omelet and a salad or some lasagna, or even just soup and a roll. They got into a schedule and things worked out well.

Chavi enjoyed scrubbing and shining the house on Friday, her day off. The rest of the week, though, she found washing dishes and straightening up to be so tedious that she pushed off dealing with them as much as possible. Often she procrastinated until it was late enough for her to convince herself that it would be irresponsible to stay up any later and the jobs would have to wait until the next day. Their apartment was still reasonably in order. With only two adults in the house, even if the dishes and laundry waited for a day or two, everything remained under control.

Shmuel's adjustment to married life was a bit more difficult than Chavi's. Chavi had been living in Jerusalem for nearly a year by the time they got married. She had settled quickly into her job and felt comfortable there. She always had her mother to turn to for help, advice, and companionship, and she had set up a small network of friends. Shmuel's situation was different. Although he had learned in Israel for two years, he had been back in America for a number of years since then. He knew the neighborhoods and the bus system, he fit right into the *kollel* program at the yeshivah he had studied in previously, and he had family nearby, but he had few familiar faces in yeshivah and his good friends were all settled in America. Even though he didn't feel out of place, he didn't feel acclimated, either.

Sheva berachos week had been wonderful, and now, as a married man, he didn't feel lost and lonesome anymore. He was glad to come home every night to someone who was interested in hearing about his day. It was difficult, though, to constantly have to consider someone else's feelings. No matter how tired he was at night, he stayed up talking for as long as Chavi wished. Sometimes, when he knew his exhaustion would make going to yeshivah pointless, he would go back to sleep for an hour or two after Chavi left. He didn't tell Chavi about that, since he thought it was important to give her whatever time she needed in the evening and didn't want to upset her by revealing that he went in late.

For the first month of Shabbosim they switched off between their parents. They spent their first Shabbos after *sheva berachos* with Mrs. Baumel. Sensitive to both the young Rosenberg couple and Gitty, Mrs. Baumel had hinted to Gitty that it would be best if she went away for Shabbos, so mother, daughter, and son-in-law were alone for Shabbos.

When Shmuel left for shul on Friday night, Mrs. Baumel and Chavi were alone for the first time since the wedding. It was relaxing for both of them to fall back into their familiar roles of mother and daughter. Suppressing her curiosity and motherly concern, Mrs. Baumel didn't ask how Chavi's married life was going. She had learned the hard way from her older two children that a new couple needed independence in order to set up its home with a strong foundation. The two women chatted lightly until Shmuel returned home.

As Shmuel made Kiddush, a tear ran down Mrs. Baumel's cheek. After they each had a sip of wine, Chavi asked, "What's wrong, Ma?"

"This is the first time a man has made Kiddush in this apartment," Mrs. Baumel replied. "It just reminded me that Abba isn't here. How happy he would have been to see you married!"

Why did her mother always have to talk about her father? Chavi wondered in annoyance. Of course, she missed him. They all did. But what did it help to mention him at every possible moment? Chavi had so much wanted Shmuel to have a perfect Shabbos. Why couldn't her mother just act normally?

She knew that the Rosenbergs were bothered by the fact that her father had died. Mrs. Rosenberg had once mentioned something about her "broken home." When Chavi had asked her what she meant, Mrs. Rosenberg had changed the subject. Later Chavi realized she was referring to Mrs. Baumel being widowed. It always embarrassed Chavi when her mother became sentimental about her father in public.

Now it was worse — if her father's death was some sort of flaw in the family to the Rosenberg parents, then it probably was in Shmuel's eyes, too. A mother was supposed to be strong for her children — to comfort, not to be comforted. Why did her mother have to mourn so publicly?

Impulsively, Chavi burst out, "I'm sick of hearing how everything reminds you of Abba. He's gone. It's time you made peace with the situation and moved on."

Both Mrs. Baumel and Shmuel were shocked by the eruption. Chavi immediately saw that her mother was hurt and embarrassed in front of Shmuel. She regretted her words at once, although, she admitted to herself, it was a relief in a certain sense to express her building resentment to her mother. "I'm sorry. I didn't mean to say that," she muttered, leaving the room to be alone for a minute.

Shmuel, confused by the uncharacteristic outburst, felt he should go after her and see what was wrong, but he didn't want to leave Mrs. Baumel alone without trying to right the situation. "I'm sorry," he apologized. "I have no idea what happened to Chavi. I'm sure it must be difficult for you to adjust to your loss."

"Sometimes people say things they don't mean, especially when they are under the pressure of being newly married and all that entails," Mrs. Baumel replied, but she was tingling with self-pity and anger. Her adjustment to her new single role was such a terribly difficult one. For forty years her husband had been the sun around whom she revolved. He decided when it was day and when it was night, protected her and loved her and supported her. They had been almost one person, and living alone was like being half-dead. Just getting through the day took a superhuman effort at times. And now had Chavi made it clear that even the small relief that expressing her pain allowed her was socially unacceptable. Left alone when Shmuel went to draw Chavi out of the bedroom for *HaMotzi*, she was keenly aware of her deepened isolation.

Chavi came back humbled and contrite and her mother accepted her unspoken words of remorse. The incident was soon forgotten and their relationship recovered its normal rhythm, as only a mother-daughter relationship can under such circumstances.

Mrs. Baumel had prepared a sumptuous meal, which Shmuel enjoyed even though it was only a few days since *sheva berachos*. When he complimented his mother-in-law, she didn't mention that she had cooked all her husband's favorite dishes on the assumption that Shmuel would share his male preferences.

After the meal, Chavi and Shmuel invited Mrs. Baumel for a walk. She declined politely. "A walk sounds lovely, but I'm in the middle of an interesting book and I can't wait to find out what's going to happen next." Her daughter and son-in-law slipped out into the brisk Jerusalem night.

Five minutes into their walk, Shmuel had the opportunity to question Chavi's outburst. "Why did you get so upset when your mother said she missed having a man make Kiddush? Was there something I missed?"

"My father passed away over a year ago," Chavi explained. "I know it's hard on my mother, but at some point she is going to have to move on. It's annoying that she's always bringing up what my father felt or did or would do in every situation. I know I said it wrong, but I think she needs to make peace with reality and live in the present. Besides, I know it's an issue with your family that my father is gone. I don't need you to constantly be reminded of that fact."

"Chavi," Shmuel began assuringly when she was finished, "my opinion of you is not going to be formulated on or even tinged by your relatives. You know that. But I can't understand your feelings about your mother. She's such a warm and caring person — that's what attracts so many people to her. A warm and caring person is a feeling person and so, of course, a loss affects her more potently than a similar loss would affect someone less emotional.

"You've told me many times how devoted she was to your father over the years. It is especially hard for a devoted wife to be missing the focus of her life."

As an outsider, he found it hard to understand the negative emotional energy Chavi had on the issue, but he spoke patiently nonetheless about what he considered a gross lack of caring and understanding on Chavi's part. He had yet to learn how deep are the feelings and sensitivities inherent in a mother-daughter relationship.

Chavi admired his compassion, and she told Shmuel, "Thank you for helping me view it that way. I think I'm learning to understand the strength of the bond that ties a husband and wife."

7

Shmuel and Chavi's first month of married life had passed, and they decided to try making their first Shabbos alone. Chavi was glad Gitty had moved in with her mother, because otherwise it would have been unthinkable for them to leave her mother by herself. Shmuel had invited three boys from his yeshivah for the Friday night meal. One was a younger brother of a close friend of his, and he had asked to bring two boys with him.

On Thursday night, Chavi set out all the ingredients she needed for cooking on the kitchen table. Looking at the table laden with chicken and meat and produce, she was overwhelmed with gratitude to God. This table full of food, which was meant to last one day for her, would have been a month's worth of food for a family living at an earlier point in history. She felt undeserving of such blessing and undeserving of all the other blessings in her life, chief among them living in Jerusalem with a wonderful husband who was devoted to learning. She whispered a prayer of thanks before she began her Shabbos preparations.

Soon the kitchen was alive with action. Pots were boiling on the stove. Vegetable peels piled up on the table. The sink filled with dishes. As the night progressed, pans appeared to cool on all the empty spaces on the counter.

Shmuel, interrupting his night *seder*, came in periodically to sample her creations and check how she was doing. She was glad to see that she had inherited some of her mother's culinary skills, as everything she tasted was to her satisfaction. She listened to a *shiur* on tape as she worked, but enjoyed the respite from her solitude that Shmuel's visits provided.

After the third visit, though, she felt herself getting annoyed when he came in. Wasn't he supposed to be learning? "Can't you sit still for ten minutes straight?" she wondered aloud.

She saw the wounded look on Shmuel's face as he turned to leave the kitchen. He had come in to visit her because he enjoyed her company so much, was proud of her cooking talent, and enjoyed the homey Shabbos atmosphere that permeated their apartment for the first time. But all those happy feelings evaporated in an instant with her biting words.

His look hit her harder than any retort could have. Feeling terrible, she told herself self-righteously that her words were right, though perhaps too sarcastic. In the other room, she heard Shmuel calling a friend on the phone. Not only had she lost his learning time, but she had also lost his company to his friend.

An hour passed, and Shmuel came back for a moment to show Chavi that everything was okay, but that was it. Chavi finished her preparations alone and went to sleep later than she had expected to, after Shmuel was sleeping.

ꕥ ꕥ

Chavi was happy with her first Shabbos meal in her own home. There was plenty of delicious food and harmonious song. Her husband gave a short *d'var Torah,* which she really enjoyed. It felt strange to Chavi to be in the background of the conversation. Although she was included as a member of the conversation, she felt uncomfortable speaking with so many men at the table. The conversation was interesting, though, and taught her a lot about the world of the *yeshivah bachur* that she had heard about but had never before experienced firsthand.

She and Shmuel ate alone the next day, which was just as well since the *cholent* didn't turn out as Chavi expected. She made it just as her mother did, but the beans were crunchy and there was way too much water. Shmuel assured her that these results were to be expected the first time and she would eventually figure it out. Abashed, Chavi brought the plentiful leftovers from the night before out of the refrigerator.

After a nap, the couple went for a walk in the neighborhood. The streets were bustling with young children playing and their mothers chatting casually. Chavi noticed a distinct absence of men on the street and assumed they were all learning. There were a few men bustling from here to there, but they walked, it seemed to Chavi, with a destination. Suddenly, she was ashamed to be seen walking with her husband on Shabbos afternoon. Now everyone would know her husband wasn't learning.

Shmuel felt the change in mood immediately and asked her what was wrong.

She answered him truthfully about something else that

also made her uncomfortable. "Shmuel, I feel lost when I'm outside. Our house is a haven of comfort and belonging, but when I go outside, I feel so lonely, especially seeing all the people who fill the streets on Shabbos. I barely know a soul around here."

"It is hard to break into a new neighborhood," Shmuel commiserated with her. "Maybe we can think of some way for you to meet new people." Together they decided that she should attend one of the neighborhood Shabbos *shiurim* to get acquainted with her neighbors.

The very next week, Chavi went to a *shiur* on the parashah that was held in a shul a few houses away from her home. She made sure to get there fifteen minutes early, so she would have time to meet any other early attendees. There weren't any, and the seemingly endless wait in the empty shul made her feel like a fool.

At the time the shiur was called for, women of all ages began coming in. They all seemed to know one another, making Chavi even more uncomfortable.

After a few minutes of agony, a woman who appeared to be in her early forties introduced herself to Chavi and then introduced Chavi to all the women in her radius. Chavi was incredibly thankful for this small act of kindness, which instantly changed what had become an ordeal into an enjoyable experience. She was actually disappointed when the speaker arrived, robbing her of her opportunity to meet new people. In the end, though, she enjoyed the *shiur* and committed herself to becoming a regular.

After that *shiur*, every time Chavi saw the woman who had introduced herself she felt a sense of belonging. She became the familiar face that Chavi searched out in crowds, an anchor which rescued her from being lost in a sea of strangers. Although they never became more than casual acquaintances, she gave Chavi the priceless gift of beginning to feel that she belonged.

Despite the weekly *shiur,* she still felt alone in the neighborhood. The main socializing in the neighborhood was done in the parks and on Shabbos walks. Chavi, having no children, felt she had no business participating in either activity. She forced herself to go to the community N'shei gatherings, where the young English-speaking women went to get to know each other. Far from family and new to the country, they came to build a sense of community.

Although she got to know more people at these gatherings, Chavi felt herself a spectator rather than a central player. It seemed that most of the women came to spend time with old friends and not to make new ones. Slowly she formed neighborhood friendships, though she was still lonesome for her old childhood friends, with whom she had comfortable and well-established relationships. As a final step in becoming a part of the community, Chavi volunteered to cook for families that couldn't cook for themselves once a month and to have a weekly *Tehillim* group meet in her house.

8

Shmuel and Chavi's first anniversary was just around the bend when Shmuel told Chavi that Mrs. Rosenberg wanted to make them an anniversary party in her house. It would be just for family, and Mrs. Rosenberg felt it was an appropriate way to mark their special occasion. Shmuel felt it was a nice gesture and assumed Chavi would take it as a sign of his mother's affection for them. He was totally unprepared for her reaction.

"Another party? Every occasion is call for 'just a little family get-together.' It's nice that you're so close knit, but I'm afraid that we're going to have to decline the offer."

"Why?" Shmuel asked, taken aback. What bothered his wife about an offer for an anniversary party? He knew that every time they got together she seemed to get insulted by something his mother said, but he assumed that was just the way mothers-in-law and daughters-in-law interacted. Since Chavi was the first daughter-in-law in the Rosenberg family, he didn't have anyone to compare her to on this matter.

"It will be a waste of your time. You have other things

you are supposed to be doing, and you don't have to miss night *seder* every couple of weeks because some momentous occasion has taken place in your family."

"I'm sure my night *seder* didn't even cross her mind," Shmuel defended his mother.

"Exactly my point," Chavi replied, clearly enunciating each syllable.

Shmuel didn't say anything, and Chavi wondered what he was thinking. She debated in her mind inconclusively about whether her comment was *lashon hara,* but felt she had had enough. How long was Shmuel going to let this abuse continue?

Shmuel understood her perspective, but, frankly, he enjoyed the get-togethers. He enjoyed going back to his familiar home environment and taking a break from his regular schedule. He was surprised and flattered by his wife's protection of his time, but he felt it was unnecessary and out of place.

They compromised by allowing his mother to make the party but agreeing to limit the number of future invitations they accepted. Despite Shmuel's verbal agreement to the indefinite deal, he doubted that he would have the interest or strength of character needed to follow it through. Deep in her heart, Chavi knew that he wouldn't do as he promised, but she pushed those thoughts away, wanting to feel that the problem was handled. She was always bothered when Shmuel didn't keep to his schedule. She knew Shmuel felt she overreacted, but she panicked whenever she thought her dream of his success in learning was slipping away.

Chavi had a surprisingly pleasant time at the party. The usually bumpy interchanges that tended to characterize the time she spent with her mother-in-law were absent. Maybe it was because Chavi softened Mrs. Rosenberg's heart by showing up in maternity clothing. She didn't really need it yet, but she was so eager to share the good news that she couldn't resist.

ॐ ॐ

Happily, things progressed as planned. Soon there was a new Rosenberg boy. The bris took place at the Ramada Renaissance Hotel, thanks to the senior Rosenbergs' generosity. As Chavi entered the hotel, thoughts of her first meeting with Shmuel, which had been at the same place, flashed through her mind. The courtship had come full circle.

When she entered the hall where the bris was to take place, she remarked quietly to her son that his bris was going to be nicer than her wedding. A number of guests were already assembled. She knew most had come because of the closeness of their relationship with them, but some were there just to enjoy the posh setting, atypical of a Jerusalem bris.

The *mohel* was also already present and anxious to begin. Chavi had arrived twenty-five minutes late. She had been pretty much on schedule when the baby passionately let her know that he had to eat immediately, and then he had needed a diaper change. Before she even had a chance to exchange pleasantries with her guests, the *mohel* announced that the bris was about to begin.

Although only a moment before her mind had been focused on being a good hostess, suddenly the importance of the event that was taking place hit her. She prayed fervently that everything should go correctly and painlessly for her baby, realizing that this was his introduction to a life of holiness and commitment to Torah. She tried to hide the tears that flowed so effortlessly and frequently since the onset of her pregnancy.

Her thoughts were interrupted as the name was announced and she heard loud sobs behind her. She turned to see her mother weeping, no doubt because her husband now had a namesake.

Chavi felt her mother's behavior was exaggerated, but she remembered Shmuel's soft rebuke of the past, that this was a manifestation of her mother's caring and tender nature. Chavi turned around and put her arm around her mother's shoulder. A surprised Mrs. Baumel squeezed her back, her sobs subsiding.

Within minutes, the bris was over. Chavi was wiping her eyes when Mrs. Rosenberg came over and planted a kiss on her cheek, telling her how thrilled she was with her newest grandson. "I was very worried that we would never see this day. I'm just so happy."

What did that mean? Was it because Shmuel wasn't married until twenty-five? Probably not. Most likely, it was because she and Shmuel had been married nearly a year and a half before Yitzchak was born. Chavi had noticed Mrs. Rosenberg glancing at her stomach every time they got together over the course of Chavi and Shmuel's first year of married life. Chavi pasted a smile on her face and excused herself to talk to her other guests.

After a few minutes of accepting good wishes, she went to feed baby Yitzchak. While she was gone, the waiters began serving the first course, small whole perches stuffed with steamed vegetables. She returned to the hall in the middle of the next course, chicken breast in mushroom sauce with salad and roasted potatoes. She washed and sat down to eat just as her father-in-law began to speak.

Dr. Rosenberg spoke of his hope that baby Yitzchak would follow in the footsteps of his illustrious ancestors and bring pride to his family. He mentioned his delight in having a grandson born in Eretz Yisrael, tying in the idea of Yitzchak Avinu, who was never allowed to leave the Holy Land.

Shmuel spoke next, giving a traditional speech on some aspect of halachah relating to the bris milah. He ended off thanking his parents and mother-in-law for all they had done for himself and Chavi and mentioned his happiness at being able to name the baby after a man as wonderful as his father-in-law. In an uncharacteristic show of sentiment, he thanked his wife for allowing him to build the life he had always dreamed of.

Dr. Rosenberg was surprised to see his son's eyes misting. On the women's side, all eyes were on Chavi to see how she would react to her husband's compliment. She simply smiled shyly at her beaming mother, who was, of course, also misty eyed.

Before long a delicious dessert of hot strudel topped with ice cream was served. As Chavi was enjoying her third bite, Mrs. Rosenberg leaned over and whispered to her, "Don't worry, dear, you'll get your figure back soon enough if you're careful with what you eat."

Chavi lowered her fork and shut her mouth. Suddenly it seemed that her scrumptious dessert had gone rancid. Her eyes sent darts in her mother-in-law's direction. Mrs. Rosenberg had trampled on a raw nerve once again.

Little Yitzchak's unexpected feeding wasn't the only thing that had caused her tardiness to the bris. She nearly had a full-blown temper tantrum that morning as she tried to find an outfit to wear. After birth she had felt so thin. She was able to bend again, even to reach her toes, and she thought she was one of the lucky ones who escaped having a matronly figure. She had spent the next week in robes, having neither the time nor the inclination to look in the mirror. That morning, with only an hour to the bris, she had scanned her closet to pick out a suitable outfit, only to find that the outfit she chose didn't fit anymore. She tried another one. Same result. Soon her bed was piled with clothes that needed rehanging, with the surplus falling to the floor. She had angrily grabbed her least maternity-looking maternity outfit and gotten dressed. Now her mother-in-law had to make it known, in her signature snide manner, that Chavi's figure flaws were obvious to all.

The rest of the bris passed with Chavi a bit more withdrawn, her anger simmering beneath the surface. She tried to focus her mind on the bris again. She looked around and noticed Gitty looking forlorn and introspective. *This must be so hard for her,* Chavi thought. *She needs to get remarried. I must remember to ask Shmuel to look around for her.*

Chavi wasn't sure if Gitty had healed enough yet to start dating, but she certainly wouldn't bring up the topic until she had a suitable suggestion. She hoped it wouldn't be difficult to find someone. Gitty came from a prominent family, she was a beautiful woman, and there were no children or scandalous stories involved in the divorce.

As Chavi sat thinking, little Yitzchak began to cry. She handed him over to her mother, who acted as if Chavi was doing her a favor by allowing her to hold him. Chavi was just glad to have a break from caring for him.

ꕥ ꕥ

When they got home from the bris, Shmuel let Chavi nap while he watched his tiny son. Until now, he had avoided holding Yitzchak. He was fascinated by the baby's very existence, but his tiny size made Shmuel nervous. What if his big hands accidentally held the baby the wrong way and broke him? But Chavi looked so worn out that he overcame his fear and told her to take a nap. He prayed the baby would also sleep until Chavi awoke.

He wasn't so lucky. About fifteen minutes into Shmuel's babysitting stint, Yitzchak began to scream. Shmuel hurried over and watched him cry for a minute, sweetly telling him to try to calm down, but the situation did not improve.

Very gingerly, Shmuel scooped the baby up and held him up as one would carry a tray full of drinks. Yitzchak began to squirm, and Shmuel quickly realized that this manner of carrying him was too risky. He let the baby rest on his shoulder and walked back and forth with him, singing softly. Almost immediately, Yitzchak calmed down.

Shmuel was surprised at the depth of satisfaction he felt over his accomplishment. He sat down after a few more minutes without daring to change the baby's position, lest he wake him up and not be able to calm him down again.

As he waited for Chavi to wake up, Shmuel's mind naturally turned to his new fatherhood. He wondered if he was up to the task. He didn't consider himself a worthy role model for this innocent child. He had so many flaws in his character. His davening wasn't what he wanted, often rushed and condensed. He didn't learn as much as he was supposed to. There was so much to correct to become a proper model for his son, but Shmuel consoled himself with the knowledge that he already loved the baby with all his heart and would do his best, no matter what.

By the time Chavi got up and acclimated to being awake, it was close to lunchtime. She took out the leftovers of a meal her mother had brought and warmed them up for herself and her husband. As the two of them ate, they rehashed the details of the bris.

When Gitty's name came up, Chavi asked Shmuel to see if he knew anyone for her.

"Do you think she's ready to remarry?" Shmuel asked.

"I don't know, but she needs to move on with her life and have a fresh start," Chavi answered.

"It won't be easy unless she'll be flexible. I'll think about it," Shmuel said, moving on to another subject.

When he mentioned his mother, Chavi's face changed from neutral to sickened. "Did something happen between you and my mother?" Shmuel asked, praying that he had misread her face but assuming he hadn't.

Chavi paused for a moment before answering to consider if it was all right to unburden herself to him. She decided that it was necessary for her to speak, since only Shmuel would be able to understand her. Also, his love for his mother wouldn't let him agree to her interpretation of the events without considering all the variables involved.

She began, "I've absolutely had enough. Every time I'm with her she has to insult me, always in the guise of an innocent remark. If she didn't think I was good enough to join her family, she shouldn't have let it happen! I'm sick of all her back-handed comments and seemingly benign pieces of advice that are camouflaged arrows sent straight to pierce my heart. Sooner or later I'm going to lose my self-control and say the wrong thing. I'm telling you, I've had enough."

"What did my mother say to you today?" Shmuel asked.

Chavi described her mother-in-law's comment about waiting for them to have children and her remark about Chavi's figure.

"Oh, Chavi, come on. Do you really think my mother blames us for not having children the first year? She was just anxious to have a grandchild from us. And I'm sure she didn't mean to be insulting about your figure. She was probably just trying to be reassuring."

Immediately, Shmuel realized that he had made a mistake in trying to play peacemaker. Chavi clutched the edge of the table, as if trying to forcibly keep herself seated. Her voice rose as she answered, "You don't understand. She didn't mean her comments innocently. I'm not basing my assessment on these comments alone. She's always insulting me covertly. I don't even like being near her anymore. She constantly makes me feel like I don't measure up to her standards. 'Chavi, I know a great *sheitel macher* who could do wonders with your *sheitel.*' 'Chavi, I have a fabulous frosting recipe that would really enhance the flavor of the cake you sent us.' 'That outfit reminds me of something I used to have ten years ago.'

"I could go on. I can never act insulted because, after all, she didn't insult me. What's wrong with suggesting a *sheitel macher*, swapping recipes, or talking about her old clothes? Don't you see what I'm saying?"

Shmuel realized that he had best convince Chavi that he saw her point — if not she might explode. "Certainly I see what you're saying," he said soothingly. "But do you really think that my mother doesn't like you? If she doesn't, why would she invite us over at every possible opportunity? Don't you see how generous my parents are to us? Take the bris as a case in point."

"The bris could have been a gift to you and the baby, and only coincidentally to me," Chavi pointed out. But her mother-in-law did often "pick up a little something" that she thought Chavi would like. It was true, they were very giving people.

"Maybe my mother just has a way of expressing herself that rubs you the wrong way," Shmuel suggested. "I know she has a hard time talking to her children's spouses. Her relationship with her first son-in-law, Ruchie's husband, got off to such a rocky start that sarcasm and self-defense just became entrenched in her personality. Part of what you're describing is the normal style of speech in her social circles, but I think part of it is like spiked armor that she wears to protect herself from attack. My mother is very sensitive — maybe she's afraid to speak in a more direct and neutral manner."

Chavi laughed sarcastically. "I've never insulted your mother. I have always been very nice. She has no reason to be scared of me hurting her."

But then she wondered. She had never been rude to her mother-in-law, but if Mrs. Rosenberg really did have a complex, especially with her children's spouses, maybe Chavi hadn't been kind enough. Maybe the barriers between them would fall a bit if Chavi went out of her way to be extra loving and gentle.

There was no way she would try it now. She was too angry. But maybe, although she doubted it, she would try it in the future. Her doubt stemmed from knowing that one comment from her mother-in-law would make her see red and toss her good intentions out the window. But Shmuel had given her food for thought.

Shmuel saw Chavi had grown pensive and knew he had made inroads in her thought process. Letting her thoughts settle and develop further on their own, he delicately changed the subject.

9

Soon enough, Chavi's maternity leave was over. It had been a glorious three months at home. She loved leaving the house at her leisure in the morning, proudly pushing her baby in the stroller as she shopped and ran errands. She loved having time to try new recipes, to get to her mending pile and other such domestic tasks that were always put on the back burner when she worked. Shmuel also enjoyed the relaxed atmosphere at home. No morning hustle and bustle. He got real meals and didn't have to help his exhausted wife clear the table. Although the baby didn't sleep through the night yet, Chavi was free to nap when Yitzchak did. She enjoyed the first vacation from work that she had since her marriage. But all good things must come to an end, and this was no exception.

She was greeted warmly when she returned to the office, her outgoing personality and problem-solving skills having become valued assets at her company. After a round of hellos, she buckled right back down to work, and soon it felt like she had never left.

She had brought lunch with her that day and decided to eat at her desk. As she was eating, Yair Katz, one of her co-workers, came over to speak to her.

Yair, a tall, muscular man who sported a goatee, was in his early thirties. He often visited Chavi at work. At first Chavi had been worried about a lack of modesty, but she soon realized that Yair never spoke to her for more than two or three minutes and the conversation generally focused on understanding a point in religion or religious culture. Often the questions were smacked with antireligious bias or based on complete ignorance, but Chavi, after consulting with Shmuel, decided to answer his questions to the best of her ability.

Yair and his wife, Nava, had been among the few representatives from her office to attend the bris. "*Mazal tov!*" he greeted her now, giving her a gift, a small light-blue sweater that his wife had knitted for Yitzchak. "I knew you would be coming back soon, so this has been in my desk since it was finished, waiting for your return."

"It's adorable — and beautiful," Chavi exclaimed, fingering the soft yarn. "It means so much to have something homemade."

She could see he was pleased with her reaction. He asked Chavi how she was feeling and how the baby was doing. She answered positively. Then there was a pause.

Chavi could see that something was on Yair's mind. She asked him if he wanted to sit down. Yair sat, but still he said nothing. Chavi asked if something was bothering him.

"No, nothing really. I mean, well, one of our neighbors started keeping Shabbat a few weeks ago. We used to go to soccer games every weekend, and now he won't go anymore.

I asked him what happened and he told me that he attended a seminar that got him thinking a little.

"There is a religious *beit knesset* in our neighborhood and my friend decided to see what it was like. After the prayers on Friday night, a number of people came over and introduced themselves, and one invited him to a Shabbat meal at his house. He accepted right away. He enjoyed himself so much that he went back a few times, and the rest, as they say, is history.

"I'm telling you this because, besides the secretary here, I don't really know anyone religious. So I just wanted to ask if you could explain how anyone could like Shabbat. The whole thing seems dreadful to me."

"Why don't you find out for yourself?" Chavi asked impulsively. "You and Nava can come to us for Shabbos."

Yair looked as if a snake had bitten him. "Uh, no, thank you. I'm not interested in being religious. I was just curious. Forget it." He got up quickly and walked away.

Chavi regretted the lost opportunity, but she was glad that he had refused the offer. As soon as the words had slipped out of her mouth, she realized she had made a mistake by not consulting with Shmuel first. Thankfully, it didn't matter now.

Much to her surprise, Yair came over to her desk again two days later. "Uh, Chavi, I mentioned your invitation for Shabbat, in passing, to my wife, and Nava got all excited about the idea. She wants to come. We don't want to be religious, you know — just want to see what it's like for a day."

Chavi gulped, but she smiled widely and told him, "I'm delighted that you've changed your mind. What week do you want to come?"

"This week is perfect," Yair said, seemingly oblivious to the fact that it was already Wednesday.

The rest of Chavi's work day went by in a daze. How was she going to explain to Shmuel that she had invited an irreligious man and his wife to their house for Shabbos without asking him? She was so apprehensive about Shmuel's reaction that she didn't even worry about how the Shabbos would work out.

As soon as Shmuel walked in the door that night, she ran to meet him. "I've done something horrible! I only hope you will be able to forgive me!"

Shmuel, seeing tears running down her cheeks, immediately became very worried. "What happened? Is everything okay? Where is Yitzchak?"

"No, nothing like that. Everything is fine," Chavi said. Not being one who could suppress her feelings until the moment was opportune, she blurted out the whole story without pause for breath.

"Great. It'll be interesting. I just wish you'd ask me first next time," was Shmuel's calm response. Chavi was floored. How wonderful of him to be so forgiving and willing to host a strange couple who was so different from them. She couldn't help but wonder if her overly dramatic tendencies had helped soften the blow. Perhaps his relief that no one was in danger made him more magnanimous.

ෆ ෆ

Chavi spent the next two days preparing the most gourmet dishes she could manage and polishing the house from top to bottom. She wondered what the Katzes would think of her neighborhood, her apartment, and, most importantly,

Shmuel. She wasn't as worried about how they would react to Shabbos. Shabbos had so much attraction that she didn't have to be apprehensive about it.

Fifteen minutes before candle-lighting time, the Katzes arrived at an uncharacteristically calm Rosenberg house. Yitzchak, bathed and dressed, was playing peacefully on the floor. The house smelled of Shabbos delicacies, and the table was already laid with the Rosenbergs' Shabbos finest.

Nava was holding a bouquet of flowers. As Chavi invited the couple in, she caught a glimpse of Shmuel whisking the flowers he had bought her off the table and into their bedroom so as not to lessen the importance of the Katzes' gift. *How thoughtful of him*, she remarked to herself.

The Katzes were more or less appropriately dressed. Yair was even sporting a *kippah*. He had been worried about what they should wear, and Chavi had explained the norms in the neighborhood to him the day before.

After showing the Katzes their room and getting them settled, Chavi went to light the candles. She asked Nava, "Do you also want to light Shabbos candles?"

Nava glanced nervously at her husband. "Um, what does that entail?"

"You just light two candles and say a blessing. They symbolize the extra light and harmony that Shabbos brings into the home," Chavi explained. "But there's no need to do it if you feel uncomfortable. I can light for you."

"That's okay. I think I would like to try."

While Chavi went to retrieve an extra pair of candlesticks from her breakfront, Nava left the room and returned a minute later with a white lace kerchief on her head, much to Chavi's surprise. She followed Chavi's lead in the lighting procedure.

After they wished each other and their husbands a Shabbat shalom, Nava asked, "Why did you light three candles instead of the two you gave me?"

"There is a tradition to light one candle for each member of the household to symbolize how each individual brings his own light into the world."

Nava stared in silence at the candles for a moment. Chavi wondered what she was thinking. Her thoughts were interrupted by Shmuel inviting Yair to shul.

Soon Chavi and Nava were left alone. They chatted comfortably about their family backgrounds, enjoying one another's company. Nava had come from a traditional family, but after her father's death when she was nine years old her mother had slowly let their religious practices slip. When Nava married Yair, the break from religion became complete. Nava and Yair were both in their early thirties and had been married for nine years. Nava worked as a real-estate broker, work that she found interesting and enjoyable.

The men came back from shul, and Chavi hurried to put the finishing touches on the table. She overheard Nava asking Yair how the experience had been.

"It was nothing like what I expected," he told her in an undertone which carried clearly to Chavi's ears. "Chaotic and at the same time warm and inviting. The prayers were loud and unregimented most of the time — it even seemed like people were saying different prayers. After the services, Shmuel introduced me to a number of people, including the rabbi, and they were all very friendly."

Both couples enjoyed the Shabbos meal that followed. Chavi's food all came out wonderful, except for one dish, a fancy vegetable casserole, which had an otherworldly green color and an original scent. No one ate it, but at least it provided some comic relief. The conversation, although serious, was peppered with laughter. The Katzes asked one question after another about the culture and mind-set of religious people. When Shmuel taught Yair a Friday-night *zemer*, Chavi was relieved that Nava did not try to join in or ask her why she wasn't singing.

After the meal, the two couples, and Yitzchak, went on a walk together to enjoy the crisp night air and the serene atmosphere that enveloped the Rosenbergs' neighborhood on Shabbos. Chavi could see that the Katzes were aware of the peacefulness, as they both spoke in lower voices than they had during the meal.

At one point, Yair and Shmuel, deep in conversation about the political situation in Israel, pulled ahead of the women. Nava used the opportunity to compliment Chavi. "You have such a wonderful husband, Chavi. He is so intelligent, warm, and gentle, and I see that you are treated well. During the meal, he kept making sure you had what you needed and complimented you sincerely on both the food and your comments.

"I hope my remarks aren't inappropriate. It's just that sometimes people don't fully appreciate what they have, and when someone points it out to them they take note. Your husband is really something special."

Chavi blushed in the darkness and thanked Nava for her kind words. Inside, she wondered if those words had been sent to her directly from heaven. She knew she tended to be harsh with Shmuel. Even though they had a close, caring relationship, she didn't allow Shmuel to feel unconditionally accepted by her. She often wondered if she just wasn't passing on her full acceptance or deep down she really didn't fully accept him. Nava was right — she was blessed with a special partner. Chavi committed herself to focusing on his good points and allowing him to know that she accepted him, even with his faults.

ꟸ ꟸ

Shabbos day was restful. Yair seemed to enjoy the *cholent*, which he said he had never tasted before. Both he and his wife became a bit antsy in the afternoon, but Chavi brought out some picture albums and a chess set Gitty had given her when she broke up her house, and between the two the problem was solved.

Nava delighted in holding and caring for Yitzchak and even watched him so his parents could sleep. As they waited for the men to come home from *maariv*, she admitted to Chavi that the day had seemed long to her, but in a certain sense she hated to see it end.

After Shmuel recited Havdallah, Yair commented, "This blessing and its reference to the non-Jewish world seems so harsh and cruel — 'He who separates between holy and profane, between light and dark, between Israel and the nations...' "

"Do you really think so?" Shmuel asked. "Perhaps look a little more deeply into the words and you'll come to a different conclusion."

Yair seemed satisfied with this answer, which respected his ability to think. "Is the blessing saying that the difference between Jews and non-Jews is the difference between light and dark?" he asked, thinking aloud. "That non-Jews are profane? It seems racist. Are the Jews different than any other nation? The whole world seems to think so. What's the difference between them?"

"Think about it some more," Shmuel said encouragingly.

While the men were talking, Nava and Chavi cleared the table. Chavi thought of sending some of the leftovers home with the Katzes, since she knew it would give them a warm feeling. She decided against it, though, because she knew they wouldn't make blessings over the food.

The Katzes left shortly afterwards, and the Rosenbergs began cleaning up. Shmuel swept while Chavi started the dishes.

When Shmuel came to sweep the kitchen, Chavi asked him if he had enjoyed Shabbos.

"Yes, it was nice. It was a bit hard to be on display all the time, but they were pleasant company. I'm glad we had them."

"So am I," Chavi said. "Nava was very impressed with you — she told me that you're really something special. And I was quite impressed with your skill in leading the conversation."

Shmuel gave her a surprised but gratified smile.

"Why didn't you answer Yair's question about Havdallah?" Chavi asked.

"I didn't think he was ready to hear that the Jews are the moral leaders of the world or that we are the chosen nation. Also, I think he'll gain something from thinking the issue through on his own, developing a thesis, and questioning further to see if it is right."

Interesting, thought Chavi.

10

It was hard to believe Yitzchak was two years old already. He was an adorable child, with thick deep brown hair that cascaded past his shoulders in waves and large round eyes the color of honey. A fearless and energetic toddler, he always had a full-toothed smile for everyone.

Chavi had adjusted to the more challenging parts of young motherhood by that point. She had learned that it wasn't necessary to sleep through the night to function the next day. It wasn't necessary to sit through a whole meal every day in order not to starve. It wasn't even necessary to see the bottom of the kitchen sinks in order to have a happy and productive life. She did her best to keep on top of everything and to be cheerful to boot, but her new pregnancy made managing all she needed to do more challenging than ever.

Yet Chavi delighted in her role. She enjoyed Yitzchak's antics and often found herself laughing aloud as she watched him. She knew he was bright and that he understood her when she spoke to him, even though he had only recently begun to speak.

Chavi was delighted when he said his first word. She hoped it meant that her worry that he had a problem was unfounded and that it would bring an end to the temper tantrums that came when she misinterpreted his hand motions and charades. Still, his vocabulary remained very limited, and they continued to play guessing games. Yitzchak stuttered terribly and it took a while for him to get words out. This was very frustrating, not only for the listener, but also for Yitzchak himself.

Whenever Chavi brought up her concern to Shmuel, he would remind her that Yitzchak was only a baby and that boys generally begin to speak later than girls do. Desperate to believe that Yitzchak didn't have a problem, Chavi allowed herself to be consoled by Shmuel's words. Deep inside, though, she knew something wasn't the way it should be.

At first, Chavi's mother also tried to assure her that all was well, but her assurances stemmed more from her need to make things right for Chavi than from any real knowledge of the situation. When Chavi insisted that something was wrong, Mrs. Baumel suggested that she take him to a professional to be tested, so that she could put her mind at ease.

It took a good deal of energy for Chavi to find out which type of doctor one went to under such circumstances. But then, everything seemed to take a good deal of energy these days. Chavi didn't suffer very much when she was pregnant, except for a deep, inner fatigue that no amount of sleep could relieve. Her day at work was enough to wipe her out. And, of course, her job wasn't all she had to worry about; she also had her housekeeping and cooking and, most important, caring for her son. Added to her list of things to be done she had finding out if Yitzchak had a problem.

She began by visiting their pediatrician, who referred her to a clinic specializing in children's speech. Then she called a man who knew which doctors were the best in their fields to find out which doctor at the clinic she should speak to. Finally, the long-awaited appointment arrived.

Chavi felt nervous about going to the doctor alone. Although she was proficient enough in Hebrew to converse with and understand the doctor, she was worried that she would need moral support if the news was bad. She was very tempted to ask Shmuel to come with her, but that would mean making him miss time from yeshivah, which was out of the question. She thought of asking her mother to go with her, but her mother's love of her children and grandchildren sometimes made her pushy and a bit abrasive with doctors. Chavi didn't want to risk a personality clash between her mother and the doctor when she felt so dependent on the doctor's abilities.

Asking her mother-in-law to go was worst of all. Chavi was scared to even admit to her that Yitzchak might have a problem. Her mother-in-law might feel humiliated at having an imperfect grandson and take out her negative feelings on the grandchild himself by lowering his favored status. Chavi often found herself answering questions that her mother-in-law directed to Yitzchak so that she wouldn't hear his stutter. This was definitely one trip Chavi wasn't going to invite her to participate in.

The whole issue was too personal and laden with emotion for Chavi to ask any non–family member to come. When the day arrived, she went alone.

The clinic was housed in a modern white building in one of the more suburban neighborhoods of Jerusalem. Chavi found it easily enough with the clear directions the receptionist had given her over the phone. Flowers and greenery surrounded the building. It was a warm day, and the bright sun accentuated the clear blue sky and the flowers. The scene had an almost provincial look to it. Before Chavi opened the heavy front door, she murmured a prayer that the visit would go smoothly and bring results that would benefit her son.

Inside, the office was clean and modern but sparsely furnished. Chavi saw a receptionist's desk with three large file cabinets behind it. Around the periphery of the room were black, imitation-leather chairs with metal frames. Two plants were placed in opposite corners, and a few children's toys and books sat on an end table. The room was empty except for a few patients waiting their turns.

After checking with the receptionist, Chavi learned that her doctor, Dr. Ben-Eliyahu, was on the upper floor. Chavi and Yitzchak climbed up the stairs to a floor almost identical to the one below it and sat down to wait. Together, they looked at a picture book she had brought with them and shared a sandwich bag of pretzels.

After about twenty minutes of waiting, their name was called. The speech specialist, Dr. Ben-Eliyahu, was a tall woman in her early fifties. Her short brown hair, large glasses hanging from a chain around her neck, beige skirt and brown blouse, and white lab coat gave her a stern impression, but once she began to interact with Yitzchak, Chavi saw that she was kindly and was impressed with her professional manner. She wasn't stern, just serious.

The appointment lasted over half an hour. Yitzchak was shy in the beginning, but he warmed up after he saw the toys and crayons that the doctor wanted him to play with. After the testing was done, Dr. Ben-Eliyahu and Chavi sat at the desk to discuss the doctor's conclusions while Yitzchak continued to play with the toys.

"Some of your son's cognitive and motor skills are underdeveloped for a boy his age," the doctor began. She explained the reasons for her diagnosis, giving examples from the way Yitzchak had played with her. At Chavi's look of confusion and fear, she continued, "He's still very young and there may be no life-long ramifications from the fact that his skills aren't developed for his age. However, I recommend that you give him therapy twice a week for at least the next year, which would include complementary exercises at home."

"What type of therapy?" Chavi asked, determined to remain calm in front of the doctor.

They discussed the various possibilities for several minutes. Then, summoning up all her courage, Chavi asked, "What are the possible long-term effects?"

"He may have some learning disabilities and the stutter might worsen," Dr. Ben-Eliyahu explained matter-of-factly. "But there is no need to worry at this point. Yitzchak is still a baby and chances are good that everything will pass with time."

This reassurance did little to allay Chavi's fear. On the one hand, she was relieved that the nebulous problem she had sensed but couldn't define was identified and that there was a possibility that it would be temporary. But on the other hand, now she actually knew that there was a problem and all her hopes that she had been wrong about her normal little boy had evaporated. She was on the verge of tears when she left the doctor's office.

Even though she always cried easily when she was pregnant, she was upset with herself for taking the news so hard. After all, he was still a perfect child. At most he had some learning disabilities and a stutter. There were people with bigger handicaps and bigger problems — much bigger problems. But, still, she needed to adjust her utopian dreams once again to reality.

She knew the news would make Shmuel nervous. Everything about the baby made Shmuel nervous. If he coughed a bit too hard, Shmuel worried he was choking. If Chavi let him climb, Shmuel worried that he would fall. Remembering how Shmuel was afraid he would break Yitzchak if he held him the wrong way when he was a newborn, Chavi smiled to herself.

There was a benefit to Shmuel's nervousness, besides encouraging a higher level of safety precautions in the house. Shmuel's weakness brought out a strength in Chavi in situations where she might have also lost her cool if there was someone else to take the role of level-headed decision maker. Chavi thought of the time that Yitzchak bumped his chin on the corner of their desk. When Shmuel saw the blood streaming from Yitzchak's chin, he panicked. Chavi, who had always felt squeamish in the presence of blood, took command of the situation. She cleaned the wound, applied pressure, and took Yitzchak for medical help. By the time they returned home after getting Yitzchak stitched up, a much calmer and very grateful man greeted them.

Chavi felt good that she was able to meet that sort of parental challenge. But a diagnosed disability was different. She wondered how she was going to fit therapy and exercises into her schedule, even though she felt selfish worrying about herself when she should be focusing on her son. Her current biggest fantasy was just to have a little bit more sleep. Her ever-present fatigue, in addition to a full-time job, toddler son, husband, and housework, made her feel sometimes that she was running on a treadmill set a bit too fast. There was the constant feeling that she had to push herself more than comfortably just to keep from slipping backwards.

Even just an hour of speech therapy would entail preparations for the visit, transportation, and waiting time. It would all add up to well over two and a half hours, she imagined. And what type of exercises would they need to do? Would Yitzchak cooperate, or would she have to spend time convincing a contrary son to do the necessary exertion involved in completing the exercises? The one thing she knew for certain was that the worry was going to be worse than the actual therapy. But worrying over the future was one of the things that she felt powerless over.

The ride home with Yitzchak was quieter than the way to the doctor had been. They had taken a taxi to the clinic, enjoying the ride and pointing out the different sights of interest that they passed. But Chavi opted for a bus ride home. There was no point in rushing home to explain to Shmuel and her mother what the doctor had said and begin life with the new issue of her son's problem. She sat silently with Yitzchak on her lap as the bus took them home.

ഉ ഉ

It was late afternoon when they got home and Shmuel was out. Rather than call her mother, whom she knew was anxiously waiting news to hear about her visit, Chavi sat down on the couch and read Yitzchak a book. As she read, she cuddled him tightly, as if trying to protect him from the world he would have to contend with.

By the time Shmuel came home, Chavi had gotten Yitzchak bathed and into bed and had supper warming on the stove. She had gone over in her mind what she would say and how she would say it to this man who cared so deeply for his son. But when Shmuel came in, tears began rolling down her cheeks before they had even said hello to each other. *So much for bravery*, she thought, feeling foolish but at the same time glad to have someone to comfort her.

They spoke over dinner, each reminding the other that everything was determined by the One Above and was for the best. They discussed the practical steps they needed to take. Once the technical issues were enumerated and defined, the situation became easier to deal with.

After the meal, Chavi and Shmuel took turns calling their parents. Mrs. Baumel was shocked at first, but recovered quickly enough. She asked for all the details, commiserated with Chavi, and then offered her help. Chavi thanked her and hung up, feeling unsure about what her mother's real emotional reaction to the news was.

As to Mrs. Rosenberg's reaction, there was no room for doubt. She was angry. First she was angry with the doctor and her obvious misdiagnosis of Yitzchak's condition. Mrs. Rosenberg knew her grandson was simply a late bloomer, and she had barely noticed a stutter. She insisted that they go to a "real" doctor for a second opinion, and she would finance the appointment.

After Shmuel reiterated the doctor's credentials and the warm recommendations they had received from different medical sources, Mrs. Rosenberg's attack on the doctor toned down, but her anger didn't. Although it wasn't directed at

Shmuel or Chavi or Yitzchak, it was clear that the situation was to her dissatisfaction. When Shmuel brought the conversation to an end, he heard in his imagination the yelling that was taking place at his parents' home as his mother related the news to her husband, and then to her daughters, and then over the phone to her married daughters and her siblings.

After the calls were made, Shmuel and Chavi decided to cut their nightly activities short and go to sleep early. They each stopped in Yitzchak's room before retiring to kiss his cheek.

11

Yitzchak's first speech therapy session was only two days after the original diagnostic appointment. The speech clinic was two buses away, a trip that took nearly an hour, but, according to Chavi's calculations, it would have cost her a small fortune in taxi fare.

She waited outside while Yitzchak met with the speech therapist for an hour. For the first half-hour, she said *Tehillim* for the success of the treatment. When she could no longer summon up the strength for concentration, she leafed through a decorating magazine that was on the table in the waiting room.

Yitzchak came out happy but tired. Chavi did her best to keep him awake on the bus ride home, knowing that a small nap would keep him up for hours past his bedtime. She needed to go to sleep as early as possible lately, and the thought of a long night with Yitzchak terrified her. She tickled him and talked to him and stood him up on her lap, all the while explaining to him aloud that if he slept now he wouldn't sleep at night. The explanation was mostly for the benefit of the other passengers on the bus, who probably thought that she was cruel not to let a tired child rest. Finally, though, her maternal soft side took over, and she let him nap on her shoulder. She blocked out the thoughts of what the night would bring and enjoyed his warmth and softness as she stroked his head.

She came home more exhausted than usual, if such a thing was possible. After getting Yitzchak settled with some toys, she ran to put together supper for Shmuel and then began the straightening up that she hadn't managed between work and leaving for the appointment.

Chavi was just about done tidying up when Shmuel walked in. She felt disappointed that he had come a minute too early, especially since she knew that whatever didn't get done in honor of his arrival was not going to get done that evening. She hadn't even attempted to put Yitzchak to sleep, and he was delighted to see Shmuel. They usually only spent a few minutes together after Yitzchak was in bed, so tonight was special to him.

A similar scene repeated itself the next evening when Chavi and Yitzchak came home from the specialist who was to help him develop the weaker areas in his brain that were not directly related to his speech. This doctor often worked together with the speech therapist. Chavi's schedule included two sessions of speech therapy and one with the learning specialist each week.

After the second speech therapy session of the week, Chavi managed to keep Yitzchak awake during the ride home. She put him to bed as soon as they came home and prepared dinner, then sank onto the couch and closed her eyes to avoid seeing the mess all around her. Toys were scattered everywhere, mixed with pretzel crumbs. Dirty dishes had overflowed to the counters. The floor in the entrance hall was sticky and black from a juice spill that had been only superficially cleaned up. A half-eaten sandwich lay on one of the chairs.

Chavi tried to remind herself that an hour and a half of cleaning was all the mess required. It was just one of those everyday messes. But even as she told herself intellectually that she was blowing the mess out of proportion, she found herself crying once again in a mixture of depression and self-pity.

Why had she chosen this lifestyle anyway? Maybe it was time to move back to America. Shmuel could get a job — his brother-in-law had given him a standing offer to join his business. She wouldn't have to work. She could have a car to drive Yitzchak to his appointments. She could live in a house and probably allow herself cleaning help.

She let the tranquility of her reverie take over as she pictured herself shopping in an air-conditioned supermarket, loading the groceries into her trunk, and driving home, with her favorite tape playing in the tape deck, to her two-story house. She would do laundry in her laundry room instead of sorting it in the hall, in full view of anyone who came to the door. She would buy the convenience foods she had loved as a child and share their delight with her children. The mornings would be free for her children — they could do projects, go to the park or the zoo, enjoy each other's company. A blissfully restful feeling overtook her horror at neglecting her obligations.

Often when things got rough, she would daydream of life in America. She knew she shouldn't picture it as a utopia, and that life in the United States wasn't simple, but physically it was easier. She used her fantasy life in America as a mental escape when life overwhelmed her.

This time, she thought, *it's not a fantasy anymore. I've had enough. It's too much for me.* Shmuel had already been learning for a few years anyway. She knew that was more than some of the girls he dated were interested in to begin with. She wasn't stealing away his learning; he wouldn't have even gotten this far without her.

Justifying her decision to change their lifestyle, she thought about how Shmuel would continue to learn at night after he went to work. He wasted so much time as it was in yeshivah. He often shared with her how he struggled just to remain in the yeshivah building, let alone actually learn. He wasn't the scholarly type, he had explained so many times. Why did Chavi have to force this on him when it seemed that it wasn't what God had intended for him?

Lost in her thoughts, Chavi got up to straighten the room. Knowing that the situation was going to be over soon gave her the strength to do what she had to. When Shmuel came home, she explained patiently to him that it was time for him to go to work and they would be moving to the States at the end of the *zeman.*

Shmuel looked confused and hurt, but automatically agreed. "Well, if that's what you want, then I guess that's what we need to do."

Chavi was taken aback at his immediate acquiescence. It angered her. Why should she be angry? He was just doing what she asked. But it strengthened Chavi's fear that he was only learning because it was important to her and not because he wanted to on his own.

In her anger, she announced in the middle of dinner, "I'm suddenly kind of tired. I'm going to bed now."

She forcefully pushed her chair away from the table and exaggerated her movements as she prepared for sleep to leave no room for doubt that she was upset.

Shmuel, confused, wondered why she was angry, but he put the issue on the back burner to deal with more pressing emotions. He chided himself for having allowed himself to fall prey to Chavi's youthful enthusiasm. He had begun to believe that he would be able to realize his dream of being a true *talmid chacham*, and he had been a fool. Truly, he was no better than everyone had told him he was. He was nearing thirty, and he still found it so hard to sit and learn for an hour straight. Chavi was right. There was no reason for her to struggle for someone like him.

He would call his brother-in-law the next day to see what was available. There was no way he could make the call that night. He was surprised at the depth of his depression. He had known this day would come inevitably. But now his dreams had been destroyed, testimony to how wrong he had been to dream them in the first place.

Chavi lay in bed, unable to fall asleep. She knew she had gotten carried away in her fatigue. There was no way she was going to give up her future. Every word that Shmuel learned meant more to her than diamonds, certainly more than a laundry room. It might be true that Shmuel only learned a few hours a day when more serious men were able to learn twelve hours a day or more, but those few hours were more precious than anything else. Even if he could only learn one minute more a day than he would while he was working, it would be worth her effort.

Perhaps there were even working men who were able squeeze in the same amount of time that Shmuel learned into their daily schedule, but Shmuel wasn't that type. She had to admit to herself that if he left yeshivah, his learning time would probably fall close to nonexistent. She also knew how important it was for a person to be in yeshivah. Even if Shmuel was just talking to his friends there, the atmosphere was one of Torah and was helping to shape her husband into a true *ben Torah*.

No, she would never be able to bear it if her husband left yeshivah. She had known she was speaking senselessly even as she spoke, although the release of her frustration felt good. Shmuel presumably understood that her announcement was just caused by one of her frequent mood swings. Peacefully, she fell asleep.

ꟸ ꟸ

When Chavi awoke in the morning, Shmuel told her that when it was a decent hour in New York he would call his brother-in-law.

"What are you talking about?" Chavi asked.

Again, Shmuel was confused by this woman that he was supposed to know so well. "Didn't you say I should do that last night?"

"Oh, my. You didn't really think I was serious, did you? I would never, ever want you to leave yeshivah. I was just tired, that's all."

Now completely confounded but deliriously happy, Shmuel continued with his morning routine and left to shul.

Was he serious? Chavi asked herself as she continued her morning preparations.

In a few hours she had put the incident out of her head. Shmuel, too, had forgotten about it by the time he came home that evening.

12

Faigy was born four months later. She was delivered three weeks early, but both mother and baby were fine. Not expecting to give birth early, as she had been overdue with Yitzchak, Chavi had scheduled Yair and Nava as her Shabbos guests for the week before she was due, which turned out to be two weeks after Faigy was born.

Of course, Yair and Nava tried to cancel as soon as they heard the good news, but Chavi wouldn't let them. This was the first time they had asked to come back since their first Shabbos together, and Chavi didn't want to lose the opportunity. She assured them that most of the food would be bought, so there was not going to be much work involved. After a good deal of pressure from the Rosenbergs, the Katzes agreed to come.

When Chavi shared the news of her expected company and her reservations about having guests so soon after birth with Gitty over the phone, Gitty offered to come for Shabbos and help. Although Gitty had first said her stay in Eretz

Yisrael would be only temporary, until the end of the school year, she had found it still too uncomfortable to return to New York and her familiar social setting. Also, her younger sister Esti had started dating, and Gitty thought it prudent to stay off the scene; a divorced sister would not help Esti's *shidduch* prospects.

Gitty had found a job as a secretary in a law office, and she often spent Shabbos either with Mrs. Baumel or with the Rosenbergs. She and Chavi felt very comfortable together, but Chavi wondered how Gitty would get along with this irreligious couple.

Worst comes to worst, she thought, *Gitty will be quiet, as she gets when she's uncomfortable.* Yitzchak loved Gitty, and she could also relieve Chavi of her hosting duties when Chavi had to rest or feed the baby. After consulting with Shmuel, who thought it was very nice of Gitty to offer and didn't see any reason to worry about the dynamics between the guests, Chavi accepted Gitty's proposition.

Gitty arrived early on Friday afternoon. Chavi was glad to see her. She had planned a simple Shabbos menu and divided the jobs among herself, her husband, and her friend.

After sending Shmuel to a nearby take-out caterer for challah, potato kugel, noodle kugel, chopped liver, coleslaw, and cake, Chavi began to prepare a soup, a fresh salad, *cholent,* a ready-made fish loaf, and a simple chicken recipe. Gitty took Yitzchak out to the neighborhood supermarket for a container of pareve ice cream and some drinks and snacks. Once the food was taken care of, Chavi went to bathe and feed the baby, while Gitty took kitchen duty. Shmuel straightened up the toys with Yitzchak's help and then washed the floors while Yitzchak read a book on the couch.

Chavi enjoyed the serene atmosphere as she gently washed Faigy in the bath. She heard Yitzchak and Shmuel laughing as they worked together and Gitty's tape playing in the kitchen and smelled the soup emitting its familiar Shabbos aroma. Everything seemed so perfect.

Chavi was glad she had told the Katzes to come for Shabbos. Her mother, her mother-in-law, and a couple of neighbors who had stopped by to offer their assistance had made it very clear that they felt Chavi was being irrational, but her heart told her she was doing the right thing. She was extremely grateful to Gitty. Besides helping with shopping and cleaning, she had a way with Yitzchak and was often able to calm him down when Chavi had given up.

If only they could find her someone. All of Chavi's constant reminders to Shmuel to ask around and all of her calls to various friends hadn't turned up anything particularly promising. She was afraid to bring up the suggestions she heard to Gitty — Gitty would feel insulted by the offers. She wouldn't want to marry a man fifteen years her senior with six children, who was the closest thing in personality and culture that had come up. Gitty hadn't even dated once in the almost five years since her divorce. Chavi knew this upset her friend, who had hinted once or twice that she was irritated that Chavi and Shmuel hadn't set her up. If only she knew how hard they tried!

Soon the baby was tired of her bath. Chavi lifted her out and wrapped her in a towel. As she was carrying her precious bundle to the bedroom to dress her, she heard Yitzchak trying to tell Shmuel something about his toys. Every sentence took so long sometimes. Yitzchak was excited from their game, which made speaking all the more painstaking. Chavi could feel Yitzchak's immense frustration at not being able to express himself. She listened to Shmuel patiently waiting for Yitzchak to finish.

Yitzchak wanted his red toy truck to go in the box of match cars, but Shmuel didn't understand what he was trying to say. The situation became tenser as Yitzchak tried again. Chavi was tempted to call to Shmuel and explain, ending her husband and son's misery. Then she thought better of it and decided to let them handle it on their own. She dressed Faigy in the children's bedroom and went to her own bedroom to relax while she fed her.

She heard the doorbell ring and the muffled sounds of the Katzes being welcomed by Shmuel. It took effort to get up, but she thought it was appropriate to say hello. After the introductions were made, Gitty brought out some cake. Then Shmuel took the Katzes to the apartment where they would be staying. By the time they got back, it was time for Shabbos to begin.

There was a lot to catch up on. When the men went out to shul, Nava told Chavi and Gitty that she and her husband had attended a seminar geared toward irreligious Israelis, similar to the one that their neighbor had gone to.

"Both Yair and I were very impressed with the content of the lectures," she said. "The seminar made us seriously rethink our attitude toward religion. Now, although I can't say I feel compelled to become religious, we've agreed to host a weekly learning group in our home, sponsored by the organization that arranged the seminar. The learning group is really terrific. I feel like my mind is going to burst sometimes from all the new information and esoteric concepts being thrown at me."

Chavi smiled. "When I was in seminary, I felt like that sometimes, too. But isn't it exciting to have your mind stretched?"

Nava nodded eagerly. "I really look forward to Tuesday night each week. We've developed a close relationship with the rabbi who gives the class and his wife. Believe it or not, we've even begun to keep kosher at home, and we decided not to drive or watch television on Shabbat to create a Jewish atmosphere in our home life." Quite openly, Nava continued, "We've recently begun to keep the laws of family purity. The rabbi's wife suggested it — she says that their merit might bring us the blessing of children."

Chavi saw Gitty smoothing her skirt out in a decidedly uneasy manner, so when Nava began to ask Gitty about her personal life in an attempt at friendliness, Chavi made sure to change the subject.

Yitzchak, who had been playing on the porch in his pajamas, came in after a while and jumped on Chavi's lap. He looked suspiciously at Nava, who was cradling his new baby sister, and then turned back to Chavi, perhaps glad that someone else was dealing with the baby for once. "Mommy, I saw a big...a big t-t-t-...." The unfamiliar word escaped him.

"What's wrong with him? Why does he speak like that?" Nava asked curiously.

Chavi hoped her son hadn't understood the question, which had been posed in Hebrew. He was self-conscious enough of the way he spoke. Didn't Nava consider the fact that she might hurt the child's feelings? But then, Chavi had encountered this often enough before. Many people would unabashedly say things in front of Yitzchak that they wouldn't dream of saying to or about an adult, assuming, often incorrectly, that he didn't understand. "He's a bit late in his speech development, but he'll be fine when he gets older." Glancing down at Yitzchak, she added, "I'd rather not discuss it further right now." Nava got the hint and let the conversation drop.

With the men's arrival home, the night meal began. Yair asked if he could make his own Kiddush, in an attempt to show off his newly developed skill. The conversation during the meal flowed smoothly. The Katzes had less questions than they had the first time. It seemed that many of their questions were answered as a result of their contact with religious people through the seminar and their learning group. They did ask how Shmuel and Chavi managed with two children, but Chavi admitted that she didn't have much to say, as she had only recently become the mother of a twosome.

ဆ ဆ

The next afternoon, Chavi and Gitty took the children outdoors while the other adults napped. Chavi enjoyed the attention she got as the mother of a newborn and gratefully accepted her neighbors' *mazal tov* wishes. She happily noted how much more comfortable she was outside now that she had children. She fit in with the other mothers and no longer felt like she was trespassing on private property.

Remembering how much she had appreciated being included in the conversation when she was new to the block, she took care to introduce Gitty to everyone who stopped to wish her *mazal tov* and see the new baby. Soon a number of women were chatting around the bench where Chavi and Gitty sat. The topic turned to Shabbos menus and desserts, and Gitty proudly described a fabulous cake with six layers, two fillings, and a crown of caramel that she had recently made.

One of the women commented, "I can tell you don't have kids. I could never make a cake like that at this point in my life."

Chavi froze. How painful that comment must be to Gitty! She knew Gitty longed for children. Hoping to save the situation, Chavi spoke quickly. "Kids or no kids, I could never manage to produce such a gourmet creation. Whenever I frost a simple chocolate cake, I feel like Julia Child. Gitty, you always had a talent for baking. Maybe you should start to give classes. I, for one, would be your first customer."

The more sensitive women in the group breathed sighs of relief at Chavi's quick thinking to diminish Gitty's mortification. One of the others, oblivious to the significance of the interchange, asked Gitty how she learned to bake and if she really might be interested in sharing her skills.

Inside, Chavi burned with anger. How dare the first woman be so insensitive to her friend's suffering? If only she thought just a little bit about how her mindless prattle could shatter someone.

Then she tried to get a hold of herself. Yes, the woman had made a mistake, but it happened sometimes. People could be insensitive. Not that they were coldhearted; they just didn't think about how another person might take their comments.

At least I'm sensitive, she soothed herself. But was she? She was sensitive to the needs of the people she was acquainted with, but what about to the feelings of her own family? How often had she trampled on Shmuel's already low self-esteem when he disappointed her? And oftentimes she would hurt him knowing full well what she was doing. Wasn't she, in a sense, worse that the woman standing a few feet away? Shmuel certainly cared more about what she said than Gitty cared about the opinion of a stranger. Chavi admitted to herself that she had a way to go in her degree of caring for others.

13

Chavi called her mother after Shabbos to hear how her Shabbos had been, but Mrs. Baumel wasn't home. Knowing her mother didn't like to go out at night, she wondered where Mrs. Baumel was.

Chavi and her mother had remained very close even after Chavi had moved out. They usually spoke at least twice a day. Chavi realized now, though, that except for a short call before Shabbos, she hadn't spoken to her mother much in the last week. Had she not called enough or had her mother not been calling her? She wasn't sure, but she didn't think her mother had any reason to be angry with her. Gitty hadn't mentioned anything about her mother being under the weather. Chavi wondered what was going on and made a mental note to ask her mother the next time they spoke.

After a minute or two of polite conversation on the phone the next morning, Mrs. Baumel invited Chavi and the kids for lunch the following day. It was Lag BaOmer, so she wouldn't be going to work. Chavi immediately accepted the offer. It would be a change of pace for herself and the kids, and it would be nice to have her mother's wholesome food again.

They reached Mrs. Baumel's apartment at twelve the next day. It was very warm outside, and, after giving his *bubby* a kiss, Yitzchak immediately ran out to the porch to ride his favorite motorcycle. Chavi put Faigy outside in her infant seat to enjoy the fresh air and went in to help her mother prepare lunch.

As Chavi set the table, she told her mother all about her Shabbos. Mrs. Baumel, began chopping a salad as she described her own Shabbos. She had gone away to a *shabbaton* at a resort hotel off the Kinneret with a group of friends with whom she volunteered at a local soup kitchen.

Since Chavi had gotten married, Mrs. Baumel had found a job as a secretary for an organization that helped English-speaking immigrants. Her job covered her cost of living. The office closed at one in the afternoon, so, with no one to run home to, she had plenty of time at her discretion. She spent the time volunteering for a few community projects. Two days a week she worked in the soup kitchen, preparing meals and serving them to the needy in an impoverished neighborhood near the center of town. One day a week she was a candy striper in a religious hospital, and one evening a week she worked as a librarian in a Jewish library.

Her schedule, though busy, still allowed her time to visit with her family and socialize with newly found and newly reacquainted friends. She had become close to a number of the women she volunteered with, and together they had planned this Shabbos getaway. Although she always said she was getting too old to travel, Mrs. Baumel told Chavi that she had

had a fabulous time pampering herself and fraternizing with contemporaries. She described the rooms, the service, the day trip they had taken on Friday after settling in, and the *shiur* they attended in detail. Chavi listened happily, excited to see her mother so alive and enjoying herself so freely.

Mrs. Baumel still mourned her husband deeply, it was true. She still weaved his name into almost every conversation they had. But her loneliness didn't incapacitate her as it had threatened to a few years before. The nights were long and terribly quiet, but her days were filled with laughter and adventure, and she looked forward to each morning and its accomplishments. Besides the amusement her pastimes provided, she felt good knowing she was self-supporting and contributing to others. Chavi was glad that her mother's life had become so full. She had spent the bulk of her years devoting herself to other people, and now, though she was still giving, she was enjoying an independence that she hadn't experienced in the past.

The two women sat down at the table to relax before calling Yitzchak in to eat. Chavi asked her mother how her job was going. Mrs. Baumel told her of a family that considered moving back to England because the husband had been seeking employment for over a year and couldn't find anything suitable. Mrs. Baumel had spent a full hour looking through the job placement file with him, praying to find an opportunity they had previously overlooked. They found a position that had just been vacated, and the man went for an interview that very day. Mrs. Baumel had found a bouquet of flowers on her desk the next morning, signed by the indebted man, who had just received word that he had landed the job.

Chavi congratulated her mother, and Mrs. Baumel went

on to tell her about a patient she had become very friendly with in the hospital over the last few months. Her situation seemed to be terminal, and Mrs. Baumel always did what she could to cheer her up. When the woman complained that she was always cold, Mrs. Baumel had knitted her a shawl, which she now wore every time Mrs. Baumel visited. She stopped talking for a minute and her face grew pensive as she thought about the ill woman.

"Is anything new at the library?" Chavi asked, turning to a more cheerful topic.

Mrs. Baumel looked straight into Chavi's eyes and cleared her throat. "Actually, dear, one of the reasons that I invited you over was because I wanted to share some news with you in person."

Chavi was surprised. "About the library?"

"Well, sort of," Mrs. Baumel began. "As you know, I've been working at the library for almost a year now. I really enjoy seeing all the new releases, and it's a calm and relaxing way to help people. Well, there is a man who comes in almost every week to exchange his books. He is a dignified gentleman who is very polite and grateful. I always did my best to help him find what he was looking for. We exchanged a few polite words every once in a while. I learned that he was a widower with four married children in America and two married children in Israel, and he knew the same type of thing about me."

Where is this leading? Chavi wondered.

Mrs. Baumel continued, "Anyway, you're not going to believe this, but the head librarian came over to me a few weeks ago and told me that this gentleman was interested in meeting me socially. I was completely shocked and told her I would think about it; but after thinking it over for a while I decided that I had nothing to lose.

"We went out for coffee one evening that week and twice more after that. I very much enjoy his company. We also have similar backgrounds — his mother and my grandfather are even from the same shtetl in Poland. Isn't that funny? We haven't spoken about it directly yet, but it looks like we'll probably take the relationship to its next stage soon."

Mrs. Baumel's cheeks were pink with a youthful excitement. Chavi assumed she was misunderstanding. "And what might that next stage be?"

"Oh, don't be silly. I hope we'll be getting married soon. I'm sorry I waited so long to tell you. I was a little embarrassed of myself in the beginning, dating at my age and all. And then things moved so quickly. I hope you aren't angry that I kept it a secret. I hope you'll meet each other soon...." Mrs. Baumel spoke without pause.

Chavi's head was reeling. Luckily, the baby had started crying. Chavi pasted a smile on her face and mumbled something about being happy for her mother. "I'll be right back as soon as I attend to Faigy," she promised, escaping to the porch.

But she didn't go right back. Holding her baby on the sunny porch, she tried to sort out her thoughts and emotions. Her mother was getting remarried? Why did that idea repulse her so? Was it repulsion she was feeling? That seemed so strong a term. But it was repulsion. Although she tended to repress the memories of her father since his death as a way of coping with the loss, she could not imagine her mother with a new husband. Replacing her father made it seem that her mother no longer cared that Mr. Baumel was gone. It was a disgrace to her father's memory.

But how dare she try to limit her mother's happiness out of her own sentiment? That certainly wasn't fair. She couldn't get angry with her mother for harping on the loss of her husband and then get angry when she tried to rebuild her life. Intellectually, Chavi understood that. But emotionally she was too shocked to process the whole situation.

By now her mother had come to find her on the porch. She put her arm around Chavi and said, "I've upset you, haven't I? Of course, I understand how you're feeling."

Chavi didn't say anything. She wished she could tell her mother that she was happy for her so that her mother could share her excitement, but she couldn't.

Mrs. Baumel stood there for a minute, waiting for Chavi to say something. When there was no response, she said simply, "I understand," and walked back into the house, her head bowed.

Eventually Chavi came in, and they ate without mentioning the issue again. Before she left, though, Chavi kissed her mother on the cheek and said, "I'm really and truly happy for you, Ima. It's just that the news came as such a surprise that I need time to digest it."

"I understand," Mrs. Baumel said again. She kissed each of the grandchildren good-bye, offered Yitzchak a lollipop for the road, and sent them off.

ဆ ဆ

Chavi could not bring herself to discuss her mother's new friendship with Shmuel until much later that night, when the idea had settled enough in her mind for her to deal with it. Shmuel was delighted with the news, though he sympathized with Chavi and allowed her to mourn the displacement of her father. Later that week, the Rosenbergs invited Mrs. Baumel and Mr. Max Schneider for dinner.

He really was a lovely man, Chavi had to admit. He was over six feet tall, significantly taller than her father had been at five feet eight. He was completely gray with a trim beard and sparkling blue eyes that accentuated his easy laughter. Mrs. Baumel laughed a lot together with him. Mr. Schneider gave the impression of being more educated than her father.

As these thoughts passed through Chavi's mind, she stopped herself. Why did she insist on comparing these two men? They weren't the same and weren't supposed to be. This was a new chapter in her mother's life.

Soon the engagement became official and the wedding followed shortly after. They were married in Mr. Schneider's rabbi's house with just two witnesses in attendance, but after the ceremony they had a catered meal in a nearby shul for their immediate family and Gitty, who by then had been adopted as a Baumel.

The Schneiders had decided that for their wedding present to themselves they would have all their children in America fly in to celebrate with them. It was especially nice for Chavi to see her older brother and sister, whom she hadn't seen since her own wedding. At the wedding meal, Mr. Schneider spoke of his joy at meeting his new life partner, and a son from each side gave a *d'var Torah* that led naturally to the praise of his parent and to the theme of marriage.

Chavi let her mind wander during the speeches. It was interesting to meet Mr. Schneider's children. Each of them was so different. One wore a leather yarmulke and dressed in a manner that exuded wealth. His wife, the only spouse who had made the trip, was dressed at the height of style. Another son was a very simple yeshivish man who resembled her own brother and brother-in-law. Of the daughters, both of whom had come from America and left behind husbands and children, one was wearing a snood and sensible shoes even though everyone else in attendance was dressed in a more festive manner, and the other looked chassidish, with a hat on top of her short *sheitel*. The two younger children seemed to be typical Israeli *kollel* men.

The Schneiders were from Chicago, which probably meant that their social and educational experiences weren't limited to one straight mold. Still, it was interesting how they had come out so different from each other. Chavi wished she had been able to meet the late Mrs. Schneider.

As dessert was served, Mr. Schneider asked to speak again. He told the children that he and the new Mrs. Schneider had decided that he would move into his wife's apartment. Because he had lived in his old apartment with his previous wife, the new apartment would be a fresh start. It was also slightly larger.

"Although it is a bit uncomfortable to discuss it, especially in a group setting like this," he continued, "we wanted to explain to all of you the financial agreement we have decided upon so that there will be no hard feelings later on. We are going to sell my apartment and the money will be put aside to be kept in my family when the time comes. My wife's apartment will remain under her name, and in case of necessity I will buy it at a fair market value, as decided by an appraiser, and that money will remain on the Baumel side. We are going to pool all other savings for our living expenses, and eventually they will be divided evenly."

These frank words made everyone a little uneasy, yet

Chavi was glad they were said. The other children, she thought, were probably relieved to hear them, too.

A keyboard player had provided musical accompaniment for the meal, and Chavi initiated a few rounds of dancing. Then it was time to present a gift to the newly married couple. One of Mr. Schneider's sons who lived in Israel had arranged for all of the Schneiders and Baumels to chip in for the gift. After much back and forth between all the involved parties, they decided on a large silver *birchas habayis* sign. The daughter-in-law who had bought the gift wrote a beautiful poem that wished the Schneiders much happiness in their new life together.

As Shmuel and Chavi rode home, Chavi realized she had not talked to Gitty much that evening. When Mrs. Baumel had announced her engagement, Gitty had decided that it was time to return to New York. She had been gone long enough that the issue of her divorce was no longer hot news, and her family and friends had gotten used to the idea of her being single again, even if they had not made peace with the issue. As much as she dreaded facing everyone directly, she missed her old home and the comfort that a familiar setting brings. Also, her sister Esti was getting married and she wanted to be there for the *simchah*. The time seemed ripe for a change. There would be a larger pool of eligible men for her to date in America, and she felt it was worth a try.

Although Chavi was sad to see her friend go, she agreed that it seemed like a smart move. She had asked Shmuel to activate his New York network and at least find Gitty someone to date, if not marry. She promised to make a few calls herself, but first she had to arrange a farewell party for Gitty.

14

The farewell party was held in the Rosenberg home one evening the week Gitty was scheduled to go. Chavi invited her mother, her mother-in-law, a few of her mother's neighbors, and a handful of Gitty's friends. It came out to fifteen women. With Faigy only six weeks old, Chavi decided to make the party potluck and asked everyone to bring one item. She also asked each of the women to contribute toward a small gift. It was hard for her to think of something that would be appropriate, but she finally decided on a fancy phone book and pen, with a prepaid calling card that Gitty could use to call Israel.

She had to ask Shmuel to buy the paper goods and the gift for her, even though she normally tried not to give him too many errands because the time they took would be borrowed from his learning time. But, for the first month or so after birth, these small trips helped her save her strength and return to normal faster. Shmuel never minded helping her — except when he had to buy things where taste was a significant factor. He knew he was setting himself up for trouble if he agreed to be her gofer for such items. Chavi promised herself that she would assure him that whatever he chose would be fine and that she would keep her mouth shut no matter what she thought of his choices.

She wrote Gitty a sweet card to go with the gift, describing how much she would be missed and how everyone hoped she would return soon. She included a list of the names, addresses, and phone numbers of all the women attending the party.

ꝏ ꝏ

Chavi's mother-in-law was happy to be invited to the farewell party, even though she wasn't particularly friendly with Gitty. It seemed to her that she wasn't invited to Shmuel and Chavi's home that often. She stopped in once in a while without a formal invitation, but she noticed that Chavi got nervous every time she came unannounced. She could empathize with her — she had felt the same way when her mother-in-law dropped by when she had been first married. But she wasn't anything like her mother-in-law. Maybe it was just a regular mother-in-law/daughter-in-law thing. She hoped so, anyway.

Although she hinted to her son and daughter-in-law that she wanted to be invited, the hints were never taken. She had to be satisfied with inviting them to her house or out to a restaurant whenever she wanted to get together with them or her grandchildren. Now, in her delight at being allowed into the sanctuary of her son's home, she offered to come early and help set up. This way she might get to spend some time with her favorite grandchildren and see what was going on in their house.

Chavi had told her mother-in-law it was unnecessary to come early, but she had insisted. When she arrived, an hour and a half before the party was scheduled to begin, Chavi was trying to get the little ones settled so she would be free to deal with the party. She was surprised to see her mother-in-law. *She said she was going to come by before the party started, but I never imagined it would be this early,* she thought, furious. *Now I'll never be able to get the kids to sleep. Yitzchak will be so excited to see her and he'll get all riled up. Well, there's nothing to do about it now. At least the house is clean for once.*

"Hi, Bubby. Come on in. You're much earlier than I expected."

"I wanted to help. You've just recently given birth, honey, and you have no business making parties. You should be resting. I came to help so you won't have to work so hard."

No business making parties.... "Okay, come in," said Chavi, proud of her outer appearance of calmness. "Let me get you something to drink."

"No, thank you. Oh, there's my angel Yitzchak in the hall. Come here, dear. Give Bubby a hug. Look what I brought you. Your favorite.... Where did I put it? Here it is. Jelly beans. A whole bag for yourself."

Yitzchak grabbed the bag and handed it to his mother to open, but she refused. "No, Yitzchak, it's time for bed. You've even brushed your teeth. You can have these in the morning. Let's go say Shema. Say good night to Bubby."

But Yitzchak was in no mood for bed anymore. As expected, there went her plans. Her son and mother-in-law seemed oblivious to her frustration as Yitzchak took his latest drawing from preschool out of his drawer to show his grandmother. After she finished admiring it, Bubby Rosenberg called to Chavi from the other room, where she was changing Faigy. "Chavi, why is he wearing these thin pajamas? I'm sure you have a reason, of course, but it's so chilly outside that he's liable to catch a cold this way."

Chavi's automatic anger reflex had been activated. *She acts as if I don't know how to dress my own child. Why does she trust me all the nights she's not here? Doesn't he seem like he's doing okay?*

Then she caught herself. This was the opportunity she had been waiting for. Her chance to be less self-centered and try to melt her mother-in-law's exterior. Mrs. Rosenberg's fake sweetness irked her to no end. *I'm sure you have a reason, of course....* She would just answer truthfully and not try to defend herself.

"You are so right. It is a cool night. But these pajamas are Yitzchak's favorite. Whenever I try to get him to wear anything else, he has a tantrum because he wants his special pajamas. So I gave up trying."

"Oh, that's the problem? Let's see. Yitzchak, do you mind showing Bubby where you keep your other pajamas? Let's go together."

Chavi heard them going through his pajama collection. Bubby Rosenberg took out one pair and oohed and aahed over it. "These are super-special pajamas, Yitzchak. Your father used to have almost the exact same ones when he was your age. He would wear them whenever you could open up the window and feel a breeze. Let's see if it's that kind of night."

Two sets of footsteps walked over to the window. Bubby Rosenberg's voice continued. "Do you feel any wind? Me, too. On a night like this, your father would put on these pajamas and feel snuggly warm. Do you want to be like your father?"

Soon Yitzchak came running, dressed in his warmer nightclothes, to show off his super-special pajamas to his mother. Strange it was. Just the night before, he was wailing so loudly in protest at the suggestion that he change pajamas that Chavi had to close all the windows so she wouldn't get kicked out of the neighborhood for disturbing the peace. And now he was prancing around in those same pajamas. Bubby had wrought a small miracle.

After Bubby had read Yitzchak a story and said Shema with him, he fell fast asleep. No asking for drinks, no needing the bathroom. Chavi actually went to make sure that he was still breathing. She found him sleeping peacefully and felt herself relax a little.

While Bubby Rosenberg cradled Faigy, Chavi set the table, arranging two tables for eating at the end of the dining room and putting a buffet table for the food closer to the kitchen.

When Mrs. Rosenberg saw what she was doing, she said, "I don't mean to get involved, really, but I would have put the food on the tables where your guests are sitting. I don't know why you are doing it this way. It's crowded in here — this room is too small for so many people. You'll have more space to move around without the extra table, and this way people can serve themselves without having to get up."

Focus on what she's saying and not on how she says it, Chavi reprimanded herself. *It's her style. Don't let it eat you up. Shmuel said she's scared of being hurt by you.*

"Thanks, that's a good idea. It looks like the baby fell asleep. Would you mind putting her down and helping me fold up the extra table? I'm glad you mentioned your suggestion."

Mrs. Rosenberg, shocked at Chavi's mild manner and wondering if she was being sarcastic, scurried off to put the baby in her crib. The two of them finished arranging the room together, both a bit uncertain about the implications of Chavi's unusual demeanor.

Before long, the guests began to arrive, and then Gitty herself came. The party turned out to be a warm and intimate event, with plenty of food and a friendly atmosphere. After Chavi read her card aloud and presented the gift on behalf of everyone, Gitty asked if she could speak. Everyone looked at her curiously. If there was anyone who was unlikely to ask to speak in front of a crowd, especially in the emotional atmosphere that Chavi's gift had set, it was Gitty. What would she say?

"The last few years have taught me a lot," she began. "As I was growing up, I thought I knew, more or less, who I was and what my life was going to be like. I had a certain plan that was pretty typical of my upbringing: I would marry someone with a good reputation, learning in the right yeshivah, and everyone would be proud of him. We would go to Israel for a few years so he could learn while my parents supported us. Then we would move back home and he would continue to learn or work. I would raise my children in the bosom of my family and friends and everyone would live happily ever after.

"Well, as you all know, things didn't work out as planned. My life became a nightmare that I never dreamed I would be involved in, let alone be its protagonist. I still blame myself, but now I know that it needed to happen. I was immature and self-centered and had a very, very limited picture of what life was about and what was important. I was so worried about what everyone would think of me that I didn't know who I really was, who I wanted to be, and what really mattered.

"These last few years have been rough. But all of you here helped me, and for that I have to thank you. You gave me the emotional support I needed, you helped me overcome my loneliness, and you even gave me a place to live." She turned to smile at Chavi's mother. "But most important, you taught me that what matters most is not where you went to school or where your husband learns or how you dress, but how deeply you can feel for others and give to them. You have been the best role models a person could ask for, and —" here she paused for a moment to regain her composure and clear her tear-choked throat, "— and I love you all. May God bless each of you with everything good and may you never have pain."

Except for an occasional sniffle, the room was quiet enough to hear a pin drop. There wasn't a dry eye in the room. Even Mrs. Rosenberg was tearing, though she squirmed uncomfortably, knowing that she was just a bystander to the moving scene that had unfolded. She pitied Gitty and at the same time admired her strength of character, wishing that she herself could be so strong and honest.

After an exchange of hugs and kisses and good-byes, the party broke up. Chavi's mother left the earliest, saying that Max didn't want her out too late.

"I'm sorry we didn't get to talk much tonight," Chavi said, "but we'll catch up on things in the morning."

"Max and I have started walking in the mornings before I

go to work," her mother answered. "After work, I'm going straight to the hospital and then home for dinner hour. But I'll call you later tomorrow evening."

Chavi kissed her mother good-bye, feeling inexplicably empty.

Mrs. Rosenberg left last, helping Chavi clean up and waiting for Shmuel to come home so she could say hello. After exchanging pleasantries for a few minutes, she wished them a good night and left. On the way out, she said, "It was a really special party. Thank you for inviting me."

Both Chavi and Shmuel were speechless.

15

At one and a half, Faigy was a beautiful and easygoing little girl. Chavi enjoyed dressing her in adorable outfits and hair bows and buying her the dolls and tea sets that had been missing from their toy collection before she came along.

She loved Yitzchak equally, but he was a different story. The four-and-a-half-year-old was very energetic and often unruly. Chavi had to be on top of him constantly to make sure he wasn't doing anything destructive or dangerous. His grueling therapy schedule continued. Chavi barely noticed any improvement, but she was assured by the professionals involved that he was progressing nicely. In addition, she had to contend with getting him to school on time and giving him the extra help that he needed to keep up with his schoolwork. It sounded a little silly, schoolwork for a four-and-a-half-year-old, but they were already learning the alphabet and he needed supervised practice at home.

To make everything a little more difficult, although the reason was certainly a blessing, Chavi had just discovered that she was expecting her third child. She felt herself a paradigm of virtue for getting through the day with Yitzchak without losing either her temper or her sanity. The problem was that she often didn't manage to get through the day without losing her cool.

One night, she was on the phone with a friend as she straightened up the kitchen. The friend was relating an argument she had had with her husband the night before and asking Chavi's advice on resolving the issue. Since this friend had a good heart but poor communication skills, she frequently had misunderstandings with her husband, and Chavi had become her sounding board.

Yitzchak, with whom Chavi had spent the last hour playing while Faigy slept, tried to interrupt the conversation. He said "Mommy" at least fifteen times while Chavi motioned to him to wait, leave the room, be quiet, or do anything else but demand her attention. He became more persistent, though, and began pulling on his mother's skirt. Chavi's caller had just reached the climax of her story, and Chavi was very curious to hear what had happened. She tried to ignore Yitzchak, but he would have none of it. Finally, she looked him directly in the eye and said, "I told you to wait until I get off the phone!" and then slapped him across the face.

He was stunned, caught completely off guard. He backed out of the room defiantly, trying to contain his emotions and be tough, but his quivering lip gave him away.

Horrified at herself, Chavi apologized to her friend and ended the conversation.

She ran to find Yitzchak. He was sitting on his bed, about to rip up a piece of paper. Before he could carry out the act, Chavi scooped him into her arms and hugged him tightly, as if the intensity of the hug would make up for her mistreatment. She held him for a moment and then said, "I am so sorry. So sorry. I shouldn't have hit you. I was just frustrated because I had asked you to wait so many times while I finished the call that was important to me. But I was wrong." She paused to kiss him. "What did you want to tell me?"

His stutter was terrible as he answered, "I just wanted to give you a present I made."

Chavi took the present from his hand. It was the paper he had tried to rip. She opened it. Inside was the word *Ima* written in Hebrew, enclosed in a colorful heart. The two letters in this short word were so hard for him to write. She forced him to practice many times. He had written them so perfectly. A tear dripped onto the paper as she stammered, "It's the most beautiful picture I ever saw. Thank you."

Yitzchak kissed her cheek and they stayed in their embrace for another minute.

As she left the room, she felt like destroying the picture herself. She didn't deserve it. She had returned his innocent love and effort with a humiliating slap across the face. She hung the picture on the refrigerator to show how important it was to her and also to serve as a reminder of what motherhood was all about.

ꟸ ꟸ

Sensing that Chavi could use a break, the Schneiders generously offered to watch Yitzchak and Faigy for a few days so that Shmuel and Chavi could go on a short vacation in honor of their sixth anniversary. A vacation was a dream come true to the young Rosenbergs, but they knew how hard it would be for people at retirement age to watch two energetic young children. After much debate and introspection, Shmuel and Chavi decided to take her parents up on their offer. They made plans to leave early on a Friday morning and come back late after Shabbos.

Chavi had a spectacular time answering advertisements and comparing hotel prices. Although their budget was limited, she soon found luxurious accommodations at a small hotel on the seashore. She carefully planned their short itinerary and began packing well in advance. The anticipation of the trip was almost as enjoyable as the trip itself. Chavi was glad they had planned it for three weeks from her parents' offer so that it wouldn't be over so quickly.

After they said good-bye to the children and profusely thanked the Schneiders, Shmuel and Chavi settled themselves into the car that Max had offered them for the weekend. The luxury of riding in a private car again was appreciated and every mile was savored. Even though they had both owned their own cars for many years, after six years without one, two days with a borrowed car was an added bonus to their trip.

Their first destination was a botanical garden for the picnic lunch that Chavi had packed. After they ate, they drove on to the hotel, which Shmuel found easily enough despite the unfamiliar roads. They unpacked and showered and, with plenty of time till Shabbos, went for a carefree walk on the deserted beach near the hotel.

Chavi enjoyed the salty mist on her face and the soft sand beneath her feet.

"It's so nice to have this time alone together," Shmuel spoke up. "Even though we do spend plenty of time together, the children are always around, the phone is always ringing, and you're usually rushing about to accomplish your tasks for the day."

Chavi nodded, thrilled to be free of such duties for two days. Shmuel continued, "There's something I've been wanting to talk to you about for a couple of days now, but I thought it would be better to wait until we were both relaxed to bring it up."

Chavi's curiosity was piqued. She had noticed that he had seemed a bit preoccupied that week. "Go on," she said encouragingly.

Shmuel started to speak a few times and then stopped. He bent down to pick up a seashell, which he dusted off and offered her. Chavi took it, waiting anxiously to hear what he had to say.

"Chavi, it's so hard for me to learn all day. I really love learning. I enjoy the process and I feel so accomplished when I'm done. But as you've seen, as we've discussed so many times, it's hard for me to buckle down and get myself started. And everything distracts me. If someone is talking next to me, I listen. If someone is shouting across the *beis midrash,* I am curious to know what's going on. Sometimes I daydream. Sometimes I'm so tired that I fall asleep right there in my seat."

Chavi nodded. How well she knew of what he spoke. He always seemed to want to do anything but learn. He was so happy when he was finished. She had a hard time understanding how he always managed to get distracted by other projects. She tried to control her constant nagging, but Shmuel sensed her disapproval, no matter how hard she tried to conceal it.

"I feel like such a failure sometimes. I know how much

some of my friends are achieving and how little I am. I know I'm wasting time. Sometimes I think about just dropping our whole plan. I could get a job and learn a bit on the side and I would be able to feel that I was doing what I needed to do and no one would think the worse of me. But then I remember my dream. And I try again and again to sit down by my Gemara and start. Sometimes I manage to and sometimes I don't. It's so frustrating."

For the moment, Chavi forgot her traditional role of reminding Shmuel how important it was for him to learn. He knew what he needed to do and often her prodding only depressed him, reminding him again that he wasn't measuring up. She felt his pain acutely.

He continued, "Well, when I went to Yitzchak's rebbe last week for our monthly meeting to assess his progress, Rabbi Auerbach, the principal, called me into his office. I only met him once before, besides saying hello when I pass him in the hall, so I was surprised that he wanted to meet with me."

Chavi interrupted, "Why didn't you tell me about this right away? What did he want? Is everything okay with our son?"

"Yes, everything is fine. I was just getting to the point. Rabbi Auerbach told me that Yitzchak's rebbe is very impressed with our devotion to Yitzchak and he has seen remarkable improvement in his development. He has taught a number of students in similar situations and none progressed as rapidly as Yitzchak is."

"How nice," Chavi said happily.

"He said the rebbe attributes his progress to our devotion as parents and the innovative system of doctors, therapy sessions, exercises, and encouragement that we — and he mentioned you also — had designed. He's seen us work through a lot of bureaucratic red tape to get the financial help we need from various government institutions."

"I'm proud of us, too. It made such an impression on him that he called you in just to tell you that?"

"Let me finish."

"Sorry," said Chavi, although it was hard for her to wait for him to get to the point.

"Rabbi Auerbach said that the rebbe's praises came to his mind when he was sitting at a convention of principals that had been convened to discuss dealing with learning disabilities in the ultra-Orthodox school system in Israel and particularly in Jerusalem. Right now, each school has its own way of handling the issue. Some schools are more effective and some less. The principals feel that by pooling their resources and ideas they can accomplish much more. Many of the technical details of starting an umbrella organization were worked out during a brainstorming session at that convention. Only one detail remained completely unsettled — who would run the organization.

"Now, Chavi, you're not going to believe this, but Rabbi Auerbach suggested me for the position. He said it wasn't certain that everyone would agree, but he would certainly push for my appointment if I was interested. And he said that he was quite sure that I would be accepted if he strongly lobbied for my appointment. Can you imagine? It's a big position. You get to meet with the biggest names in education and politics. And I could really contribute to the progress of so many suffering children. I can't believe he offered the job to me."

Chavi bit her tongue so as not to immediately voice her protest. He belonged in *kollel,* and, as far as she was concerned, accepting such a post would most certainly be more than his first foot out the door.

But he was so alive and full of energy. She hadn't seen him this way in years. He was getting worn down by the responsibilities of life and a family, in addition to the stress he felt at not accomplishing enough in yeshivah. It was quite a compliment that they thought of him. He really was very talented in many areas that the job required. He was organized, energetic, caring, intelligent, and creative, and he had become quite educated in learning disabilities and their treatments. She could at least let him enjoy his moment in the sun before they discussed the issue practically.

"They picked the right man, for sure," she said. "You certainly have what it takes to found the organization they want. It's a real compliment that they chose you, and it makes me very proud."

Shmuel basked in her praise, a pleasant change from her disappointment in him. "Do you think I should take the job?" he asked.

"There are so many issues involved. I need to let the idea sink in for a while. We'll discuss it over Shabbos, okay?"

He agreed. As they continued walking, Chavi noticed him occasionally smiling to himself. She was indeed proud of him.

ಐ ಐ

The relaxing Shabbos took a new twist. Instead of having nothing to do but enjoy each other's company, the Rosenbergs began their Friday night meal by debating the pros and cons of Shmuel accepting the job offer.

The gefilte fish they were served was almost as good as

Mrs. Schneider's, but Chavi barely noticed it. "Shmuel, I don't think you should take the job," she said firmly. "Six years ago we agreed that we would do our best to allow you to develop in Torah. You've only been in *kollel* for six years, and it's too early for you to leave yeshivah."

There was no response from Shmuel, though his face had settled into a frown. Chavi absolutely despised his quiet responses. She would rather him protest, rant, and rave, but not brood. She was never sure what his silence meant, but it made her feel terribly left out.

"Are you upset?" she asked. More silence. "I know you're upset. What's bothering you?"

"I don't have anything to say" was all Shmuel replied.

The rest of the meal was tense and silent. Chavi was angry at his self-imposed isolation and knew it was her fault.

After the meal, she invited Shmuel for a walk. Shmuel acquiesced emotionlessly. They strolled on the dark beach for a while without saying much.

Finally, Chavi blurted out, "Fine. Do what you want. You're obviously excited about trying out for the position, so just do it."

Shmuel's aggravation was apparent. "Listen, Chavi," he whispered in a voice that yelled at her, "I will never do anything that you're not happy about. I just don't see how you have a right to make decisions for me without blinking an eyelash. You act like you're my mentor. It's true that you have a right to have a say in the matter, but you didn't even ask me how I felt about the issue, and it's my life, too. I told you what the offer was. You told me what you think I must do. As if I'm a child that needs to be told what to do because I don't have enough brains to make my own decisions."

But wasn't that the way it always was? Chavi wondered. She would nag, cajole, and push her husband into doing what she thought was right. That was the routine they had fallen into. It had never dawned on her that she was degrading her husband with her assumption of the role of pedagogue. But she had to admit that he was right. If she told him what to do, she was implying that she thought he was incapable of making his own decisions. That wasn't what she meant to suggest. She was just sharing her opinions with him, as she wanted him to do with her.

"I'm sorry, Shmuel. I didn't mean to come across that way. What do you think is the best decision?"

"Of course I do. But you don't have to use that authoritative tone with me, as if you are my teacher and not my wife. I want your opinion. I value what you have to say. But can't you at least offer it as a suggestion and not as a verdict? And don't you think your opinion should take into consideration, at least to some degree, how I'm feeling?" Shmuel ended sarcastically.

His words rang true, and Chavi's attitude, which a moment before had smacked of smug self-righteousness, quickly became one of shame for her self-centeredness. Humbly, she apologized. "Please forgive me. I truly didn't mean to come across that way. Can you tell me how you feel about the job?"

She sensed Shmuel relaxing. His stony facade melted and he began: "Yeshivah is really a challenge for me. I enjoy the challenge; I am not giving up on it. But the learning doesn't come easily to me and I fail myself often. The failures leave their mark on my motivation. I feel I need a change. I need a new challenge to keep me excited and stop my learning from getting stale. I thought of other options before this came up —

switching yeshivahs or tutoring a younger boy or other things like that. But those options don't seem like enough of a change.

"This job opportunity is exciting to me. I'll use different talents that I hope I have. I'll meet new people. I'll get to run around a bit and be creative. And most important, I'll be helping people in a tangible way and leaving my mark on society. I'm not sure I could get the job, but I know I want it.

"Will my learning suffer? Maybe — I don't know. I do know it's time for me to move on from my regular schedule. I'll only agree to the position if it will be part time. I still hope to learn at least one or maybe two *sedarim* a day. I know you're not happy with what I'm saying, but my heart tells me it's right."

Chavi realized his mind was made up. She could see that he had thought the issue through seriously, and she respected that. Should she try to fight him? She wasn't sure she wanted to. On the one hand, she was afraid that this was the end of his life as a yeshivah student. On the other hand, though, she agreed that Shmuel needed a change — something to put a little zest into his life and give him the motivation and desire to deal with life's daily challenges. She was worried because this was the first step in a major change of lifestyle, but it had become obvious that the change was going to occur sooner or later.

"I'm glad you've made up your mind," she finally answered his unspoken request for a response to his soliloquy. "I know that if you get the job, you'll do great."

The rest of their vacation was most enjoyable, but underneath the surface serenity, they were both uneasy about where life was taking them.

16

Shmuel went through a few grueling interviews with various parties involved with the decision making and funding of the new organization. He prepared himself well for the interviews. Before officially applying for the job, he worked with Rabbi Auerbach, the principal of Yitzchak's cheder, to develop an outline of what he intended to accomplish and how.

Chavi laughed to herself as she heard Shmuel practice his presentation in front of their bedroom mirror. His Hebrew was a very yeshivish, American Hebrew with a smattering of popular Yiddish words. She wondered how the interviewers would react to it. But they seemed not to mind his pronunciations because he got the job.

The first major difference in their lifestyle was that Chavi was able to cut her workload significantly once they had Shmuel's salary coming in. She was thrilled to be able to spend three and sometimes four days a week at home with the children. Suddenly, she was free to actualize some of her parenting dreams and try out her theories. The mornings were quiet, with just Faigy at home. Chavi was able to take her to the park and nap herself when Faigy did. She was also able to get a good portion of the housework done in the morning, so she was much more relaxed and available to Yitzchak in the afternoon. Shmuel started eating lunch at home on the days that Chavi didn't work. It was a treat for him and Yitzchak to be greeted by the central woman in their lives in the middle of the day, with the table set and a hot meal ready.

The only problem with having more time for housework was that Chavi did more housework. She started to pay more attention to the details of the aesthetics of her home. Once she began investing time in cleaning and beautifying her home, she began to get more aggravated when her work was undone. Suddenly, every toy that was played with, instead of being a source of pleasure and development, became a potential mess. Spilled milk was no longer a shame but a calamity.

Chavi noticed herself nagging and yelling at her family, and it hurt her that she was acting that way. Finally, after feeling her blood pressure rise when Yitzchak innocently brought out his Lego to play with one afternoon, she realized that things had gone too far and sat herself down for a talk.

She really loved having an orderly home. The last couple of years had seen a serious deterioration in her home management. Shmuel had commented a number of times that he also enjoyed the way the house was taking shape. At the same time, though, she hated the shrew of a mother she was becoming. As much as she would miss her well-kept home, Chavi decided that she would have to loosen the reigns a bit and settle for mediocrity in her domesticity.

It was not easy to implement her resolution. She was delighted to finally have a home that could rival her neighbors' and not be an embarrassment when visitors came unannounced. Yet she was determined to make the change back to her old ways for the sake of her children. Little by little, she got used to saying no when her inner voice urged her to straighten up. Besides freeing her emotionally, it also left her with much more time for interacting with the children. Although Chavi wasn't totally comfortable with her new attitude, she reminded herself that just because she was lucky enough to have time at home that didn't mean that she should use it any way she wanted.

And so the days passed in the park, doing art projects, reading books. Chavi felt herself finally growing into the mothering role she had envisioned for herself before their financial realities took hold. But there were darker days, too. There were days when her body ached to stay in bed past the children's six o'clock waking time. There were days when she longed to just sit on the couch with a cold drink and read a novel. There were days when Yitzchak's rambunctious behavior made her excuse herself to the refuge of a locked bathroom for a few stolen minutes of peace.

Sometimes she just wanted quiet, but the children didn't seem to care for her personal wants. No matter how nauseous or exhausted or depressed she was, they went about their business as if everything was par for the course. At times like those, she felt resentful of her children. Didn't they sense she needed a break? Why didn't they pick up after themselves, just for the day? Would it be so terribly difficult for them to get their own drinks of water? They were so self-serving and their selfishness bordered on cruelty.

So went her thoughts. But the rational Chavi that still

lurked behind the scenes reminded her that they were children whose job was to be egocentric and to take. Sometimes that voice of sanity calmed her and sometimes it left her angry but guilty to boot.

She thought of allowing herself a couple of hours a day to be alone. She could ask one of the teenage girls on the block to take the children to the park or let the children play by themselves in front of her building as many of the neighbors' children did. She often considered both options. Watching the baby-sitters in charge of other families in the park in the afternoon made her wary of the first option. The teenagers chatted with friends and did their homework while the children played without the constant supervision she would have preferred. The baby-sitters weren't irresponsible, but Chavi cherished her children too much to leave them playing on their own so she could relax.

She also knew she could never let her children out alone until they were much older. What if they forgot to be cautious for a moment and ran into the street? And she had seen so many bored kids looking for trouble and sometimes finding it, leaving the adults on the street clucking their tongues and saying, "If only their mothers knew what they were doing!" So Chavi just let the rough times pass, knowing that if she ever really needed a break she could look for more professional baby-sitting help and pay the price.

What did give her a great deal of satisfaction in her role of parent was watching Yitzchak's progress. Yitzchak was much calmer of late, his stutter only making an appearance when he was very excited or upset. He was doing well in school and, with some extra help, had no trouble keeping up. Although he was far from enjoying his academic experience, it was bearable and no longer torturous.

She was very thankful to the doctors and experts that worked with him. She was also blessed that Yitzchak was under the tutelage of such a devoted rebbe. Yet in her heart of hearts, she wondered if a good deal of his advancement was due to her being home and giving him the necessary time and calmness that he needed to advance. She knew his problem wasn't her fault, but perhaps she had exacerbated it with the constant rushing and preoccupation that her full-time employment had necessitated. Her guilt would have been devastating had she known that she contributed to Yitzchak's problems. But only the One Above would ever know the answer to that question.

She did her best with each situation as it presented itself and prayed with all her might that her imperfections wouldn't harm the futures of her children. Being a parent was so much more complicated than she had imagined. The issue of Yitzchak's development wasn't the only thing that made her lose sleep — there was always another issue popping up on the scene that had to be dealt with.

She remembered a lecture she had heard about child raising when she was newly married. A well-known *rebbetzin* spoke for the better half of an hour on the important issues involved in raising children. However, when it came to her concluding remarks, she said, "When all is said and done, the only thing — and I mean the only thing — that will make a real difference in how your children turn out once you try your best is the help of Heaven. So pray and pray some more."

Those words had stuck with Chavi over the years, even though at the time she had thought them to be almost ridiculous. Of course you had to pray and realize that God was running everything behind the scenes, but everyone raised children and generally pretty good ones at that. She was sure she would have no problems in that area. She was a thinking and deeply spiritual person, and both she and her husband came from stable, religious families. What could be so hard and complicated?

Boy, had she been wrong! Each child was so complex, with his own personality and will that were different from her own. It was hard enough to understand them, let alone know what the best course of action was in each situation. You couldn't be too harsh or you would crush them. You couldn't be too easy or you would teach them to be slovenly. Every minute was a tightrope and she found herself horribly unequipped to deal with each issue that came up. And so she prayed and prayed some more!

Even though she was often at a loss, Chavi enjoyed the challenge of having children. She knew they were still young and wondered how she would handle the bigger issues that would develop as they grew.

ﮮ ﮮ

Before she knew it, she had another son to care for. Since it was Chavi's "turn," according to the Rosenberg tradition, to choose the baby's name, she picked Elchanan, her great-uncle's name. She thought the name was beautiful: "God has given grace." That was how she felt about her treasure. With each birth, her awe at the miracle of the creation of a new human being grew.

Little Elchanan was a happy and carefree child. He wasn't as wild and energetic as Yitzchak nor as sweet and refined as

Faigy. Even as an infant, he didn't let much ruffle his feathers. It was funny watching him first learn to crawl. More than once, he ran straight into a wall, but instead of crying or giving up, he just bounced off and moved in the other direction.

The same thing happened when his siblings tormented him. He would just move away and continue going about his business. Sometimes Yitzchak tried to rile him up, but unless the situation took on drastic proportions, he would remain calm, giving himself the sweet revenge of seeing Yitzchak's frustration at his lack of response.

Faigy, after getting over her initial jealousy, took on a protective, motherly role with him. If he cried, she would run immediately to tell her mother or try offering him a bottle herself. In return, Elchanan often turned to Faigy for solace and was generous in showing his appreciation for her caring.

Watching the threesome interact and carve out their respective roles gave Chavi unlimited satisfaction and entertainment. She saved her stories to share with Shmuel during the brief time they spent together at night. As planned, Shmuel did stick to learning two *sedarim* a day, working only in the afternoons. But besides the time allotted for his work, all of his free time was used to further develop the cause that his job was devoted to. Whenever he was home, he received call after call from parents seeking help. Chavi rarely had uninterrupted time with him.

One day, while she was in the park with the children, a little girl came over to Faigy and grabbed her sand toys. When Faigy protested, she threw a handful of sand in Faigy's face. Chavi was horrified at the other child's violence. The other mother was sitting right there and didn't say anything.

Chavi, livid at the abuse her daughter had suffered, didn't

know what to do. She packed up their things and left, feeling like a coward. Perhaps she should have protested to the mother or rebuked the child, but she was afraid of ruining her cordial relationship with the woman, with whom she often crossed paths. She arrived home distraught and unsure if she had handled the situation correctly.

She needed to relate the story to someone who shared her protective love for her daughter. She tried her mother at work, but Mrs. Schneider wasn't available. As she replaced the receiver in the cradle, Chavi noticed the light on the answering machine was flashing. She played the message. It was Shmuel, telling her not to wait for him for lunch. He had just found out the municipality zoning committee was meeting that day. The issue of his organization receiving a building was sure to come up, and he wanted to be there in person to plead the case.

Tears welled up in Chavi's eyes as she listened to his eager voice explaining how much he hoped that the committee's decision would be in their favor. Her frustration at the park was a small incident, insignificant in the scheme of things, but right now it was important to her and her emotions needed to be expressed for her to move on. Alone, she was left with no way to release her feelings other than through crying.

And so she did. As Faigy and Elchanan slept soundly in their cribs, Chavi sat on the couch with a stack of tissues and wept. Then she got up and went on with her tasks.

For years, Chavi had complained that her husband was home too much, but now that he was busier, she longed his company and his assistance. There were so many things she wanted to share with him, but by the time they got together there were more pressing issues to deal with. In addition, most of the jobs he had once helped with around the house now fell on her shoulders. Small errands like picking up a package at the post office were now her responsibility, and she had to do them in the company of three children. Sometimes she still asked Shmuel for help, but she knew that her help was coming at the expense of his learning or his community service — if it wasn't forgotten and left undone. She forced herself to be strong and more self-sufficient and to continue moving along.

Although she managed with the extra physical burden pretty well, she found herself so lonely at times. Her acquaintances from the neighborhood would listen politely to stories of her children's genius, but they weren't really interested. Gitty was gone, and in a sense she had lost Shmuel's companionship. She was proud that he was so busy and doing so much, but she had to fight for time with her confidant and best friend.

Her relationship with her mother had also changed. Her mother's life now focused around Max, instead of Chavi. Of course, Chavi was thrilled to see her mother blossoming. Besides having someone to share life with again, it seemed that Max helped her mother feel accepted in a way that the life of her youth hadn't allowed. He accepted her as she was and made her see how special she was. She no longer felt that she had to measure up to anyone else's standards, and her youthful insecurities were slowly falling away through Max's approval.

It was both fascinating and delightful to see, but, at the same time, it made Chavi feel a little jealous and neglected. Her mother had always been there to give unconditionally.

She had always tried to anticipate Chavi's needs even before Chavi realized she had them. And now she had her own life that Chavi was a part of but nowhere near its main character. The new Mrs. Schneider was learning to live for herself.

For Chavi this meant that she wasn't always there to give her a listening ear when she wanted to share an anecdote or ask advice. She couldn't be relied upon to baby-sit anymore. Max liked quiet, so Chavi had to call before she visited and invitations for Shabbos had stopped coming. Although her mother was still caring and involved in Chavi's life, her pampering was a thing of the past. It surprised Chavi anew each time until she learned to adjust her mind-set.

To a certain extent, Chavi had lost her parents, her spouse, and her best friend all within two years. She realized that she stood on her own, her childhood clearly at an end. She could no longer rely on others to care for her, and she still had to care for others. The realization hurt.

17

Since Chavi's life was full, she didn't spend much time harping on what she was missing. She had her job, her children, community projects that she took upon when asked to volunteer, and both Nava and Gitty to keep her busy.

Nava was becoming more and more determined to take the leap to full observance. At regular intervals, usually twice a week, she would call Chavi to ask her questions. She had to visit relatives who didn't keep kosher. What should she do? Her mother had invited them to a family reunion to be held on Shabbos in honor of her brother, who was visiting from France. How should she handle the situation? Could they go for Shabbos? No one religious would be there and her mother wouldn't understand. Were they allowed to travel on Shabbos for *shalom bayis*? How could they miss the party?

They would discuss the various angles involved, and Chavi would empathize. Sometimes she called a *rav* for guidance and then did her best to work out a solution or offer a helpful perspective on the topic at hand. She enjoyed helping

Nava and took pride in her growth. She also learned a lot from Nava's clear thinking and questioning. Her relationship with Nava partially satisfied her need for distraction from the home and her craving for a deeper human relationship.

One day Nava called, this time without a question. She asked if she could come visit one morning soon. At first Chavi was hesitant about giving up her morning quiet and nap, but if Nava was asking to come she knew there must be a pressing reason. She told Nava that she had to work the next day, but the day after was fine. Nava said she'd arrive at around ten.

On the morning of the visit, there was a knock on the door at five to ten. Chavi went to answer it. To her surprise, it was Nava, wearing a light purple scarf that matched her outfit on her head. Nava smiled, obviously enjoying the effect that her appearance had on Chavi.

"Nava, you decided to cover your hair? When did this happen?" Chavi asked as she ushered her guest into the house.

"I'm really not sure if I can do it yet," Nava explained as she sat down and Chavi served her coffee. "The rabbi's wife suggested that it is time for me to start. Everything I've done until now has been pretty smooth, because I'm doing it at my own pace and the changes are subtle. No one really knows what I'm doing. But I've always felt that I couldn't even consider covering my hair."

"Why?" Chavi asked. "Many of the other things you've done are so much more difficult and involved."

"I know, but they were private. If I start covering my hair, it's as if I'm wearing a sign for the whole world to see saying that I am now a religious woman. Even though I keep religious traditions, my identity to a certain degree is still with my old ways. By covering my hair, I will be switching my cultural allegiance and everyone will know that I've taken that leap."

Chavi found her words fascinating. She had never thought of covering hair as such a symbol, but it was. "But now you are going to?"

"Oh, no," Nava answered. "I don't know if I'll ever really be able to do that." As she spoke, she pulled off the scarf.

Chavi felt very uncomfortable. Although she had always seen Nava's hair before, now it seemed like she was revealing something that should be kept private.

Nava explained, "I just wanted to try it out, to see what it feels like. You live in a religious neighborhood, and I wanted to see whether I would look natural if I came with my hair covered or if people would realize I was an imposter. No one stared, though. Did I look authentic?"

"Yes, very much so," Chavi assured her. "The way you tied the scarf around your head was very pretty."

Balling the scarf up and stuffing it into her purse, Nava asked, "Why is there a mitzvah for a married woman to cover her hair?"

"Because of modesty," Chavi told her.

But Nava rejected that idea. "If it's because of modesty, why don't single religious women cover their hair? Besides, some of the wigs religious women wear are certainly more attractive than hair pulled back in a ponytail, like I usually wear."

Chavi stammered some sort of answer, but realized that she didn't really know. "I've never really given the matter much thought, Nava," she admitted at last.

"Really?" Nava said, raising her eyebrows in surprise. "Well, do you have any way of finding out?"

Chavi was about to say that she'd ask Shmuel when he came home, but she thought the better of it. She could never be sure of time with Shmuel. "I'll call someone and ask for you."

"Thank you," said Nava. The two women chatted for a few more minutes and Nava played with Elchanan, whom she had only met briefly before.

When Nava left, Chavi thanked God for having allowed her to be born into a religious family. She didn't know if she would have the strength of character to so completely question and change everything that she had always taken for granted as normal.

Chavi's other project was Gitty, who had been settled back in New York for over three years by that time. She called Chavi once a week so they could update each other on their respective lives. In particular, they discussed Gitty's dating experiences.

Gitty had dated a couple of nice men and, in spite of her careful checking, a couple of creeps. At least she was dating, thought Chavi, with renewed hopes that something might actually happen. But the whole procedure was torment for Gitty. During her first appearance on the dating scene, her parents had done the investigating for her. This time, it was her own responsibility. She had considered asking her parents to assume their roles again, but she knew that the suggestions she got would be too distasteful and hurtful for them to deal with. Besides, she was old enough to handle things herself.

Although sometimes the information she sought on the

shidduchim suggested was clear and available, sometimes the references were hard to reach, vague, or unhelpful. By far the worst, though, was when complete strangers on the other end of the line became annoyed with her questions. At times they would imply or even state outright that they thought she had her priorities mixed up and that a woman her age, in her position, should stop thinking that everything had to be perfect. Perhaps she was more particular than she had a right to be, but who were these people who had never met her to judge?

Worse than the calls were the dates themselves. Not infrequently, she would know that there was no hope for a relationship to develop after the first thirty seconds of greetings, and then she had to endure a few hours of pointless conversation with someone whose company she didn't enjoy. Chavi urged her to just have fun anyway. Chavi had liked to date; Gitty's personality was very different. Meeting new people was anything but fun. Yet she knew what she had to do, and she faithfully made her calls and went on her dates, with no end in sight.

After every conversation with Gitty, Chavi would hang up the phone, slump into the nearest comfortable chair, and sigh, "I wish I knew someone for her!" Then she would spend ten minutes reviewing all the eligible bachelors that she had ever met or heard about, trying to find someone suitable.

One Monday afternoon, with the children playing contentedly on the porch, Chavi hung up the phone and sat down to review her list of men again. Suddenly, she bolted out of her chair as if struck by lightning. She rushed to the phone and dialed Shmuel's office with her hands trembling with excitement.

Shmuel's secretary answered. Chavi asked to speak to her husband.

"I'm sorry, he's in a meeting and left me clear instructions that he not be disturbed. May I take a message?"

"This is his wife."

"Oh, is it an emergency? Should I interrupt the meeting?" the secretary asked, knowing that she rarely called him.

"No, thank you. Just tell him I called and ask him to call me at his earliest convenience."

For the next hour, Chavi alternated between anxiously pacing the floor and attending to her duties perfunctorily, with her mind full of thoughts of Gitty's future.

Finally, after what seemed like an eternity, the phone rang. Chavi leaped for it eagerly. But it was only a survey. Restraining herself from slamming the phone down, she told the caller that she didn't have time to answer her queries and resumed her pacing.

At last, the awaited call arrived. Shmuel was taken aback by the delight in Chavi's voice at hearing him on the phone. He wasn't accustomed to such a reaction anymore.

"Oh, Shmuel, I'm so glad you called. How was the meeting?" she asked.

"It was fine. What's going on? Why did you want me to call?"

"Remember a couple of weeks ago we were discussing some of your old friends from yeshivah and how differently everyone's life turned out?"

He didn't really remember. "What about it?"

"I suddenly remembered that you said one of your friends in New York got divorced last year. His wife had terrible postpartum depression and could no longer function. You told me how another friend of yours, Dovid, I think, was saying how hard it was for him to take care of the baby and still work and take care of the house. But you said that if anyone could do it, he could. That he was the nicest guy in the world. I don't remember his name...."

"It was Aryeh Zilberman." Where was this leading? he wondered.

"Right! What do you think about him for Gitty?"

"Interesting. Someone told me he's looking for someone who wasn't married before."

"What girl who wasn't married before is going to go for a guy who is divorced and has a baby? He's been dating for almost a year already."

"He didn't ask my opinion. I know he has dates."

"But he sounds like he could go for Gitty. They have such similar backgrounds. And she would probably be willing to go out with someone with a child."

"Maybe."

"Shmuel, would you call him?"

"I'll think about it."

"It's really important to me. Gitty needs to get married. We both know that. Here is a good possibility. Will you call?"

"All right, I'll call."

"Can you call now?"

"Now? I'm at work. How can I make a long-distance call at work? Besides, I have a million things to do."

"It's the perfect time to call America now. He'll be at work if you try when you come home. You can use our calling card number. Please. It won't take long. I'll remind you of all of Gitty's details. I have numbers he can call about her right here. How many times have I bothered you at work? I'd call, but our only chance of pulling this off is if a friend of his calls. Please do it."

"Oh, all right. Give me her details again. I'll call information to get his number."

"Do you have a pen?"

"Yes, I have a pen. Doesn't Gitty want someone in yeshivah?"

"Don't worry about it. She went to Bais Yaakov of Boro Park for high school and then...."

Soon the call was made and the only thing left to do was wait for an answer.

18

A week went by and Chavi could no longer wait for an answer. She urged Shmuel to call Aryeh again, but he said he didn't want to be a bother, especially for a shot in the dark. He rarely rushed to do Chavi's bidding these days, especially for something that he didn't really want to do anyway. After a few days of nagging, Chavi became so exasperated that she called herself. She knew her impetuousness might ruin things, but she was afraid that nothing would ever happen if she didn't get the ball rolling.

Aryeh was very cordial, but said that he hadn't gotten a chance to check the name out yet. Crestfallen, Chavi almost hung up, but then she decided she might as well give the *shidduch* her best shot. She spent the next fifteen minutes singing Gitty's praises, explaining why she was so perfect for this man she had never met and trying to eradicate all his doubts. Finally, perhaps just to get her off the phone, he said that he would make sure to have an answer by the next day.

Bright and early the next morning, Aryeh's phone rang.

He knew who it was. For a minute, he thought of telling Shmuel's wife that he wasn't interested in meeting Gitty just to get rid of her. He hated dating. Between working and taking care of his daughter, Chana, he barely had a chance to breathe. A date meant a rushed night and finding a baby-sitter. In the beginning he had dropped Chana off at his parents' house, but that meant he had to fill them in on his dating experience both before and after the date, which took more effort than arranging a baby-sitter. Usually his upstairs neighbor had a daughter who was available to baby-sit, so it wasn't too bad, but it was still a hassle. His more rational side reminded him that the one person he did manage to call about Gitty had said the same things that Mrs. Rosenberg had told him. She sounded like a wonderful person. And he did want to get married.

Aryeh left Chavi elated when he agreed to meet Gitty. She was positive that she had found Gitty's *bashert*, and she immediately picked up the phone for another long-distance call, this time to Gitty. She shared her news and began to explain why she thought the *shidduch* was right. "I know you want someone learning full time, but he's a real *ben Torah*. You should hear Shmuel talk about him. He learns well and even though he has to take care of his daughter, himself, and the house and go to work, he is always careful to attend his daily *shiur*. Can you imagine! You know with a man like that that you will always have a home of Torah. He is also kind and caring. What kind of man could take care of a baby from right after birth on his own. I heard she is just the most delicious thing in the world....

"Yes, I know it would be difficult to care for someone else's child. But she's still a baby. Soon she'll be like your own.

And imagine the *chesed* of knowing you provided this innocent baby with a mother. I know it's not what you pictured, but look at the substance, not the outside issues. I really think it's worth a shot. I don't know why, but I have a very good feeling about this. Gitty, are you there?...

"Yes, I know I'm talking a lot, but I'm just so excited.... Here are some numbers for you to call about him. As far as I'm concerned, you don't have to call anyone. Shmuel has known him for years and can't think of one bad thing to say about him.... Of course it makes sense just to call. To put your mind at ease.... Yes, here are the numbers...."

ℵ ℵ

Sooner than anyone but Chavi would have imagined, a date was scheduled. On the day of the date, Chavi arranged for a neighbor to watch Elchanan after she dropped off Yitzchak at cheder and Faigy at play group. She went straight to the Kosel. Oh, if only this would work!

Between each date, Chavi walked around on pins and needles. She didn't take no for an answer from either side, always there to explain to them how the points that concerned them weren't valid or at least weren't significant enough not to give the relationship another chance. Even without considering her intervention, things seemed to be going pretty smoothly. They liked each other's personalities. They each looked forward to their next date. They shared common goals. Chavi's hopes were soaring high.

At dinner one Sunday night, Shmuel watched with surprise as Chavi jumped to answer every call. Usually, she groaned at each new ring and waited for Shmuel to answer, assuming it was another business call for him. "Chavi, why are you so anxious to answer the phone?"

"I'm expecting an important call."

"Who?"

"Aryeh Zilberman is supposed to call me after last night's date. I'm hoping it's a clincher."

"You got him to go out with Gitty?"

"Go out? This is their eighth date. Oh, am I nervous!"

Eighth date, Shmuel mused. He was impressed that his wife had managed to pull the *shidduch* off. But he also felt terribly left out. His old friend was going out with Gitty and his wife was the *shadchan* and he hadn't even known about it. He did remember Chavi telling him that Aryeh had agreed to meet Gitty, but it had slipped his mind, so he had never asked what happened. It was funny, though, that Chavi hadn't told him.

Just then the phone rang. It was Aryeh. Before he had a chance to say a thing, Chavi asked him if he had sent the flowers. He said that he had, and Gitty was really touched. She even called him to say thank you — and that was a big step. But....

Chavi's heart stopped. The tone of his voice for that "but" boded bad tidings. "But what?" she nearly screamed into the phone.

"Mrs. Rosenberg, this date didn't go so well. I don't know what happened exactly. We were discussing divorces in general. And I think I said something about how people really have to work it out unless it's an extreme case like mine. I didn't mean anything about her. I was just talking in general. And she got very offended and insulting. She started yelling at me. In public. Yelling at me — that I had no right to judge her. I tried to get her to calm down, but then I got upset. She has some temper, let me tell you.

"Listen, I like her a lot. I was sure it was going to go. But right now, I don't think I could go out with her again. I'm scared of getting involved with someone who gets angry like that. I'm a pretty nice guy, but I don't want to have to watch every word. What if she gets angry like that with my daughter? I don't think I'd ever forgive her."

Whoa. The change of direction hit Chavi hard. She was totally unprepared for this, having spent the morning daydreaming that he had proposed. She was speechless. Aryeh would have probably found that amusing if he hadn't been so irate.

Finally getting her voice back, Chavi said, "I understand that you're upset, but I've known Gitty for over a decade and I have never once seen her angry. I'm going to call her to see what happened and then get back to you."

"No, you don't need to get back to me," Aryeh said adamantly.

Chavi hung up the phone, stunned. Shmuel asked her what had happened. She was afraid that filling him in on the whole story would involve *lashon hara,* so she said simply, "It's off."

Shmuel saw her incredible disappointment and knew he should remain silent. A few minutes later, Chavi got up and said she was going to call Gitty. Shmuel had to leave by that time anyway. He wished her luck as he grabbed his hat and jacket, and Chavi began to dial.

"Hello?"

"Hi. It's me. What happened last night?"

"Chavi, I just don't know. We went out. I was really, really looking forward to the date. He sent me flowers for Shabbos and...."

"Really? Wow."

"Yes, I was quite touched. I knew it meant that things were moving in the right direction. I was so happy. Well, our date was set for last night, *motza'ei Shabbos*, as you know. All day I felt sick, but I didn't want to cancel. I really wanted to see him and thank him in person for the flowers. I had called him, but still I wanted to see him in person."

"You called him? That was gutsy."

"I wanted to show him that I really appreciated the gesture and that I thought the relationship was getting serious. I've never called a man socially before. Anyway, all Shabbos I was feeling under the weather. My day ran according to Murphy's law. Everything that could go wrong went wrong. The worst part was that for some stupid reason I decided to tell my mother about Aryeh. I never tell her about my dates. Every time we discuss anything related to marriage she starts to browbeat me and bawl me out. She still says that I caused the divorce and irreparably destroyed my future.

"But I was there for Shabbos and I thought it would be insulting not to tell her about Aryeh after seven dates. I was thinking about it all day, but I couldn't bring myself to tell her anything until after I got home after Havdallah and got dressed for the date. I thought she'd be thrilled. Instead, she asked me if I was sure I was ready to get married. Maybe I was going to be as immature as I was last time. Was there something wrong with him that he was interested in marrying a divorcee like myself? She went on and on like that.

"I tried to get off the phone, but she wouldn't let me. She insulted me over and over again. I wanted to hang up on her, but she is my mother, so I just listened until I heard the doorbell ring. By then my head was spinning and I felt ill, but, as they say in show business, the show must go on.

"The date was okay. The beginning went well, but then he brought up divorces. I lost my cool. He seemed to be saying what my mother had just finished yelling about. Was he trying to drop me? I actually lost my temper. He told me to stop yelling. I wasn't yelling, but I was angry and I guess that's what he meant. He really touched on a raw nerve. You know I don't usually get angry. I hope he wasn't upset. Did you speak to him yet?"

"I wanted to talk to you right away. I'll get back to you with his answer."

Not only did the *shidduch* seem to be over, but Gitty didn't even realize it on her own. How would Chavi ever tell her? She'd have to give it one last shot.

Chavi sat down to think over what to tell Aryeh that would vindicate Gitty's anger without incriminating her mother. After half an hour, she came up with a plan — she would say that Gitty rarely got angry, but a Shabbos host had yelled at her about getting divorced, and she hadn't been feeling well, and so forth.

When she called with Gitty's story, though, Aryeh said that he understood but he had thought it all through and he couldn't continue seeing her. He thanked Chavi for her time and effort and hung up.

Chavi couldn't believe it was off. She had been so sure that their engagement was imminent. How would she break the news to Gitty? She couldn't do it. She decided to wait until the next day to call. Maybe by some miracle Aryeh would have a change of heart.

But he didn't call. Chavi made the hardest call of her

life, and the story was over. As hard as it was on her, she knew the one who was really broken was Gitty. In addition to having her dream of marrying Aryeh destroyed, she had to contend again with the feelings that she had caused its destruction.

The only way Chavi managed to get through the day was by completely pushing the whole issue out of her mind.

19

When Shmuel came in for lunch the next day, he put the mail on the table as he usually did. A large vanilla-colored envelope addressed in calligraphy caught Chavi's eye. It was an American invitation.

She opened the envelope to find herself invited to her sister Rochel's oldest child's bar mitzvah, the first bar mitzvah in the Baumel family. Chavi's mother had been filling her in on all the arrangements as they were planned, but the reality of the upcoming event didn't strike her until she got the invitation. If only she could go and see her family again!

Shmuel came to look over her shoulder at the invitation. "The bar mitzvah is in three and a half weeks. Are you going to go?"

"Can I?" she asked.

"I don't see why not."

"It's expensive. And who's going to watch the kids?"

"It's important, and it's worth the money. We can't all afford to go, though, so I'll stay home with the kids. I'm sure my mother will help. Maybe you can take Elchanan. That way, the kids will be in school in the morning, and we'll all come home together. We'll find a baby-sitter for the afternoon. And I'll take care of the nights. I know how hard it would be for you not to be there."

"Thanks," said Chavi, overwhelmed at his thoughtfulness. "I guess we can work everything out. I appreciate you letting me go."

Soon the arrangements were made. With each passing day, Chavi's excitement grew. She would be flying alone with one-and-a-half-year-old Elchanan. Her mother and Zeidy Max were flying a week earlier. Chavi didn't want to leave her family for a Shabbos, so she was going to be missing the Shabbos bar mitzvah festivities. She would arrive on Sunday, in time to get rested for the main event on Tuesday night.

Shmuel's mother offered to come every morning to dress and feed the children while Shmuel went to shul. Chavi carefully cooked, labeled, and froze meals for Shmuel to warm up while she was gone. She left detailed instructions taped to the refrigerator to make things go smoothly.

Arranging a baby-sitter for the afternoon was surprisingly easy. Chavi found a responsible newlywed who had just arrived in Israel and was looking for a steady job. She was happy with the extra money that the Rosenberg job would give her and more than willing to help Yitzchak with his homework, take the children out to play, bathe them, and get them ready for bed. Chavi made sure the children got to know the baby-sitter before she left and informed Yitzchak's therapists that he would be skipping the sessions that were scheduled to take place in her absence. Shmuel would put the children to sleep.

It all seemed well planned out, which alleviated some of Chavi's guilt at leaving. This was the first time she was going to be away from home since her marriage and her first time back in the States since she had moved to Israel. She only planned on being away for five days, including travel time, but it was a big trip for her nonetheless. Her days revolved around her family and her job, so this was certainly going to be a change of pace.

Yitzchak and Faigy seemed a bit nervous about her leaving and asked about her plans again and again. Their bedtime stories centered around either her trip or the arrangements for their care while she was away. Chavi wasn't sure if she was doing the right thing by preparing them so thoroughly. Perhaps it would have been better if she had surprised them when the time came so they wouldn't have to worry ahead. But eventually she decided that even with the worry, this method was better. Her children would know in the future that they could trust their mother to inform them if there were to be any major changes in their daily routines.

The older children also thought it was terribly unfair that Elchanan got to go with her. Chavi explained to them that they went to school, and that was special. So Elchanan, who was a baby, got to go to the bar mitzvah. She promised she would bring them presents and pictures, and that mollified them a bit. Still, they were nervous with the uncertainty that a new situation entails.

Shmuel was also nervous, truth be told. It all seemed simple and easy, but he had never been in charge of the family before and the responsibility worried him. At least he could always rely on his mother in a pinch.

As plans were being made, Shmuel's mother called them

to invite them for the Shabbos before Chavi was to leave. Although Shabbos at her in-laws didn't excite Chavi, the offer was a tremendous relief. Her flight was due to depart four hours after Shabbos and she had been concerned about how she would finish her trip preparations, cook for Shabbos, and clean up after Shabbos was over before leaving to the airport. Now that would all be taken care of and she could leave the house in order on Friday and focus solely on her journey. They had also just finished adding a small bedroom and bathroom where a porch had been, and Chavi wanted to make sure she had a chance to clean up the construction debris before she left.

The addition was a story in itself. A group of the families in their apartment building had jointly decided to add on to their homes. Getting permission from the building council for the addition was the biggest hurdle, and once this had been handled by one of the veteran owners, the building residents seized on the opportunity to expand their cramped quarters. Shmuel and Chavi had debated at length over whether they should be included in the plans for the addition.

Had they chosen not to, the foundation for future expansion would be laid, but the work would remain unfinished. A house addition was way beyond their budget at that point. Yet their apartment was certainly smaller than what they had been accustomed to in America. Although by Israeli standards their three-bedroom apartment was more than ample for their five-person family, it would be a pleasure to have a larger place. In addition, if they didn't build on with the other owners, the cost would be nearly double if they decided to go about it individually in the future.

They decided that, even in the absence of available funds, it was a good investment and they would find a way to finance it. They applied to a number of banks for mortgages and soon accepted the best offer. Although their budget seemed to be stretched to its limit, they were sure that somehow they would manage to meet the monthly payments.

The work had taken over three months, during which they were subject to much noise and rubbish, but was finally done. Chavi loved the extra space and looked forward to putting it to good use. The extra storage area would free their apartment of some of its clutter, and they now had plenty of room for guests. Chavi was relieved that, with the Shabbos preparations off her head, she would be able to do a thorough job of cleaning up the sand, grit, electric-wire snippings, and odds and ends left in the workers' wake.

She began to feel homesick for her children as she packed the house for Shabbos, even before she left. She laughed at herself for being so attached to her children. After all, she would be gone for less than a week. As they loaded their things into a taxi, she ran through a mental checklist and made sure that everything was in order, since she was to be leaving to the airport from her in-laws' house.

Shabbos preparations at her in-laws' were much more relaxed than they were at her home. Her mother-in-law had cleaning help, and much of the Shabbos food was bought from a popular take-out place in the center of town. The younger Rosenbergs entered a clean and delicious-smelling house.

Mrs. Rosenberg kissed both Shmuel and Chavi lightly on the cheek in greeting and embraced each of the grandchildren tightly. Soon the children were enjoying cake and juice with their *zeidy* while Shmuel and Chavi unpacked. They hadn't come to the senior Rosenbergs for Shabbos in a while.

Shmuel was delighted to be at his parents' home. The fact that he was relieved of his usual jobs was reason enough to be happy, but he also found a certain comfort in returning to his old, familiar environment. He enjoyed the aromas from the kitchen that foretold of his favorite foods to be served later that evening, and he enjoyed catching up with his father on the family news and politics. These were pleasures he seldom had the chance to enjoy, now that his schedule had become so full and the family had grown larger. Soon he was sitting on the couch next to Chavi looking at pictures that his parents had taken at the bris of the newest Rosenberg grandchild, while his father, looking over their shoulders, told them what was happening in each shot.

Chavi heard Faigy singing a new song she had learned in school to her *bubby* in the kitchen. She was also enjoying the relaxed, warm atmosphere, but she worried over what the rest of the Shabbos would bring. She always felt so uptight around her mother-in-law. She reviewed to herself Shmuel's words from so long before. Perhaps her mother-in-law was insecure, and her sharp style of speech was a result of the combination of her cultural background and that insecurity. Chavi secretly vowed to be more amenable than usual.

Later that evening, with Elchanan soundly asleep in his portable crib and Yitzchak and Faigy having drifted off to sleep on the couch in the adjoining living room, the adults enjoyed the end of the Shabbos meal. The conversation had been congenial and natural. It had been a while since the four of them had a leisurely and casual conversation, and there was plenty to discuss. Over dessert, Chavi thanked her mother-in-law for having them for Shabbos and for all the help she had offered for the duration of her trip abroad.

"You're welcome," Mrs. Rosenberg replied. "As soon as I heard your plans, I cleared my calendar. I knew that I would be bearing the brunt of the work in your absence."

She knew she would bear the brunt of the work! Chavi fumed. Had Chavi asked anything of her? She knew she shouldn't have come for Shabbos. She didn't want to be a burden and she certainly didn't want to be made to feel like one. If her mother-in-law was doing anything, it was because Shmuel had asked her to. Chavi hadn't asked anything of her and certainly didn't want anything from her.

Shmuel saw that Chavi was upset, but he continued to eat his pie. If there would be any veiled verbal sparring, it was par for the course.

Chavi's conscience got the better of her right before she stormed away from the table in protest. Hadn't she been waiting for a moment like this? It was almost physically painful to swallow her wounded pride. But had her pride really been wounded? she asked herself, trying to be rational. An inner conversation took place so rapidly that no one else noticed a lull in the conversation.

First of all, Chavi pointed out to herself, her mother-in-law wasn't complaining. She had just said that she knew a trip meant she would have to work hard. She didn't even say that Chavi had forced it on her. That was an insinuation that Chavi assumed to be there, but maybe it wasn't. Either way, truthfully, Mrs. Rosenberg was doing a lot — having them for Shabbos, coming every morning and caring for the children, and also pitching in if other emergencies would come up. Maybe Chavi hadn't felt enough appreciation for what she was doing. Perhaps her mother-in-law wasn't expecting any appreciation, but she would probably be tickled pink to get a bit.

"I really do appreciate your help," Chavi told her mother-in-law warmly. "You really always do a lot for us, and you'll be doing even more now that I'll be away. I hope we don't take advantage of your generosity."

Both Dr. Rosenberg and his son stopped chewing midbite at this unexpected thanks, quite a change from the acidic retort that Mrs. Rosenberg's comments tended to elicit, especially from her children-in-law. They were so taken for granted that they fazed no one, including Mrs. Rosenberg herself. This new manner was a bit uncomfortable because it was so different, but at the same time it was most pleasing.

"Of course not," Mrs. Rosenberg said. "You know how much I love to help you. It means a lot to me to get to spend time with my grandchildren. If anyone needs a break, my dear, it's you with your schedule and all, not me."

Maybe Shmuel was onto something, thought Chavi, enjoying the success of her experiment. It reminded her of Gitty's good-bye party. Now if she could only make it a habit!

ꟻ ꟻ

When Chavi came in with the children the next afternoon, after spending almost two hours outside to give her in-laws some quiet time to rest, she was greeted by her mother-in-law's exclamation, "Ugh, those children are absolutely black! Did everyone see them walking around like that? What did you do — stick them in the gutter?"

Chavi's blood began to boil again. It was true that Yitzchak and Faigy looked a little dirty, but so what? They had been out for a long time. Couldn't she at least say hello first? It wasn't like Bubby Rosenberg was in charge of their laundry. And did it matter if her neighbors saw her grandchildren dirty? Couldn't kids get dirty? It was certainly no reflection on her. But, as usual, all she cared about was what everyone thought of her.

Chavi overran her irate thoughts by talking over them. "How did you manage to entertain your children outside and still keep them clean? I could sure use your ideas."

Mrs. Rosenberg was flattered. The tone of her reply was decidedly more cordial than her original attack had been. "It's almost impossible to keep kids clean sometimes. My children used to get filthy, too. Don't tell anyone, but sometimes I would keep the kids in, just to preserve their clothes. Really, though, that's not right. Clothes are made to be lived in, don't you think?"

Chavi smiled to herself and ushered the children into the bathroom to wash up. Her new way of interacting with her mother-in-law was both fun and enlightening. What a shame it was that she had let things drag on for so long the way they had.

She was even a bit embarrassed at herself. How much emotional energy had been inappropriately used in getting upset over nothing?

20

Chavi's flight was, thankfully, uneventful. Elchanan slept most of the way, and Chavi even managed to sleep for a few hours herself. Her excitement over the upcoming family reunion, in addition to her nervousness over Elchanan's possible awakening, made her sleep fitful.

Her sleepiness vanished as the plane prepared for landing in Newark, New Jersey. Her brother Dovid was there to meet her at the airport. They had a long ride to Lakewood and plenty to catch up on. But with Elchanan tired of sitting, Chavi spent most of the ride trying to entertain and distract her son.

Even this could not detract from her enjoyment of the ride and of being in America again. The vast plains and busy highways, even the tollbooths and the variety of races that made up the population, revived long-buried fondness for the country she had once called home. The cool morning air was fresh with dew and Chavi enjoyed feeling it as she looked out the window.

It was good to see her brother. It had been three and a half years since they had last seen each other in person, at their mother's wedding. He still had the rosy cheeks and twinkle in his eye that endeared him to everyone, but now there was also a streak of gray in his beard and some smile lines around his eyes. He looked more dignified. His impish cuteness was still there, but he looked, well, older.

As much as Elchanan allowed, they shared the news of their children's developments. Dovid described the Shabbos of the bar mitzvah. He said that Yanky, the bar mitzvah boy, had done a wonderful job with the *leining*. He hadn't spoken, but was slated to do so at the Tuesday evening party. The entire extended family had eaten the Shabbos meals together in the shul hall, and a few times people had commented that only Chavi and her family were missing. Of course, he mentioned, they all missed Abba, who would have been so proud to see his oldest grandson *lein*.

Chavi noticed that her brother looked a bit uncomfortable when she asked how Max had enjoyed the festivities. Dovid told her, "Everything went smoothly. He was so warm and friendly that he fit into the family right away. Ima looks happy and content." He paused, and then admitted, "It was strange seeing someone else at her side at a family *simchah*. It's bad enough having Abba gone, but it's worse having him replaced."

Chavi knew her brother was a sensitive man. Since her nature was different and because she was more involved in her mother's new life and her relationship with Max, she herself no longer felt particularly emotional about Max's joining the family. She understood, though, that it was hard for her brother, and she expressed her awareness and empathy.

Soon they were at his house, where she would be staying. Their mother was staying at Rochel's house and other relatives had been placed at various other families' houses. When Chavi entered the house, her nieces and nephews greeted her quite energetically and helped her with her bags and with her son. In a minute, her sister-in-law, Bracha, came out of the kitchen, wiping her hands on her apron and demanding that her children give their aunt "some room to breathe."

Chavi couldn't get over how the children had grown, particularly the three youngest whom she had never met. The children were indeed a clear reminder that time had passed. Bracha, on the other hand, looked exactly as Chavi remembered, tall, thin, sprite-like, and simple looking. She wore a brown tweed skirt and a vanilla-colored blouse with a ruffle down the center, covered by a flowered apron and a light brown snood. She still wore timeless sensible shoes, and a touch of pink lipstick gave her color.

Bracha scooped up Elchanan and looked him over. As if to voice her approval, she planted a kiss on his cheek and twirled around with him, making Elchanan giggle with delight. Then she leaned over to kiss Chavi, welcoming her to the country.

After half an hour of settling in, Chavi sat down to drink coffee in the kitchen with her sister-in-law, while the children played with Elchanan on the floor nearby. Elchanan was ecstatic, due in part to all the attention and new toys and in part to being overtired. Either way, his excited responses to his cousins' attempts at entertaining him were ample encouragement for them to continue.

Chavi looked around her brother's townhouse kitchen. The Formica floor was very worn in a few spots and the dark wood of the cabinets gave the room a heavy, tired look. The old shag carpet in the dining room that was adjacent to the kitchen complemented the style of the furniture there. They were both old and had seen better days. In her mind, Chavi contrasted the home to her bright white and airy apartment. She enjoyed the sparser furniture there, which gave a crisper, fresher impression. But her brother's home was cozier and much roomier. She had to admit that the atmosphere was inviting and comfortable.

She knew Rochel's house was different. Rochel knew how to decorate and carefully cultivated her home. Any extra available, and sometimes not-so-available, funds were invested in her home and her family's grooming. Rochel liked pretty things. When Chavi stepped in to say hello that afternoon, Rochel's immaculate housekeeping and the elegant atmosphere that the house exuded impressed her. She spent about an hour in the black-and-white, modern kitchen, saying hello to each child and to the other relatives milling around the hosts' house.

Rochel looked mature and sophisticated, even in the robe she was wearing. She had put on a few pounds since Chavi had last seen her, but they had done her good and left her looking healthy and matronly. She didn't share that observation with Rochel, who most probably wouldn't have taken it too fondly, but she felt it sincerely.

Later, she fell soundly asleep, comfortably ensconced in the familiarity and love of her family. Elchanan slept through the night, except for one waking, during which Chavi placed a quick call to Israel to let Shmuel and the kids know that she had arrived safely. The next morning they were both energetically ready to face their first full day in America.

Chavi spent the morning at Rochel's helping her decide on the seating arrangements and filling in place cards. During the afternoon, she went shopping with her mother in Dovid's car, while Bracha graciously watched Elchanan.

It was a special treat to be alone with her mother again, especially since she was unencumbered of worrying about her children. They drove about forty-five minutes to the mall, where the two of them took pleasure in window shopping, going from one outlet store to the next. It was hard for Chavi to pass up so many beautiful things and so many bargains, but their budget didn't allow for any impulsive purchases. Her mother treated her to an exquisite outfit that was at a reduced price. Chavi immediately decided to wear it to the bar mitzvah. It was flattering to her figure, and the soft peach material accented her natural coloring. She had brought with her one of the outfits that she had bought for her own *sheva berachos*, but it had grown just a bit too small and the material had pilled in a few places. It certainly could not compare to this fresh, modern-looking new outfit.

Chavi and Mrs. Schneider picked up a few basic necessities that were significantly lower in price than they were in Yerushalayim, and Chavi found some presents for her children. They stopped at an eating area before they left and each bought a soda to enjoy before they began the return trip.

"Do you ever miss living in America...the shopping...the cars?" Mrs. Schneider asked Chavi.

Chavi admitted, "Honestly, I do. But at the same time, I'm really happy with my life in Israel. I never thought I'd say this, but thank you for being the impetus for the change. It probably never would have happened without your initiative."

"I'm also very satisfied with the move. The longer I'm settled in Eretz Yisrael, the more I appreciate it. I should have done it years ago." Mrs. Schneider's eyes focused on some faraway spot as she finished speaking. Chavi knew she was thinking of Abba. In some strange way, she was glad that her mother still thought of him.

"It's hard to be away from the family," she broke in on her mother's thoughts. "I didn't realize how much I missed everyone and how long it's been until I got here. My own nieces and nephews barely know who I am. I feel like Dovid and Rochel are building a life together and I'm left out. I have you and Shmuel's family, so I don't feel alone, but I still feel like I'm missing out."

"I certainly know what you mean. It's even harder for me, since they are my children and grandchildren."

Their words were enough to convey their shared feelings. They spent the next few minutes sipping their drinks silently, watching the passersby.

Chavi glanced at her watch. "We'd better be going. Elchanan is probably going to get crabby soon and I don't want to take advantage of Bracha's kindness."

ᘓ ᘓ

The next day, Chavi shared a lazy morning with Bracha and her children. In the early afternoon, they bathed the children and put them to sleep, leaving some time for a short rest themselves. As the evening hours approached, everyone dressed for the bar mitzvah. They drove to the hall an hour before the affair was scheduled to allow time for pictures before the guests arrived. As the photographer arranged the family, Chavi thought of her children and wondered how everyone was managing without her.

The guests began to arrive as the last shots were being snapped. Chavi had a wonderful time meeting long-forgotten relatives and friends. It was fascinating to see how each of her contemporaries had settled into her chosen lifestyle. A particularly talkative friend of hers from high school, who had settled in Lakewood and traveled in Rochel's social circle, had become even more talkative, controlling and directing the conversation, peppering her words with questions and breaking in with superlatives before the answer was finished. She was so friendly that Chavi barely minded, and her manner brought back memories of their shared time together in school. A cousin who had always been rather scatterbrained remained so, but now, instead of trying to mind her schoolbooks, she was busy trying to tend to her energetic children. It was amusing to see her friends and relatives with the same characters they had had as young teenagers, now being applied to their adult roles. Chavi wondered what they were thinking of her.

It gave her a warm feeling to be embraced by her mother's old cronies. For the moment Chavi felt that she was back in the protective cocoon of childhood. She was so happy to have come.

After an hour of hors d'oeuvres and soft music, the guests were invited to wash and find their seats, as dinner was about to be served. While Chavi enjoyed her fruit plate, she had more time to study the affair. As expected, everything was quite elegant, from the hors d'oeuvres being served by gloved and tuxedoed waiters to the violin and piano combination playing softly in the background. The tables were laid with starched white linens, accented with smaller golden mesh cloths. A tall, thin vase holding white gladiolas and gold-painted wildflowers stood at the center of each table, and the china, a standard white with gold trim, matched everything perfectly.

As Chavi ate the second course, creamy artichoke soup, she noticed that the walls were painted with raised pastel flower arrangements and gold trimmings, while the carpeting beneath her feet was a light mauve. The whole atmosphere was so tranquil and distinctive that Chavi felt for the evening that she was of royal descent. She had attended many fancy affairs before, but it had been over eight years since she had been at an American affair, and she viewed everything through fresh eyes.

She made a mental note to relay her compliments to Rochel. But although she felt happily spoiled, she was also uncomfortable. She couldn't help but add up how much the evening must be costing her middle-class sister and brother-in-law. True, it was nice, but it seemed such a waste. After all, she really wasn't of royal descent and, as far as she knew, neither were any of the other party goers. It didn't seem appropriate to be acting as if they were.

Even the outfits of the immediate family of the bar-mitzvah boy seemed out of place. Rochel actually wore a tea-length gown, as did her daughters. Chavi wondered what could have been done with the thousand dollars that it must have cost just to outfit the family. She pushed her thoughts away, reminding herself that someone else's expenditures were none of her concern.

She found it curious, though, how her mind-set had changed without her notice over the years. She remembered with amusement the tears she had shed over the simplicity of her wedding. It seemed that more of the Israeli culture had seeped into her way of thinking than she had realized. She wondered what else about her was different. She had noticed that it had become difficult for her to complete an idea completely in English without groping for words. That was acceptable to her, though, considering that her Hebrew had improved to the extent that she could almost be called fluent.

It was time for the bar-mitzvah boy to speak. Despite his age, Yanky had a wonderful command of the audience, knowing how to pause for effect and even deliver a well-timed joke or two. Chavi noticed her mother crying, but it didn't bother her that much, especially as she recalled the tears she herself had shed at Yitzchak's preschool graduation party. If she could get so emotional over such a milestone, it was certainly within a grandmother's rights to do so at a bar mitzvah. Chavi wondered what Yitzchak's bar mitzvah speech would be like. His stuttering was much improved, but it was still very noticeable at times of nervousness and excitement. Delivering a bar-mitzvah *derashah* most definitely fell into both categories. There was plenty of time until then, though, so there wasn't much point in worrying now.

Between the speeches that followed Yanky's there were interludes that allowed for socializing. One of the cousins at Chavi's table remarked, "It's so nice that you were able to come, Chavi. I'm sure you miss your husband, but it must be great to have a vacation from the housework!"

Chavi laughed along with the other women, but inside she knew the opposite was true. She missed her daily routine a bit, but Shmuel was becoming less and less of a focus in her life.

ꙮ ꙮ

Chavi's last day in America was spent in Brooklyn. She got a facial and manicure that Mrs. Rosenberg had insisted on treating her to, and then she met Shmuel's sisters Ruchie and Freidel for lunch in a quaint dairy café. The conversation was pleasant but stilted, as each lady carefully chose what to say and what not to say. They shared pictures and anecdotes. Chavi told them about Shmuel's organization and Yitzchak's progress and filled them in on other family news that they hadn't heard yet.

Before they left the restaurant, Chavi asked them for gift suggestions for their mother.

The younger of the two, Freidel, said in a voice that dripped with sweetness, "How considerate of you to think of that, but it's really unnecessary. Ma comes often, and we know that money is an issue for you. I'm sure she'd be upset if she knew you spent money on her when it will probably mean that you have to be without. Just forget it. I'll make sure to mention to her that you thought of getting her something. Buy something for her grandchildren instead."

"Please don't say anything about the gift to your mother," Chavi said, thinking, *The apple sure hasn't fallen far from the tree.* She was tempted to ask them sarcastically if they had any extra *maaser* money they could share with her, but she held her tongue. She could behave herself for a few hours every eight years or so, couldn't she?

She'd have to decide on her own what would be appreciated. She hoped she wouldn't insult her mother-in-law by a gift that wasn't to her liking. Numerous times, Chavi had heard her complain about presents she had received. "That's what they think of me? If I wanted that sort of thing, I would have gotten it myself," she'd say. Chavi decided to risk the criticism, wanting to show her appreciation for all that her mother-in-law did for them.

A few minutes later she spotted a boutique that sold a variety of gift items and picked out a pretty wicker basket containing bath oil, lotion, scented perfume, a loofah sponge, and other things of that nature. With luck, the feminine, personal gift would go over well.

Afterwards, Chavi bought herself a new robe and then spent an hour visiting two of her closest friends, who had settled in New York. Elchanan spent part of the day with her and part of the day with his Rosenberg cousins. They took the bus back to Lakewood as darkness began to descend on the city.

Back at Dovid's house, Chavi packed quickly and prepared for her midnight flight. Bracha made a light supper for the whole Baumel crew so they could spend a bit more time together. Soon it was time to bid everyone a tearful good-bye, made all the more emotional by the fact that no one knew when they would be together again.

21

Back in the Rosenberg home, the first day of Chavi's absence went smoothly. Shmuel got a little annoyed before bedtime when Faigy asked him for the tenth time what Mommy was doing and how much longer it would be until she and Elchanan came back. Inside, though, he commiserated with her. The house was so empty with Chavi gone.

The next afternoon, when he checked the mailbox on his way up with the children, he was surprised to find a postcard from Chavi. Knowing there was no way it could have gotten across the ocean that fast, he checked the postmark. It had been mailed at Ben Gurion Airport in Israel. *How thoughtful of her,* he thought. *She really is a terrific mother.*

After they got upstairs, he gave the kids the postcard, which showed an El-Al plane, to look at while he set up lunch. Before long they came after him, begging him to read the postcard to them. In childlike anticipation, he scanned the postcard for mention of his name. It wasn't there. He felt disappointed, even though he knew it was a mother's gesture of consideration for her children and that he should be too mature to expect a postcard.

It was hard for Shmuel to be in charge of the children as soon as he came home, but at the same time he enjoyed it. Since his regular schedule was so busy, he rarely spent much time discussing the children's days with them. Sometimes Chavi would share a cute anecdote from one of them with him during dinner. Now he had a chance to experience their wit and charm firsthand.

By the second night, he and the children had figured out a mutually agreeable routine for their evenings together. Shmuel made sure to stop at a candy store or a toy store on his way home each day to have a bribe ready, in case any unforeseen circumstances should arise. When he got home, he would sit on the couch with his clean, fed, and pajama-clad children and discussed the day's events, went over notes from school, or read a book together for half an hour. Then he would carry them to their room in their position of choice — Faigy liked to ride piggyback, and Yitzchak preferred to be carried upside down. They would say Shema together, and he would kiss them and shut the light.

The bedtime routine continued for close to another hour, with the children coming out to get a drink, use the bathroom, or share a story that they had forgotten about. Shmuel waited to eat dinner until he was sure that they were really asleep.

He didn't bother warming up the food Chavi had left with her meticulously prepared schedule. Instead, he would rummage through the refrigerator, hoping the baby-sitter had put away some leftovers from the children's dinner. If he couldn't find anything, he would eat a bowl of cereal or a sandwich and tell himself that the next day he should pick up a falafel on the way home.

Dinner was especially lonely. The house was perfectly quiet. The first night, he shut most of the lights, as no one needed them. Although he did it to save electricity, it was also out of a subconscious desire for a physical sign of the frigid atmosphere. With the house dark and uninviting, he felt more justified in his forlorn feelings. At least he had been able to convince his night-*seder* learning partner to come to his house for these few nights. It broke the stillness for an hour or two.

The days went by quickly enough, though, and soon it was the day of Chavi's scheduled arrival home. Shmuel, Yitzchak, and Faigy looked forward to the homecoming with great anticipation. They had barely spoken to Chavi since she'd left. After she had called to say that she had arrived safely, they hadn't heard from her. Shmuel had called Dovid's house to see how her trip was going, but Chavi was out, so he just left a message.

In anticipation of Chavi's arrival, Shmuel left work early and relieved the baby-sitter of her duties. He had the children make "welcome home" signs and tape them to the door. Shmuel set the table for five and warmed up one of the meals he had neglected to warm up for himself so that it would be ready when Chavi came in. He was happy that he had thought of having a meal for her to enjoy as soon as she came home.

Finally, he heard the children, who had been glued to the window in search of her taxi, squealing with delight, "Mommy's home! Mommy's home!"

Shmuel asked the children to wait upstairs while he went

to help Chavi with her bags, but his request went unheeded. The three of them hurried down to the street together. After a few moments of greetings, Yitzchak and Faigy took charge of Elchanan and Shmuel took the two suitcases. Together they escorted Chavi, carrying only her hand luggage, back upstairs.

"Oh, look at these beautiful welcome signs!" Chavi exclaimed upon seeing the front door. When she entered the house and looked around, though, she was taken aback at how small her apartment looked. It was hard to believe that this was the livable dwelling she had left just a few days before. She knew that she had to readjust after being in larger American homes, but her apartment suddenly looked very cramped — almost miniature — and dirty. There were crayon markings on the kitchen table and jelly stains on the refrigerator door and at least five toys sticking out from under the couch.

The house smelled good, though, and Chavi decided to keep her negative comments to herself. She reminded herself that it was just her exhaustion from the trip that made her so critical, and the house was sometimes significantly messier under her care. It very easily could have been worse. "It smells delicious. Did you cook something? Lasagna?"

Shmuel told her proudly, "I warmed up one of your meals for dinner."

"You didn't eat them? I was careful to make sure you had meals every night. It took me a long time to figure out that schedule," she said, disappointed.

"Oh, I ate a lot of them. They were great. But sometimes I was too tired to defrost and heat up food for myself. At least now you won't have to cook for a day or two!"

Chavi was annoyed that her well-designed plan hadn't been followed. What was so hard about warming up a prepared meal? She had done the hard part. She felt her work hadn't been properly appreciated.

By now, her two oldest children were talking to her simultaneously and the noise was becoming overwhelming. Shmuel was standing nearby, eager to converse. Her exhaustion and disappointment, combined with her family's needs, were becoming too much for her to handle.

Chavi smiled at the children and waited for them to finish their sentences. After nodding to show interest, she said to Shmuel, "I know you've had a hard job watching the children the last few days, but I'm so tired from the flight. Would you mind letting me go rest for a bit? I think it would make everything a lot easier for me."

"Okay, go ahead," Shmuel said, knowing how draining flying could be. Personally, he would have preferred her company and her cheery attitude, and he had thought her arrival would be the end of his parent-on-duty stint. But he knew that it was only right to let her go.

Chavi rushed into the bedroom, quickly changed into a robe and snood, and lay down in bed. She shut her eyes and willed herself to sleep to avoid thinking too many depressing thoughts. Soon, she was blissfully oblivious to the world.

She awoke two hours later, groggy and dazed. The clock on the nightstand read 7:30 P.M., and though she had fallen into a deep night sleep and wasn't physically ready to awaken, she knew she had to or she wouldn't be able to get back on schedule. As she walked to the bathroom to wash up and then felt the cold water on her hands and face, she slowly returned to her normal waking awareness. The nap had greatly improved her mood, though she still felt a bit disoriented. Her house felt foreign and unfamiliar, but, knowing that a day or two would change that, she went out to the living room to see what was going on.

The children jumped on her as she entered the room, but now it felt welcoming rather than annoying. Shmuel offered her the cold leftovers of the meal they had eaten during her rest, apologizing for not having waited. Chavi sat down at the table, suddenly quite hungry. Her own cooking tasted great to her and she was glad to be served, cold or not.

After she had eaten a few bites, she unzipped her suitcases to find the gifts she had bought for the children. Yitzchak was happy with the model plane sets and immediately began assembling one. Chavi had been tempted to buy him a handheld video game. They looked like so much fun and the prices were less than a third of what they had been when she was a child and wanted one. Yet she passed them up, afraid that they would distract Yitzchak from his studies. Although he was only six, learning didn't come easy to him and Chavi did her best to encourage him to keep up, complimenting him whenever she could find an excuse and rewarding him with small gifts whenever she noticed progress. Distractions would certainly not be helpful at this point.

Faigy received a doll set that came in a large box and included two doll outfits with shoes, a bottle, grooming tools, a tea set, and a few imitation grocery items, as well as a set of costume jewelry for the owner of the doll. Thrilled, Faigy took the toys to her room to try them out on her doll collection.

Elchanan was given a toy electric piano so that he wouldn't feel left out and banged away in creative ecstasy, so involved that Chavi had to send him into her bedroom to play behind closed doors so she would be able to hear herself think.

Only she and Shmuel were left at the table. Shmuel brought out two cups of coffee and a plate of store-bought cookies. Chavi enjoyed her drink, thinking that Shmuel's domestic stint had had a positive effect on him. This was the first time she could remember him offering her a drink of his own accord.

"Thank you for the drink, Shmuel," she said out loud. "And thank you for taking care of the children while I was away."

"I barely had to do anything," he replied warmly. "You arranged everything for us. So how was it?"

"Really nice. Thanks for letting me go."

"Of course you had to go."

Silence.

Shmuel broke the silence by asking, "How were the flights?"

"Kind of long, but quiet. For the first few hours, I enjoyed just sitting and doing nothing. But then I started to get stir crazy as the hours dragged on."

"How was the bar mitzvah?"

"Just beautiful. Rochel did a nice job. The bar mitzvah boy's speech was charming. Everything was perfect."

Shmuel wondered in the silence that followed what had happened to his wife. She was usually so talkative. He couldn't remember her attending any event, no matter how insignificant, without filling him in on every detail almost as soon as she walked in the door. She never even seemed to notice if he was interested or not. Now, though, the silence was uncanny. He made one more attempt.

"What did they serve at the bar mitzvah?"

"Since when are you interested in that sort of thing?"

"I was just trying to make conversation."

"Oh," she answered laconically.

"Chavi, is everything okay?"

"Yes, why would you think not? The trip was terrific. I'm glad to be back."

"You seem so distant, and you're usually much more talkative. You describe everything so vividly that after you go somewhere I end up feeling like I was there, too."

"When was the last time that happened?"

Shmuel was surprised. They always reviewed their days together; it was part of their routine. What did she mean? As he puzzled over Chavi's comment, it struck him that he couldn't remember a recent time that Chavi had relayed one of the reports that he took for granted.

"Strange. Now that you made me think about it, you're right. We don't talk as much as we used to anymore."

"It's okay. I got used to it."

Now what in the world did that mean? Finally, it hit him. He had slowly become separated from the family. He had realized it initially on the first night that Chavi was gone. It felt foreign to him to sit around and talk to the kids. When they spoke of their teachers and friends, he didn't recognize most of the names.

He had wondered why Chavi hadn't called while she was away. He had wanted to speak to her but for some inexplicable reason didn't want to be the initiator of the interchange because he sensed that she wouldn't call if he didn't and that made him uncomfortable. Out of desperation, he made one feeble attempt at reaching her and then conceded defeat. And now Chavi had clearly said that she was used to not talking to him.

He had thought they were a close and happy family. He had thought they had a good marriage. They were both happy. Chavi was generally upbeat. Things were fine. The disagreements that had been so frequent during their first years together were almost nonexistent at this point. Was it because they had worked things out? Perhaps it was just because no one cared anymore. Although he had attributed the harmony in the home to the former reason, he now started to realize that it was a combination of the two.

Maybe things weren't fine. Or maybe they were fine, but not great. He didn't know. This was the first time that he had even realized things were amiss. He also didn't know how Chavi felt. He realized that her unnaturally placid attitude meant that she was hurt, but to what extent? He had been so lonely in her absence. Maybe she was always that lonely, if she felt that there was no one to talk to even when he was home. How often was he home anyway?

Shmuel knew he would have to work on rectifying the problem, but he wasn't sure how deep it ran or what it would take to make things better. The whole issue scared him, which was one reason why he had allowed things to get this way. Besides enjoying the preoccupation that his outside life offered, Shmuel was still uneasy with emotional closeness to a certain extent. He always worried that he would say the wrong thing or be misunderstood and feel rejected. But now he had no choice other than to bite the bullet and try to deal with the issue. His relationship with his family was too important to him to let it suffer the slow death that he had just realized had begun. Everything else mattered, but only against the background of a close, fulfilling family life.

"Chavi, I was thinking that the children haven't been to

the zoo in quite a while. Do you want to take them on Sunday?"

"That would be nice. I was thinking about getting there soon. Before I left to the bar mitzvah, my friend Rena and I discussed going together one afternoon. That way we could split the fare for a van and enjoy each other's adult company. Thanks for reminding me. I'll call her tomorrow and see if she's free."

"I meant maybe we could go as a family." Why hadn't she understood the question? Maybe because it was so out of the ordinary. The last time they had gone out as a family had been nearly two years before, if he remembered correctly. And besides, it wasn't vacation time now — no wonder it hadn't dawned on her that he would go.

"How are you going to have time?"

"I haven't missed a day at work in a while. I'm sure it won't be a big deal."

"Well, the children will certainly like it." She got up to rinse off the empty mugs.

He went to stand next to her. "Chavi, I really missed you when you were gone."

"Thanks," she said, without looking up from the suds in the sink.

Shmuel left the kitchen with his shoulders slumped, like a child who had just discovered a picture he had made for his mother in the garbage.

ꟸ ꟸ

The minivan from the local taxi company honked in front of their building at three. "The children are so excited you'd think they're flying internationally," Chavi chuckled to Shmuel. This was the first time in a long time that Yitzchak and Faigy were going to have both their parents to themselves. Plus, they were vacationing in the middle of the school year. This was a day they would always remember.

Chavi and Shmuel loaded the children, stroller, and bags into the cab. Chavi had packed a picnic dinner and all the essentials for traveling with children. She had recovered from jet lag quickly after a calm and restful Shabbos at home and was happy at her children's joy in a family outing.

Yitzchak and Faigy didn't stop chattering all the way to the zoo. Eagerly, they pointed out buses, buildings, and trees as if they were all new and not the things they saw outside their window every day. Chavi did her best to sound excited over each of their discoveries, although the cab ride for some reason made her queasy. Shmuel sat silently, holding Elchanan.

At last, they arrived. While their parents paid the driver and unloaded the taxi, the children ran around the entrance. Shmuel stretched his legs and went to pay the entrance fee, leaving Chavi to calm everyone and get organized. A few minutes and a bathroom stop later, they were enjoying the animals and nature.

Chavi still enjoyed the zoo as much as she had before her marriage. Now she shared her delight with the children, telling them the name of each animal they passed and everything she knew about it. Shmuel fell a few steps behind them, taking pleasure in watching the children run and laugh. Chavi's patience and competence as a mother amazed him. He found himself laughing out loud at the children's antics and walking proudly with his family.

He did feel a bit of an observer, though. The family

seemed to have a rhythm of its own. They were all aware of the family routine and rules of conduct, but he wasn't an integral part of the family dynamics. When they discussed which direction to go in, he wasn't consulted. Chavi decided when it was time to eat and rest. The children naturally ran to her with their questions and suggestions. Chavi was well mannered enough to ask Shmuel his opinion or how he was doing at regular intervals, but so would any good host.

He became the hero of the day when he treated everyone to ice cream from the refreshment stand. As they ate, the children sat on the grass watching the surrounding animals, while Shmuel and Chavi sat on a nearby picnic bench.

Shmuel said, "I'm really having a nice time. I'm glad we came."

"Yes, it's a special treat for everyone."

"Chavi." He waited for her to give him her undivided attention. When she turned to him curiously, he began, "Your trip made me realize something that I can't believe I didn't notice before. I don't even know how it happened. I guess I let myself slip bit by bit, until all the small acts of neglect added up to a big problem."

Chavi was watching him intently. Encouraged by her apparent interest, Shmuel continued, "I feel like I've lost my family. Of course, you're still here and so are the children, and you are each so special. But I feel like I am not really a part of you. And now that I realize what's happened, I miss you. I am suddenly terribly lonely. I guess I was so busy running that I never stopped to catch my breath and see where I was running to and what I would end up being when I got there. I don't exactly know what to do now. But I want to try and repair some of the damage I've caused."

"Okay," Chavi responded apathetically. Although she felt anything but apathetic, she was afraid of getting her hopes up. The disappointment of having things remain the same after she let herself believe they might be different would be more painful than her trained indifference.

She saw Shmuel's face fall and knew that her response had hurt him acutely. A vicious part of her was glad he was experiencing some of the incredible pain she had suffered and repressed over the last few years. But her love for her husband was stronger and she knew she had to show him how much his confession meant to her.

"I really appreciate what you've said, Shmuel. I've been hurt and lonely for a long time. I tried to tell you in the beginning a few times, but you implied that I was being immature and selfish in needing you around so much. So I decided that I wouldn't share my weakness anymore. Even more, I decided that I wouldn't be weak anymore. I was determined to be self-sufficient. It worked, to a certain degree, but deep down, there is an unfilled void." A tear escaped her eye against her will.

Shmuel squirmed in his seat. It was uncomfortable to see her raw emotions, especially in public. He couldn't ignore the issue now, but he was scared to continue under the circumstances. "I'm really going to try to make things better. I'm going to work on being more of a partner and friend to you. We'll talk more later, okay?"

"Okay," Chavi agreed, glad to let the issue rest for now. She had shared her feelings and would leave the next step to him.

ɛ ɛ

By the next day, Shmuel told Chavi that he would be making some changes in his schedule. He would make sure to be home for lunch and dinner every day, and the answering machine would pick up phone messages during that time. He would also call Chavi at least once a day, just to check in. Though the changes weren't major, they required some effort on Shmuel's part. And, almost immediately, their impact could be seen in the harmony of the home.

22

A week after the Rosenbergs' trip to the zoo, Nava called to welcome Chavi home. "Are you going in to work tomorrow, Chavi? I would like to meet you for lunch one day."

She must need to talk, Chavi thought, noting the slight hesitation in Nava's voice. "Yes, I am, Nava. Why don't you pick me up at the office at one o'clock?"

"Actually, I'd rather meet you in a restaurant. I don't want to bump into my husband at the office."

Chavi's initial suspicion about Nava needing a listening ear was confirmed. "Let's not meet for lunch then. Come to my house in the evening, and we'll have more time to talk."

Nava came later that night. The two younger children were already in bed, and Yitzchak was up in the living room, practicing his Chumash reading. He sounded out each word carefully, thrilled whenever he found a word that he was sure he had pronounced correctly.

Chavi and Nava sat at the dining room table, out of Yitzchak's earshot. Chavi brought out some light refreshments.

Nava took a small wooden box out of her purse. "I brought this for you," she said, handing it to Chavi. "I just wanted you to know how much I always appreciate that you're there for me. No matter how busy you are, you always make time for me at the drop of a hat."

"Oh, Nava, we're friends. That's what friends do," Chavi answered. She opened the box and found an assortment of herbal teas. She inhaled deeply, relishing the fragrance that the teas emitted, and looked through the colorful packets. "Mmm, these smell good. I always wanted to try herbal teas. Let me boil up a kettle of water and we'll sample them."

As soon as they had each taken a sip of tea, Nava characteristically got straight to the point. "Yair and I aren't talking to each other," she said.

"Oh, no. What happened?" Chavi asked.

"Well, it's not really that we're not talking to each other. I'm not talking to him. He's prepared to just drop the whole topic of our disagreement and move on, but I am not." Nava took another sip of tea and continued, "You know that we've been trying so very hard to have children. We've been married for a long time. We've tried all sorts of things, from expensive, painful medical treatments to superstitious home remedies. It's been draining physically, emotionally, and financially, and nothing has come of it. We are both ready to give up hope and accept the fact that we will never be parents to our own children.

"I really want to nurture a child, though, and if I can't have my own, then I would at least like to raise someone else's child who needs love and care. I told Yair that I want to adopt. He firmly and stubbornly refuses to even consider the idea. I feel an emptiness inside that only a child can fill, and I can't accept his decision."

Chavi knew better than to get directly involved in a disagreement between a husband and wife, especially over such a personal issue. But with Nava sitting beside her, brokenhearted and dejected, Chavi knew she had to say something. "I understand how hard it must be for you," she commiserated. "Perhaps adoption will alleviate some of the pain and emptiness, but you certainly can't do it without Yair's agreement. Maybe if you just leave the issue on the back burner, Yair will get used to the idea and eventually concede."

Chavi ended a little lamely. Her response seemed most unsatisfying to her, but she could not think of anything else to say. Nava seemed calmer, though. Before she could reply, Yitzchak approached the table to ask Chavi if he had read a word correctly. Chavi worked out the difficult word with him, hoping that Nava didn't mind the interruption.

After he went back to the couch, Nava commented, "It's so beautiful to see you working together on reading the Torah's words. I just attended a *shiur* last week on the importance of Torah study. The lecturer explained that the learning of little children is what sustains the world, because they are free of sin. You're so lucky to be part of the momentous event of having your son beginning to learn Torah!"

Chavi first thought this response to helping her son sound out a word was a little melodramatic, but then she realized how true and important Nava's words were. Her daily interactions with her children sometimes made her lose sight of how significant her job was. It was good to be reminded.

ၷ ၷ

Chavi's trip to America was soon all but forgotten as she was pulled back into her hectic routine of mothering, keeping house, and working. The days passed and turned into weeks, and the added factor of nausea and fatigue slowed her down. Although Chavi realized the probable cause of her poor health, she didn't confirm her suspicions medically, not knowing if she was ready to hear the news.

She felt gloriously happy as she made her way home from work one day, her physical condition far from her mind. The sun was shining, but it wasn't too hot. Instead of taking the bus home, she had decided to leave work a drop earlier than usual and walk. As she passed by the common sights of everyday life in Jerusalem, she took pleasure in the feel of the city she called home.

Rows of small stores dotted the neighborhood her office was in. She peered into each window as she passed it, though she knew she didn't need to buy anything. She watched her fellow pedestrians as they crossed paths. There was such a mixture of people, but each was dear to her and she felt a part of the crowd. The neighborhood was a well-to-do secular one, but its business strip was filled with many different people from all walks of life.

She noticed a photographer snapping pictures of the scene she was part of and agreed to herself that here was a perfect spot to catch the beat of contemporary life in Jerusalem. Young couples sat at the scattered cafes, some enjoying drinks or meals at outdoor tables. Casually dressed businessmen in sandals and checkered shirts, identifiable by their briefcases, walked briskly in both directions. Religious men and women came in and out of various stores and offices, clearly the minority yet not looking out of place. Tourists looked for souvenirs and gifts, and students from abroad met with friends. The place was alive with the stream of humanity.

The streets were too crowded to allow her the luxury of intense daydreaming, but she enjoyed the familiarity of the scene. She glanced at the newspapers at a newspaper stand, hoping that the news would be peaceful. The headlines revolved around some sports event, so she knew that things were quiet.

Chavi left the business district and soon reached the open-air market. Although it would have been significantly faster to avoid it, she walked through the narrow aisles, relishing the exotic smells and sounds. She breathed in the smell of fresh fruit mixed with pickles and olives and raw fish and cold cuts, listening to the stand owners calling customers to buy their bargains. A sudden hunger washed over her and she bought a small bag of freshly roasted peanuts.

Leaving the market behind, Chavi found a bench on a secluded side street where she sat down to enjoy her snack and rethink the day's events. As soon as she was finished she jumped up, realizing that her break had made her a bit behind schedule. Now she had to rush home to relieve the baby-sitter on time.

When she got home and got settled, she tried to talk to the children, but she found herself too distracted. She let them busy themselves as she went to prepare dinner. After a minute of reflection, she decided to make one of Shmuel's favorite dishes to add to the festive atmosphere.

ぷ ぷ

Shmuel noticed that Chavi had something on her mind when he reached home. She greeted him enthusiastically and implied that she had news to share. He figured he knew what it was, but it would have to wait until the children were in bed.

They sat down to eat after the children were settled down for the night. Shmuel relished the meal but was more interested in hearing the good news that Chavi wanted to share.

He was totally unprepared for what she had to say.

"Shmuel, I was promoted at work today. Do you know what that means? I am now going to get my own office, a secretary, and three times — yes, you heard right — three times my salary. Can you imagine? My own office. A secretary. My boss called me in this morning and told me that he was very impressed with my work and that he had thought I deserved a promotion a while ago, but he was waiting for a suitable position to open up. Honestly, I was getting bored at work. The challenge was gone. I more or less know what to do by rote. The clients that we program for generally have similar businesses and problems, and I no longer need to use my creativity. But now I'll be moving into a managerial position, and I'll need to employ a whole new set of skills. Oh, isn't it wonderful? I practically danced the whole way home. Now we won't have to worry about paying for the room addition or Yitzchak's tutors or anything. You see how God provides for us when we need it?"

Chavi's words sounded like one long, run-on sentence to Shmuel. It took him a moment to digest what she was saying. He was certainly happy to see his wife so energized. It had been a long time since he had heard her speak in such an animated fashion. He wasn't sure yet, though, if he wanted to share her excitement. "That's great. Were you expecting this?"

"No, not at all. Last week, one of my coworkers was called in to the boss and given a raise. I was upset that I hadn't also been, but I told myself that it was all for the best and if God wanted me to get a raise, I'd get a raise. And now look. I was jealous over an eight-percent raise and a few days later I got a two-hundred-percent raise! Look how silly it was for me to be envious."

"Are you going to have any extra obligations with this job?" Shmuel asked, gently broaching the subject that was unnerving him.

"Oh, sure. I'll have to start coming in every morning to make sure that things are running smoothly in my department, but my boss said that I could leave an hour earlier every day. I'll also have to be on call for emergencies."

Shmuel didn't say anything. He didn't feel like he was being asked to say anything. Chavi seemed to be presenting him with a done deal, a deal that he frankly wasn't interested in.

"Well," Chavi pressed after his silence became uncomfortable, "aren't you happy for me? What are you thinking?"

"Sure, I'm happy. It's a big compliment to be offered a promotion. It's just...."

"Just what?"

"I don't know if you are interested in my opinion."

"Of course I am."

"Well, um, do you really think you can handle going back to a full work week? The kids need you at home, it seems to me. I know how hard it is on you as it is. Imagine almost doubling your workload."

"This is something that really invigorates me. I want to do it. It's a lot of prestige and money and it's intellectually stimulating. Are you asking me to give up on an opportunity of a lifetime?"

"Did I say I'm asking you anything? It's your decision. I'm not going to stand in the way of your accomplishments. It just doesn't seem like the right decision to me. I think we both need to let the idea sink in a little before making any rash decisions. It's great for your career, but is that where your priorities lie? If it's not right to do, money or honor or even intellectual challenge can't tempt you. You have to decide if it's a wise decision."

He had touched upon a sensitive topic. In the back of her mind, Chavi knew that the extra workload would negatively affect her home life. But she wanted the career advancement so badly that she ignored the inner voice that told her that it was not the time to add to her responsibilities outside the home.

"And anyway," Shmuel continued, "you've been more tired than usual lately. It could be that it might be a particularly inopportune time for you to take more upon yourself, if you know what I mean."

She did know what he meant. And she was doing her best to ignore that new development in her family life also. She was angry at him for putting a damper on her plans, especially because she knew his points were all too valid.

"I really don't think you have a right to tell me to curb my desire for career advancement. You're no one to talk. Look what's happened to you. You started off deciding to devote a few hours a day to your job, and hypothetically that's what you've done. But in reality, your work has taken over your life. How many times have you canceled *seder* in order to attend an important meeting? You have been trying a little to spend more time with the children, but exceptions have become almost as common as the rule. Your idea of spending more time with me means a phone call from work to see how my day was, often with the conversation ending with an apology that you'll be home later than expected.

"I can only wonder what has happened to your davening. We used to learn a short *mussar* piece about davening with each dinner. Remember that? We both agreed that we needed to improve our prayer and we saw that the learning helped us. When was the last time you had a chance to sit with me and do that? Do you know I've kept up our tradition alone? Probably not, because it never crossed your mind to ask. I'm already on my third *sefer.* If you could drop our learning without noticing, I assume it means that your davening improvement has been put on hold. How dare you tell me about curbing ambition? I really don't feel you have a right to talk."

Shmuel was confused by the rapid change in the subject of the conversation. A minute before they had been discussing the pros and cons of accepting Chavi's promotion, and suddenly she was ranking him out about his davening. He wanted to remind her that he wasn't the topic at hand, but his need to defend himself was stronger. He wanted to tell her how wrong she was, that he was keeping to learning two *sedarim* a day. But he knew deep down that she was right. He was letting his work become the focus of his life. It was easy and brought him immediate satisfaction, and he was helping people, people who really appreciated him and openly expressed that appreciation.

To save face, he told her she was wrong anyway. "I have been keeping my *sedarim*. Once in a while there is an exception, when someone needs something important. What do you want me to do? Should I tell them that I'm busy and can't help them? These are people's lives we're talking about, you know."

"Yes, I know you're helping people. I feel it's wonderful

that you are. But there are other people that you have to help also. If you ask these people from work to wait until you're available, they will either wait or find someone else to help. If you push off your own children, there will be no one else to help. They are your primary responsibility."

Once Chavi had started, she couldn't stop. "More importantly, you have to take care of yourself. You might get more immediate gratification from your *chesed* work, but if you don't take care of your personal *avodas Hashem*, no one will do it for you. We both know that one of a man's primary goals is to toil in *talmud Torah*. You can't let the rest of your life push its way into your learning. Soon you will end up with nothing."

"Maybe my main purpose in life is not to learn. It's hard for me. Really hard. I love the learning itself once I start, but it is torture sometimes to get myself into my seat with my Gemara open. You've never tried it. You don't have the *yetzer hara* pulling you away from it — how can you judge? At least I am using my time to help people. I've always accepted you with your faults and personality quirks, but I don't feel you've ever really accepted me for who I am. Why can't you just accept me?"

"Why do you sell yourself so short?" Chavi asked. She knew he gave up on himself too easily. True, it was hard for him, but if he pushed himself, he could do it. He had the mind and the ability to learn. He needed to believe in himself and his ability to overcome obstacles.

But something in his words did ring true. He always made her feel accepted the way she was — flaws, idiosyncrasies, problems, and all. Did she accept him unconditionally? Truthfully, when he didn't measure up to her standards of propriety she got angry with him, and sometimes she was even disgusted at her own temper. Was that fair? She felt so good knowing that he appreciated her no matter what she did. Didn't she owe him the same?

The knowledge that she was withholding from him one of the basic things a person expects from his spouse, unconditional love and acceptance, hurt her. Yes, he was wrong in his actions, but she was wrong in her attitude. She wondered if she should share her feelings with him, but she decided against it. She didn't want to reveal that she really didn't fully accept him the way he was. The validation of his suspicion would probably hurt him more than her regret over her attitude would comfort him.

Shmuel also had mixed emotions over Chavi's words. A part of him wanted her to leave him alone so that he could do what was comfortable. He didn't want to feel that his wife was breathing down his neck, following and analyzing his every move. It hurt his ego and therefore exasperated him, often leaving him not wanting to listen to her just because of the mentor-like tone she took on.

At the same time, he delighted in her respect for his abilities. They both agreed that Torah learning was of utmost importance and needed to take precedence over almost anything. Although Shmuel was often able to excuse himself for not putting all his efforts into his learning, Chavi constantly reminded him that he could accomplish what he truly wanted to and that he shouldn't fall prey to lame excuses.

The conversation was at a standstill, with both Shmuel and Chavi upset, humbled, and unable to grant themselves a certain gratification they longed for. After several minutes of silence, Chavi said, "Let's discuss this promotion more later."

"Okay," Shmuel said.

Chavi hoped the points she had raised to Shmuel about his own job would give him food for thought, but she knew that pressing the point any further would only be counter-productive.

Later that evening, after she had gone to bed, Chavi tossed and turned in an effort to shut off the flow of thoughts that was robbing her of her sleep. After a few minutes she saw Shmuel sit up in bed, obviously having the same trouble.

"Can't you fall asleep?" Chavi asked.

"Not yet," Shmuel answered.

"Neither can I," she said. "I was thinking a lot about what you said. I think you're right. It wouldn't be right for me to take more work on myself at this time. I'm not saying for sure yet — I want to at least enjoy the possibility a bit more and make sure I'm making a decision I'm comfortable with. But I guess I got carried away earlier tonight. I'm glad you spoke up."

"I know you'll make the right decision," he said. "Good night."

She knew he was thinking about her comments about his job, too. Oh, why couldn't he give her the satisfaction of telling her that he was glad she had brought up the topic and was considering her words? She knew that he needed his space, but it was hard for her not to demand that admission from him. Although she was unsatisfied with his reticence, Chavi wisely decided not to say anything.

23

The next day was a hard one for Chavi. She told her boss that she couldn't accept the offer because she couldn't work any more hours. To her surprise, her boss asked her to consider moving up to management (with the accompanying change to an office) yet continue working the same hours, while being on call for emergencies. The pay raise wouldn't be as steep but would still reflect her added responsibility.

Chavi said that it sounded good to her but she wanted to think about it for a day. She didn't tell her boss the real reason she didn't accept on the spot: so that she could discuss the offer with her husband. She had learned once again that her exuberance could lead to rash decisions and that she needed Shmuel's tempering perspective.

In the end, Shmuel did agree, and to show his pride in her accomplishments, he bought her a nameplate and business-card holder for her new desk. Chavi was very touched by the gift, and he was glad.

In terms of her personal life, though, she could no longer

ignore the signs of the upcoming event and finally confirmed her suspicions with her doctor. She was expecting a baby in a little over half a year.

Hanging up the phone after hearing that the blood test was positive, Chavi knew she should be thrilled, but it was difficult to be excited. Although God was giving her a special blessing, she didn't know if she was ready for it. She thought of the aches and pains of pregnancy, labor, nighttime feedings, pacing the floors with an inconsolable baby, and the dieting that would inevitably follow the birth. She remembered the effort it took to keep up with her regular responsibilities in the face of exhaustion. It wasn't a good time to go on maternity leave from work.

She told herself to stop being petty and to look at the big picture. She was to be entrusted with one of God's special treasures. Once again, she would be a partner in the creation of the world.

In an effort to raise her spirits, Chavi reached for her special book of prayers and found the one that she had said so many times. "Let it be Your will, O God in Heaven, that we appreciate the greatest gift that You have given us, that You have entrusted us to care for Your holy souls and to raise them in Your service. Help us to know how to raise them, when to be soft and when to be firm.... And please help us never to feel that raising children is a burden, for we know the importance of our efforts and the goals that we can achieve...."

When she finished, she sat on the couch wondering where this new development would lead and soon nodded off into a light sleep. In case of any doubt, that served to confirm that the blood test results were accurate.

The ringing phone awoke her. It was Shmuel from a pay phone at his yeshivah. He wanted to know if she had found out the results yet. When she told him that she was indeed expecting, she heard the elation in his voice. His enthusiasm helped kindle hers, though she also shared her worries with him.

Shmuel told her that she didn't need to worry. They could get cleaning help if she wanted...and babysitters...and he would help more....

She was a little upset that there wasn't anything she wanted to get out of him. Now would have been a very opportune time — he was willing to give her the world. When she hung up the phone, she felt more content. Since the situation was as it was, she might as well try to focus on the positive.

ꙮ ꙮ

Just a few weeks later, Chavi started to experience complications. There was worry that her pregnancy might come to an end. Chavi found herself davening passionately for the health of her unborn child and the success of the pregnancy. The scare helped her realize that she was very happily anticipating the arrival of her new child. Her worries were real but secondary, and she now knew that she had to keep them in their proper place.

Her pregnancy continued, but there was still concern that the problems weren't over. Her obstetrician prescribed bed rest until he was sure that the pregnancy was viable and without complications.

His decision hit Chavi like a ton of bricks. Who would care for her children? Who would take care of the house?

How would her boss react to her absence? It seemed to her that it was impossible to fulfill her doctor's wish, and she told him so. He firmly replied that if she was interested in the health of her unborn child, there was no choice.

The impossible happened, and somehow life went on. Chavi was confined to her bed for an unlimited amount of time. She made good use of the phone and arranged for help with both the children and housework. She was very satisfied with the women she found, who were both competent and of good character. The only real problem was financing all the extra expenditures.

At least she had gotten a raise from work and her leave of absence was covered by her medical benefits. Maybe this was the reason God had arranged for her to get the raise in the first place. She had hoped that her raise would mean an improvement in her standard of living or at least a chance to save some money, but now it was going to be applied to partially cover the extra help she needed. Where the rest would come from, Chavi had no idea whatsoever. She was still worried about the mortgage they had taken out to cover their room addition. But she knew there was no need to worry. He who had taken care of her since she was a newborn until that very day would continue, no doubt. How that would work was yet to be seen.

The financial worry wasn't the worst of it. Chavi found it incredibly difficult to rely on others for everything. If she needed a drink of water, a book from the living room, or a robe from the clean laundry, she had to ask for them. She felt terribly dependent. And she hated watching her house being run, in her full view, in a way that was contrary to her desires.

She couldn't complain; things were the best they could

be. But when there was a mess, she could do nothing about it. When the meals weren't as nutritionally balanced as she would like, she tried not to comment. Since she couldn't contribute to the fulfillment of her requests, she thought it was unfair to criticize.

Bored and physically uncomfortable, Chavi renewed old friendships over the phone, read every book that was delivered to her bedside, and even took up the knitting that she hadn't done since she had been in high school. Still, the hours crept along and the days even slower. How she wished she could get up and do those chores that she detested at times!

She remembered something one of her Israeli neighbors had said to her one day when they were discussing the trials and tribulations of motherhood and housekeeping: "Motherhood isn't hard. It's constant work, but it's not hard. It's hard when you don't have children or can't take care of them. That's hard."

Chavi was annoyed at the time by the comment. It was hard for her many times, and it often took all of her strength and determination to pull through. Was her neighbor being dishonest or was Chavi just not as strong as she was? She often felt the development of an inferiority complex when she compared herself to her Israeli neighbors. They generally had significantly more children than she in significantly smaller apartments. Yet these women always looked put together, their houses were spotlessly clean, and they didn't seem weighed down by life. How did they do it? Why was it so hard for her?

Now, however, she understood the wisdom of her neighbor's words. Child raising and housekeeping took tremendous effort, but if you had the right attitude, it wasn't a struggle. It was torture for Chavi to lie in bed and watch life go on without her input. How she longed to be able to care for her children herself now. It was all a matter of attitude, she saw. Yes, her life took energy, but if she focused on being thankful for the energy she was given and the opportunity to feel satisfied with her accomplishment, the bitterness of the exertion would disappear.

For now, though, she had to learn to appreciate the lesson that she had gained from what she termed her incarceration and endure the prolonged period of inactivity.

As she lay in her monotonous state one morning, the ring of the phone diverted her attention from analyzing a crack in the ceiling. The ringing phone was one of the highlights of her day. Besides the occupation it provided, the initial suspense of not knowing who was on the other end of the line thrilled her.

To her surprise, it was Gitty. A quick calculation of the hours told her that New York was well into the early morning hours that most people call night. "Gitty, what in the world are you doing up at this hour?"

"I have something to tell you. Are you sitting down?" Gitty asked.

"Very funny. What's going on?" Chavi asked, her curiosity piqued.

"I'm engaged!!"

"*Mazal tov!* How wonderful! Oh, Gitty, I am so happy to hear!"

"Aren't you going to ask me to who?"

"Good point. Who's the lucky guy?"

"He's a terrific person — great *middos*, a *ben Torah*, fun to be with. The *shadchan* is also a super lady. She was involved but not too pushy, and her patience helped everything work out."

"*Nu?*"

"My *chassan* is Aryeh Zilberman."

"No way! How in the world did that happen?"

"One day he called me up directly and told me that he thought he had been too hasty in stopping our relationship. He realized that sometimes people act out of character and, if things seem pretty good, there is no reason to stop a *shidduch* because of one incident. I was really surprised to hear from him, but I was happy to take him up on his offer to continue dating. You know how I felt about him from the start. Anyway, as they say, the rest is history."

Chavi plied her friend with questions on how the dating went, where and when the *vort* was to be held, and the wedding plans. After fifteen minutes of excited conversation, Gitty said, "I can't keep my eyes open anymore, Chavi. I'll call you next week at a more decent hour — but I figured you deserved to hear right away. We can't thank you enough for your help in making this dream come true."

Chavi tried to brush off the thanks. "No, it's true," Gitty insisted. "Aryeh and I are putting a check in the mail tomorrow — it's *shadchanus* that you more than deserve."

When Chavi heard the amount the couple was sending, she nearly dropped the phone. "That's much more than necessary," she protested.

"We're happy to send it, and you should watch the mail for the check," Gitty replied.

After Chavi hung up, it struck her again how God had provided their needs as they arose. She said some *Tehillim* in gratitude to God for His constant caring for her and for Gitty's engagement.

24

By Chavi's sixth month of pregnancy, she was allowed, to her incredible relief, to resume her normal activities. Soon she was back in the throes of managing her career and housework, and most significantly tending to her children's needs. Both Faigy and Yitzchak were happy in school, but Chavi made sure that either she or Shmuel was always in touch with their teachers, both to make sure that any problems that arose were attended to and to show their gratitude and interest in the effort the teachers were investing in their children.

When they were let out for summer vacation, Chavi arranged some tutoring for Yitzchak and signed him up for a camp program. Faigy's preschool had its own summer camp, which was really just another month of school, but in a more relaxed atmosphere. Elchanan, who was already two years old, had become more active than ever before, and Chavi found a summer play group to keep him well occupied.

The summer months passed peacefully, and Chavi had a chance to prepare herself for the upcoming birth. She used her spare time to clean and organize the house and sort through her collection of children's clothes to find the newborn items. She baked and froze a freezerfull of desserts so that she would be prepared to host a *kiddush* or *shalom zachar*.

The baby was born on his due date, three weeks before Rosh HaShanah, and the next few months revolved around reorganizing the family dynamics to make little Tzvi part of the schedule. The older children took to him at first as if he were a treasure to be guarded and cared for. Those feelings slowly turned to a nervous jealousy as they realized that this time-consuming addition to their family was there to stay. But faster than Chavi had expected, Tzvi was accepted as one of the gang.

ℵ ℵ

Eight months passed. Elchanan was no longer the baby of the family, and Chavi began planning his *upsherin*. Although Yitzchak had been taken unceremoniously to the barber for his first haircut, Chavi wanted to have a proper party this time, similar to the ones her friends made for their children. She looked forward to taking Elchanan to various *rabbanim* for *berachos* and then to the cheder to lick honey off the letters of the *alef-beis*. She would then host a get-together for friends and relatives in her home. She practically had the menu for the party decided upon in her mind when she shared her plans with Shmuel to get his approval.

To her surprise, he adamantly refused to allow anything more than having his parents and hers over for dinner after the trip to the barbershop.

"Why are you so set against a party? I really feel it will be a moving and meaningful way to bring our child into the world of Torah and mitzvos."

"It's not my *minhag,*" Shmuel said. "As nice as it seems, people are not supposed to introduce innovations into their religious practices."

"But your family has a number of chassidish *minhagim.* Why can't this be one of them?" Chavi pressed.

Shmuel didn't concede. "If a *minhag* is yours, it is a wonderful and necessary enhancement of the laws of the Torah, but if it is not your *minhag* the addition is dangerous. Tradition is tradition and it should not be tampered with."

ꟹ ꟹ

Another summer vacation was over, and rambunctious Elchanan was ready to enter cheder. To Chavi's relief, his rebbe found him charming and charismatic and gave him plenty of room to play freely. Eight-year-old Yitzchak walked his brother to cheder each morning, filling the role of big brother well.

Chavi wondered if her two older boys were going to be compared and contrasted in their rebbes' minds as they passed through the same classes. They were so very different. Yitzchak had developed into a calm and sweet boy who had trouble learning. Elchanan was more precocious, but wild and energetic. She was glad that Yitzchak was progressing so well and hoped that his label of being a slow learner might eventually become a thing of the past. He had finished his speech therapy and only went to the clinic once a month to have his abilities monitored. He was tutored by a young man for an hour each day, but that was the extent of his outside help. The school's internal assistance made sure that his situation was supervised and improved.

Tzvi's first birthday was fast approaching. Chavi called her mother a few days before the event to invite her to an informal birthday dinner in the little boy's honor. She was surprised when she wasn't able to get through, even after calling a few times during the early morning and late afternoon hours. When no one answered well into the evening, she became worried.

Shmuel told her that her mother and Max were adults and may have gone away without informing her of their plans. But Chavi knew that although that was a possibility, it was uncharacteristic of them and highly unlikely. She tried her mother's number again and again, every quarter of an hour, and with each call, her nerves became more frazzled.

Finally, at about ten in the evening, the phone rang. It was Mrs. Schneider.

"Oh, Ima. I'm so glad you called. I was terribly nervous that something bad had happened. I've been trying you all day. Where have you been?"

Chavi's relief was short-lived. "Chavi, I have some bad news to share," Mrs. Schneider said, her voice cracking.

"What's wrong? What happened?" Chavi asked, her heart beating wildly.

"Max had a severe heart attack last night.... We rushed him to the hospital as soon as he complained of pain...but by the time the ambulance got him there, he was unconscious.... He held on until this evening...but he passed away an hour ago...."

When Chavi said nothing, her mother continued, "He didn't suffer much. It wasn't like your father where things dragged on and on. I was glad of that.... But this is such a shock. Yesterday, we were both fine and went about our business as normal. Who would believe I would be attending his funeral today?"

Again, Chavi said nothing. A tear trickled down her cheek, with another following in its wake. Memories of Zeidy Max flashed through her mind. He had been a kind, loving, and accepting man. Over the years, he had become not so much of a father figure, but more of a grandfather to her. He was always available for advice or a kind word or to listen to a story. It was hard to believe that, suddenly and without warning, he was no longer in this world.

Chavi wondered how her mother was going to handle the funeral and shivah again. Another heart attack. Another spouse's funeral. What would her mother's life be like now? She had never lived alone before. What was going to happen?

The first thing to take care of, Chavi realized, was the funeral. It was already ten o'clock at night. In Jerusalem, funerals take place on the day of death, no matter how late in the day. Rousing herself from her thoughts, she said, "Ima, I'm so, so sorry. Is there anything I can do to help you? What needs to be done for the funeral arrangements?"

"Max's son Asher was in the hospital with me all day. He knows the system here better and he said he would make the arrangements."

Just as she finished speaking, a car with a loudspeaker came down Chavi's block announcing that the funeral was to take place at eleven-thirty at a local funeral parlor. A shiver went through Chavi as the car passed slowly by. What if she had heard the announcement before speaking to her mother? "Where are you now, Ima?"

"I'm at home," Mrs. Schneider said.

"Shmuel is due home any moment. I'll get a baby-sitter and we'll be right over," Chavi assured her.

Except for her working hours, Chavi spent every morning the following week at the shivah house, leaving Tzvi at a baby-sitter. Max's children had all flown in to be together, and the apartment had a steady stream of visitors. Some came because of the relationship they had had with Max, others came for his children, and some came for her mother.

It was interesting to hear the history of Max's life and the ways in which his soft manner had touched many people. Chavi enjoyed seeing the familiar faces that passed through the doorway of the apartment. She and her mother reminisced together about their lives as each visitor that came to visit Mrs. Schneider reminded them of times past.

Chavi noticed that although her mother was sad, this shivah was very different than shivah had been for her father. Max had been older. Although his death was sudden, it wasn't considered as tragic by society as her father's youthful demise had been. In addition, Chavi saw that there was a difference in her mother. Although she had developed a strong bond with Max, the loss of the spouse of one's youth, after forty years of marriage, was much more acutely painful. No matter what sort of love developed between two married people, a relationship that was forged by two young people navigating their lives together from the onset of adulthood had a much deeper dimension. In addition, her mother was much stronger now and more independent. Her loss left her lonely but not broken.

This was the first time that the Rosenberg children experienced the death of someone they were close to, and they had many questions for Chavi. What surprised her initially was the nonchalance with which they asked their questions. Their direct style, bereft of heavy emotional content, made Chavi realize that the children were a clean slate and that their attitude to death, and the resulting attitude to life, was going to be a result of how she approached the topic. One night before bedtime, two nights after Max's funeral, she sat down on the couch with them to talk.

"Children," she opened the conversation, "how do you feel about Zeidy Max's dying?"

"I'm very sad," said Faigy.

"I'm very sad, too," Elchanan agreed. Yitzchak said nothing.

"Why are you sad?" she asked them.

Elchanan answered first. "Because Bubby cried."

"And that makes you sad, that Bubby is sad?" she clarified.

"Yes, that makes me sad, and I also want to cry and to hug Bubby so she will feel better," he said.

Chavi was touched by his sensitivity and took him on her lap to hold him as they continued talking. "Faigy, why are you sad?" she asked.

"I am sad because I miss Zeidy Max, and you said that we won't see him until Mashiach comes and all the dead people come back."

Elchanan answered before Chavi could say anything. "But Mashiach can come tomorrow or the day after that. Don't be sad."

"But I don't want to wait," she answered him, partially comforted by his words. "Mommy, where is Zeidy Max now?"

Chavi didn't know how graphic to be. She said, "Zeidy

Max's *neshamah* went back to live with Hashem. His body was put in the ground."

"Oh," was all Faigy said, not seeming particularly disturbed.

"What's a *neshamah*?" asked Elchanan.

Faigy told him, "It's what makes you you. It's what tells you what to do and how to feel. It lives in your body so it can do things. Mommy always calls me her '*neshamahle,*' because she says that that is the part of me that matters. Right, Mommy?"

"You explained that perfectly," Chavi said, leaning over to kiss her daughter's forehead.

"Is Zeidy Max also sad?" Elchanan wanted to know.

"Zeidy Max is very happy because he gets to live with Hashem," Chavi told him.

Yitzchak sat silently all through the conversation, listening without saying a word. Later, after everyone was in bed, he came out to the living room to ask his mother, "Mommy, how does Hashem decide when it's time for a person to die?"

"Are you worried, Yitzchak?"

He nodded.

"Come sit down at the table," she said, trying to think of a suitable answer for this impressionable eight-year-old in her care. They sat down on opposite sides of the table and she reached across the table to touch his hand, tempted to promise him that everyone he cared about would live to a ripe old age and that death was something he would never have to deal with. But what if his future held the pain and suffering of losing someone he was close to at a young age? He would never trust her on anything if she promised something that ended up being false.

"Yitzchak, no one knows how long they are going to live or why God gives people a certain number of years. When Hashem decides that the person has accomplished what he needs to, He takes that person's *neshamah* back to live with Him where the *neshamah* is totally happy. Even though no one knows how long their life will be, one thing is for certain — God gives each person the amount of time that is best for him and the people around him. It hurts when someone dies, but the situation is good." She paused. "Do you know what I mean, Yitzchak?"

"I think so," he answered. "It's like when you moved to Eretz Yisrael from America before I was born. You were sad to leave your relatives and friends and they were sad that you were leaving, but you knew it was good to live here, and you were glad to come."

Chavi was surprised that he understood so well. "That's why there is never a reason to be scared or worried about what's going to happen in the future. You know that it will be good and you will be happy in the end that things came out the way they did," she said.

They spoke a bit longer, and then Yitzchak stood up on his own initiative and went to bed. He left Chavi alone to think. She wished that she had the simple belief her children had. Mashiach was an expected event. Death just meant moving to another stage. Of course, she fully knew that these things were true, but her children's emotional simplicity was something she hoped to achieve one day.

Her thoughts drifted to her mother. For the week of shivah, she had Max's children staying at her house. What would she do after that? Perhaps she would want to live alone. But she had never lived alone before. Chavi wondered how things could be made more comfortable for her mother. Maybe one of her older grandchildren in America could come live with her for a bit until she got settled. That wouldn't work, though, because the school year had already started. Then it struck her. She would have to discuss her idea with Shmuel, but it seemed like the perfect solution.

When Shmuel came home that night, she broached the topic. "My mother is going to be living all alone when shivah is over," she began. Shmuel nodded. "She's never lived alone before, and the loss of her husband is so fresh. It's going to be so hard on her to live alone, to have to take care of everything by herself and to mourn her husband's passing."

"Yes?" said Shmuel patiently.

"I was thinking that maybe we should offer her the option of moving in with us. We have our extra room with its own bathroom. We don't put it to any important use now. It would probably be hard to adjust to another adult in the house, especially one we have to respect, but I think it could work out. What do you think? Is it feasible?"

Shmuel didn't answer for a few minutes as he considered the pros and cons of her suggestion. Chavi waited quietly, realizing that asking someone to have his elderly mother-in-law move in with him was no small request.

Shmuel answered faster than she expected him to. "I think it's a great idea. You are right that there will be many difficulties to overcome in order for everything to work smoothly, but it's the least we can do for a woman to whom we owe so much."

Chavi was very impressed with his expansive soul and was filled with a deep admiration for the man she had chosen to share her life with. "Thank you, Shmuel," she said, overcome with gratitude.

ꕥ ꕥ

The next morning, Chavi announced her plan to her mother. "It would be such an honor to have you live with us, Ima. Think how much the children could gain from having you so close." Seeing her mother's hesitation, Chavi continued, "We'll allow you all the privacy you need — you'll have your own bathroom, and we can install a new phone line, a small refrigerator, and burners in your room."

Mrs. Schneider smiled. "I appreciate the offer and your welcoming attitude, dear, but for now I want to be home. I've been thinking of my options, too, and I've decided to maybe take in a boarder for company."

Chavi was both disappointed and relieved. She tried to convince her mother to take them up on the offer for another few minutes, but then she decided to just leave the option open and give her mother the freedom to decide without undue pressure.

25

After the week of shivah was over, life returned to normal. Chavi's mother found two single American girls to live with her. She hoped their company would bring life to the apartment and was happy to have the extra income.

Rosh HaShanah, Yom Kippur, and Sukkos passed in quick succession. Chavi invited her mother over as much as she could, hoping to alleviate some of her loneliness. Their lives settled back into routine as three months slipped by.

Before they knew it, Shmuel and Chavi were approaching a milestone in their lives, their tenth anniversary. They didn't have any grandiose celebrations planned but gladly accepted Mrs. Schneider's offer to baby-sit one evening so they could have some time alone. They chose to go to the Kosel and then out to dinner in a fancy restaurant.

Chavi looked forward to their evening out. She tried to think of an appropriate gift to give Shmuel to show how much their relationship meant to her. She picked a gift carefully and made sure it was wrapped and ready for the evening she needed it.

On the night of their anniversary, Shmuel and Chavi took a taxi to the Kosel and thanked Hashem for their years together and all the many blessings He had given them. Then they walked through the Old City to a restaurant that was located right outside the city's walls. The Old City always had a captivating charm, especially in the evening and especially this particular evening. Although it was a chilly night, Chavi felt warm inside. She marveled at the history, artistic creativity, and original spirit that intermingled in the streets of the Old City, giving it its almost magical appeal. They didn't talk much. It was good just to be together and enjoy the warmth of a relationship that had become so comfortably stable.

The restaurant's atmosphere, in contrast to that of the Old City, was ultramodern and affluent. Shmuel and Chavi were seated and began to read their menus. The exotic foods listed captured Chavi's attention and she carefully read the descriptions of the foreign-sounding items. The waiter asking for their orders interrupted her reading. After Shmuel ordered his meal, she pointed at her choice, too embarrassed to say the name out loud lest she mispronounce it.

While they were waiting for the food to arrive, Chavi took out her wrapped package and handed it to Shmuel.

"I didn't expect you to get me a gift," he said, unwrapping it. Inside there was a beautiful professional portrait of their children, already in a silver frame. "What a wonderful gift! The photographer did a super job of capturing the essence of each child's personality," Shmuel said warmly. "I think I'll hang it in my office so that I'll be able to see the children whenever I want."

"I really appreciate the attention you give the family, even though your schedule makes it difficult," Chavi told him.

"It's my pleasure," said Shmuel, glad that his efforts had been noticed. He drew out a small box from his pocket and handed it to his wife.

Chavi, who hadn't been expecting a present at all, was shocked when she saw what was inside. She looked up from the sparkling diamond earrings to her husband. "They're just exquisite."

"I thought they would look nice on you," he replied, smiling.

Just then, the waiter reappeared with their meals. They both began to eat, but after two bites Shmuel put his fork down and said, "I have another surprise for you, Chavi." He took a paper out of his jacket and passed it to her.

It was a letter from the group of educators behind Shmuel's project. The first paragraph sang Shmuel's praises. The group wrote that they marveled at his abilities to devise a project, research the best method for implementing it, and then make it become a reality. They described him as "a man of vision and talent," and Chavi's heart swelled with pride.

In the next paragraph she read that principals from other schools around the country had approached the Jerusalem educators. They had witnessed the success of the Jerusalem network project and they begged the administration to start similar programs in their cities that would connect as one large organization. The educators were interested in expanding their efforts to a national level, and maybe even an international one. They knew who to ask to spearhead their efforts — Shmuel. They were offering him the position of head administrator of the network of school programs.

"Wow, that's some honor," Chavi said when she finished reading. "I'm really proud of you."

"It will be so exciting to travel around the country and see the different cities and schools."

"You're going to take it?"

"How could I not?"

"It sounds like a full-time position, though."

"Of course it is. It's a lot of responsibility."

"You're leaving yeshivah?"

"I've been waiting for a while for something like this to come up. I'm thirty-five, and I've been in *kollel* for ten years. I don't think any of my friends are still learning. It's time to move on. I thought it was obvious."

It hadn't been obvious to Chavi. She hadn't had an inkling that her husband was looking for full-time work. "Why do you want to leave?"

"It's time. What were you thinking, that I'd learn forever? I tried. It's not for me. I'll still learn at night or before work. Don't worry. Right now, I just can't sit anymore. My job excites me and I feel I'm doing something I'm good at."

"Oh," was all Chavi said.

Maybe she just had to face reality. He had been in *kollel* for ten years already — that was something. She had to accept the fact that although all her crying, yelling, and nagging over the years had technically kept him in yeshivah, she hadn't succeeded in changing his attitude. True, her tenacity had given them ten years, but there was no longer a fire in his heart to grow in learning. It was hard to face that fact. All at once, she felt a failure.

They tried to take pleasure in the rest of their evening together, but the underlying tension made it impossible. Shmuel was upset at Chavi's lack of understanding, while she was trying to face her unfulfilled aspirations.

Mrs. Schneider was surprised to see them home earlier than expected and in such gloomy moods. She didn't ask but silently gathered her things and went home in the cab waiting below.

Both Shmuel and Chavi dropped the issue and pretended that it had never come up. The board had told Shmuel that they didn't need a commitment for another few months, so the Rosenbergs pushed off a definite decision.

The planned turn of events was constantly on Chavi's mind, though she feigned apathy in Shmuel's presence. She decided that she would do her best to save the situation. Instead of relying on *mussar* and pressure, it was time to turn to Heaven and, at the same time, use her brains.

Chavi asked her baby-sitter to watch Tzvi on her next day off from work so that she could take the morning for herself. Her first stop was back to the Kosel. She didn't get there much; it was hard to find the time to go frequently. Today, though, she found herself slowly approaching the holy wall, hoping that she would be able to express what was in her heart and to beg for Divine assistance.

Whenever she went to the Kosel, there was some event going on that distracted her from her prayers. Sometimes it was a rowdy bar mitzvah, sometimes a military ceremony, sometimes it was a deranged woman shouting at the crowd. Today, though, she was so preoccupied with her own issues that she didn't even look around. She paused momentarily, as a sign of respect, before entering the plaza and then entered.

She found a seat and took out the siddur she had brought along. After collecting her thoughts for a minute, she turned to the *Tehillim* in the back of the siddur and began. She recited several chapters and then stopped to speak in her own words. "Hashem, You are the master of the world and can do anything. There is nothing too small or too big or too hard for You.

"I am turning to You for Your help. My husband, Shmuel Yosef *ben* Ruchama Leah, has been trying for the ten years of our marriage to devote himself to the study of Your Torah. He spent years in yeshivah before we married. Even though it's a struggle for him, he gets up every day to face the battle anew. But he still doesn't feel satisfaction in learning. He still doesn't feel accomplished. He is about to leave the yeshivah to pursue his job, where he can feel like a success.

"I know he wants to learn, and he will feel that he didn't meet his goals if he leaves now. But he is too frustrated. If he leaves he will be honored, his family and friends will think he is being sensible, our financial situation will be much more comfortable. But even though he says that he is ready to leave, I know, and certainly You know, that deep down he isn't comfortable with his decision." Here, she began to sob quietly.

She was surprised that tears came. Ever since she had been a little girl, she had been careful not to cry in public. Once or twice, since she had entered motherhood, she had cried with emotion over her children's accomplishments, but never out of despair or desperation. "Hashem, I beg You, help him to find satisfaction learning Your Torah. Make it easier for him. Help him spend his days in yeshivah — for the sake of Your Name and for the sake of the Torah, for which You created the entire universe. Thank You for listening to me, and thank You for the ten years that You have given us thus far."

She sat silently for a few minutes, letting the tears flow and feeling that God was listening closely to her words and would help them. She had done what she could. She prayed for another few minutes for the welfare of her family and again thanked Hashem for the many blessings He had generously showered on her. Ending with a prayer for the rebuilding of the Beis HaMikdash, she made her way out of the plaza toward the steps that lead up to the Old City.

At the top of the steps, Chavi stopped momentarily to admire some colorful lithographs for sale and then found a table at a small outdoor café and bought a cold drink. She sat down, took out a pen and paper, and began phase two of her plan. It was time for her to act wisely. Sermonizing Shmuel about the value of his learning hadn't been effective. She remembered all the seminary speeches she had heard so many years before about a woman's role in shaping the home. She had been told again and again, "Your husband will be adverse to accepting your words of *mussar.* Your job is not to lecture, but to set up an atmosphere where Torah is primary...."

What did that mean practically, though? She couldn't remember being told that. She sat for a few minutes reminiscing about her seminary experience but then remembered that she had work to do and pulled herself back to the task at hand.

She thought of the story of Rachel, the wife of Rabbi Akiva, and how she had encouraged her husband not to be embarrassed by the taunts of the small boys he had to learn with when he began to learn at age forty. When he became self-conscious of how little he knew, she didn't push him back to the cheder with threats and screaming. She patiently set the scene so he would see that the children's ridicule would be short-lived and that they would soon be used to his presence during the study sessions. Her planning was brilliant, thought out, and patient. And she had built Rabbi Akiva.

Chavi thought of the prophetess Devorah. She had also built her husband into a scholar without lecturing. She made sure that he spend time in the presence of the Mishkan and the holy Levites by sending him each day to deliver her homemade wicks for the Menorah. She let the environment influence him, not using words. She, too, was patient and well planned. And she, too, built a *talmid chacham* through her ways.

But what did that mean to Chavi? Chavi decided to let her ideas flow freely, writing down whatever came to mind without analyzing each idea's merit or feasibility. She began: "Encourage him to start learning with someone who works at his office to bring learning into his workplace. Make him a fancy party when he makes a *siyum*. Look for high-paying *kollel*s. Find out about *semichah* programs."

She wrote down everything and anything that came to mind. Nothing struck her as particularly exciting, but she continued brainstorming for a full hour.

After ordering a second drink, Chavi looked over her list. She finished her drink feeling frustrated and paid the bill.

As she was gathering her things, an idea came to her — the first one that really seemed good. She would have to think it through some more and think about the best way to implement it, but there was still an hour left until she had to head home. The perfect amount of time. Chavi walked through the Old City deep in thought, developing her plan for the better part of an hour. As she headed for the bus, she whispered a thank you to the One Above and asked again for His assistance.

Later, at dinner, she presented her plan to Shmuel. "Shmuel, I came up with an idea that I think will really help our son."

Shmuel wondered which son and what he needed help in. Everything seemed to be going well. "What do you mean?"

"Yitzchak has just begun learning Gemara in cheder. It's not that easy for him and so far we've been paying Rabbi Cohen to learn with him, which is working out all right. But the arrangement has its drawbacks. First of all, we are paying a small fortune for his services. But more importantly, as long as Yitzchak has a tutor he still feels that he needs remedial help. It's not that great for his self-esteem. Imagine what it would do for him if we could show him that he has moved beyond tutoring."

"But he hasn't."

"Okay. Let me finish. We both know Yitzchak is very bright, but he has learning disabilities that make it hard for him to accomplish in his normal school setting. It happens to be that we have an expert on the topic living right in our home. That's you, of course. If anyone knows how to deal with a child like Yitzchak most effectively, it's you. Through your work, you have gathered ideas and experience. And you have a knack for reaching kids who don't do well in a conventional setting. Right?"

Oh, what did she want? he wondered nervously.

"I was thinking that maybe we could drop the tutor, and you could work with him at night. You could come up with an appropriate plan. We would save money. Think of how good Yitzchak will feel if we tell him that he doesn't need any tutoring anymore and he has graduated to learning with his father. He'll be so honored. And the quality of his tutoring time will be vastly improved, I'm sure.

"Besides, I know it sounds silly to worry about it at this stage, but I am worried about him getting accepted into a quality *yeshivah ketanah*. Competition is so fierce. It will be much easier to send him to the place that we think is best if he doesn't have a tutor. And we have to worry about where Elchanan is going to be accepted, too. I've heard that the yeshivos check into the older brothers when deciding whom they should accept. This plan could save us an awful lot of grief in the future."

Shmuel was impressed that his wife spent so much time thinking about their children's futures and trying to make things good for them, but he thought her worries were a little extreme. Everything was going fine. The boys were still only eight and a half and three and a half, respectively. He had to admit, though, that she had brought up some good points about Yitzchak. "I'll have to give up my night *seder* with my *chavrusa* if I learn with Yitzchak. Obviously, the level of my learning with him won't compare to learning with an adult. Do you think it's worth it?"

"I do."

"Okay, I'll think about it."

A couple of days later, Shmuel said he would try it. Chavi smiled and expressed her appreciation.

The first thing to do was to find Rabbi Cohen a replacement job. Chavi soon heard of an older boy in the neighborhood who needed two hours of tutoring a night. She asked Rabbi Cohen if he would be able to switch from helping Yitzchak to helping the new boy. He said he was happy to get the extra hours. Chavi paid him for his work and added a bonus with a note thanking him for all the help that he had extended to their family.

The first night of their new arrangement, Chavi prepared some drinks and cookies and sent her men into the extra bedroom where Yitzchak was tutored to begin their session together. Earlier that day, she had prepared Yitzchak for the change, and he felt appropriately honored.

Chavi nervously busied herself with housework as she waited for the hourly session to come to an end. Forty-five minutes later, the door opened and they both came out.

She acted casual, deciding to wait until later to hear how things had gone. But she saw from Shmuel's face that the session hadn't gone so smoothly. As they were preparing to go to sleep that evening, she asked him how the tutoring had gone.

"I don't know how long it's going to last," Shmuel told her frankly. "It's funny, but I have so much patience for other people, but not for my own son. In the middle of our learning time, we both got frustrated. He also asked me a few questions that I couldn't answer. I'm going to try to look up the answers tomorrow morning. I've learned this stuff before, but I never thought of these things."

Success! Chavi thought to herself. "I'm sorry it was hard on you both. Hopefully, you'll find a rhythm together soon. I really appreciate what you're doing."

26

The tutoring continued. Sometimes the sessions ended early. Sometimes Chavi heard yelling from behind the closed door. Sometimes, the breaks Shmuel and Yitzchak took were longer than the actual time they spent learning. But sometimes, they would go past their allotted hour. And sometimes Chavi would hear them discussing something to do with the Gemara in the morning or after lunch. One time Chavi saw Yitzchak run to ask Shmuel a question about the Gemara right before he went to sleep.

Two weeks after Shmuel and Chavi's eleventh anniversary, Chavi realized that it had been a full year since her husband and son had started learning together. She was very happy with how things were working out. Shmuel had started preparing for the learning sessions to make sure he had a clear enough grasp of the Gemara not to be stumped by one of Yitzchak's basic questions. In trying to anticipate anything that would come up, he would delve deeper and deeper into the subject. Chavi saw him take out *sefarim* that he hadn't used in years. He had also started writing things down to organize his thoughts. He was still learning his regular *masechta* in the morning, and reviewing morning *seder* had to be squeezed in after he finished with Yitzchak at night. When the time had come for Shmuel to inform the cheder network of his decision regarding the job offer, he had decided not to take the job. Instead, he switched his position to consultant for the national project, keeping his daily schedule the same.

Chavi baked and frosted a cake and left it in Shmuel and Yitzchak's learning room in honor of their one-year anniversary together. The bigger surprise came, though, when Yitzchak came home that afternoon. He handed her a *sefer*. She read the Hebrew description that his rebbe had written inside. "Dear Yitzchak: This book is being given to you in appreciation of the effort that you have put into your learning and the depth of understanding that you have shown. May you continue to go from strength to strength."

Chavi was speechless. She warmly embraced her son and said, in a voice laden with pride, "Oh, just wait until Tatty sees this!"

ꙮ ꙮ

Faigy, a sweet first grader, was doing well academically, with none of the problems her older brother had had at that age. Chavi was disappointed, though, in her daughter's teacher, a stern young woman who was determined to whip her charges into shape. At the first parent-teacher meeting of the year, she told the parents that she tolerated no nonsense and did not hesitate to reprimand any girl who misbehaved. Chavi did not like the sound of that, but luckily Faigy was not a troublemaker by nature, so she made the best of it.

Toward the end of the year, Faigy began to have trouble sleeping at night and pick at her food at mealtimes. Chavi pressed her daughter to share with her what was wrong, but Faigy insisted that it was nothing.

After about three weeks of such behavior, an elegant invitation, printed on card-stock paper, arrived in the mail. It invited Chavi to "a moving evening of song and dance" to be performed by none other than her daughter and her six- and seven-year-old friends. "Wow, Faigy, look at this invitation!" she exclaimed. "It looks like a real wedding invitation. This sounds like it will be some show!"

Faigy did not share her excitement, though. She didn't even look at the invitation. Obviously, something was wrong.

Chavi tried to engage her in conversation. "What kind of songs are you singing?"

Faigy said matter-of-factly, "I'm not in the choir. Mrs. Golden said that only girls with good voices are allowed to sing on stage. I am in charge of props."

It was true that singing wasn't Faigy's forte. She could hardly carry a tune. Still, Chavi thought, how could the teacher put down her daughter like that? Faigy must be feeling terrible. Couldn't she at least have been told that she was in charge of props because that was her strength, not because she couldn't sing? Besides, did it really matter how a choir of first-graders sounded? How could Mrs. Golden leave girls out of this main event?

For several months already Chavi had been noting the absence of positive notes and encouraging remarks on the papers Faigy had been bringing home. She had kept quiet so as not to ruin the good terms Faigy was on her teacher. But this was too much.

"Faigy, is anyone else not in the choir?"

"Yes, three other girls."

After keeping the story in for so long, Faigy seemed relieved to share it. "We all had to try out in front of the class and then Mrs. Golden told us what we would do. We didn't get to say what we wanted. I want to be in the choir, but I can't. And Esther Lowey doesn't want to be in the choir."

Chavi had never heard the name of this particular friend before. In a minute she found out why. "She is embarrassed to sing in front of all the mothers. She likes to just be quiet all the time. Sometimes we play together, but usually she plays by herself at recess. Mrs. Golden made her try out also. She started crying, but Mrs. Golden said that she had to be like everyone else. Mrs. Golden held her hand and kept telling her we were all friends and it would be all right. She stopped crying and sang, but it was very hard for her.

"She really has a pretty voice. Kind of like yours, Mommy. She sounds like a lady almost. The teacher told her how nice she sounded and told her, 'You see, there was nothing to be afraid of.' She even has to sing alone now during the show. Every day, I see her get sad when we start to practice. I wish I could switch with her because I love to sing. But I can't ask Mrs. Golden to do that — she'll yell at me or punish me."

Chavi was horrified. Why hadn't Faigy told her about this earlier? It was scandalous. Later that evening, she called Mrs. Golden at home, but her complaint on her daughter's behalf fell on deaf ears. Mrs. Golden crisply explained that their production was to be professional and each child had her part to play. She had been teaching for a number of years and knew what she was doing.

Chavi brought up the topic of the girl who didn't want to

sing. She heard the anger in Mrs. Golden's voice as she replied that the personal affairs of another child were certainly none of Chavi's business. With that, Mrs. Golden ended the conversation.

Chavi replaced the receiver grimly, thinking, *It's a good thing the year is almost over.*

Chavi asked Faigy periodically over the next few weeks how the preparations for the show were going. Faigy said there were a lot of fancy costumes and they practiced for a long time each day. Chavi asked about her shy friend. Faigy told her that she had been sick lately and absent from school. *No wonder,* Chavi thought.

During the week of the production, Faigy uncharacteristically began fighting with her brothers and ignoring her mother's requests. Chavi, blaming Faigy's behavior on Mrs. Golden, was glad the dreaded production was almost over.

The day finally arrived. Chavi was surprised to see Faigy excited, but she realized it was a big day for the class. They had put a lot of work into making sure the evening would be perfect. Chavi escorted Faigy, dressed all in black for her job as stagehand, to the neighborhood shul where the performance would be held. Faigy disappeared backstage and Chavi sat down with the other mothers to wait for the performance to begin.

Fifteen minutes after the performance was scheduled to begin, Mrs. Golden introduced it with a poetic recitation about the theme, the lofty ideals to which a Jewish home must aspire. The mothers clapped and the show began.

Chavi marveled at how well her daughter's classmates performed. Their actions were well coordinated, and they sang in harmony. Each song was introduced with a two-line rhyme about the topic of the song to follow, which Chavi found to be written in inappropriately mature language. She searched for Faigy and once caught a glimpse of her between scenes. She waved enthusiastically and got a smile in return.

The lighting changed to set the mood for each scene. The costumes were exquisite. Chavi wondered how much they had cost and where they had come from. The lights dimmed as the last scene began, after an introduction to the effect that it was about Jewish tradition being passed from mother to daughter throughout the generations. The piano player began a slow melody and the curtain parted to reveal the choir dressed in head scarves and aprons.

Slowly a frail-looking blonde girl walked to the microphone, her gaze on the floor. For a moment, she looked up with terror-stricken eyes at the audience. Then she looked at Mrs. Golden, who had been standing near the piano throughout the production. Chavi was certain that this was Esther Lowey.

The little girl stood there as the piano continued to play, looking from the floor to her teacher and back. Finally, she started to sing. The first word came out softly, and then she stopped. The piano continued its music. Mrs. Golden inched closer to the stage, her back to the audience. The girl's lips began to quiver as she tried to hold back her tears. Time seemed to have stopped. Chavi wondered what the other mothers were thinking. She prayed that God would give the young child the ability to sing.

Suddenly, to her great amazement, she saw her daughter, dressed in black, but with a *tichel* on her head, step out from behind the curtain and stand next to the petrified soloist. Faigy took the girl's hand and smiled at her gently. Chavi wondered what she was doing.

Faigy looked at her teacher and then straight out into the audience and began to sing with all her heart and soul. Chavi heard a woman a few seats away from her giggle. It was true that Faigy's energy only accentuated her lack of talent, but to Chavi, there had never been a more beautiful song sung since the world began. Her daughter was displaying incredible strength of character in trying to save her classmate from embarrassment. She was terrified of her teacher and did whatever she could to avoid having to face her wrath. And yet here she was, standing up to Mrs. Golden in public!

Chavi continued to watch the drama unfold. From Mrs. Golden's posture and frantic arm gestures, Chavi knew she was saying something, but she didn't know what. Faigy took no notice and kept on singing, all the while holding the mute soloist's hand. Soon the solo came to its finale and the stupefied choir joined Faigy in finishing the song as per the original plan.

The choir sang its finale song. Faigy was absent from the scene. The audience applauded, and the curtain closed. All the mothers rose and made their way in an excited throng toward the stage to congratulate their daughters on a job well done. As Chavi walked behind stage, she noticed a few mothers had gathered around Mrs. Golden to compliment her on the wonderful show. Chavi felt nauseous from the scene.

She found Faigy folding costumes and packing them in their appropriate boxes. "Faigy?" she called, hurrying over. Faigy turned toward her. Chavi scooped her up and hugged her tightly. Stroking her hair, she said, "I can't believe that I am so fortunate to have you as my daughter. How did you do it?"

"I just felt so sorry for Esther and I didn't even think

about Mrs. Golden," Faigy said in a muffled voice.

Just then they heard someone asking where Faigy was. A moment later, Mrs. Golden was facing them, her hands on her hips and her brows knitted. Chavi put Faigy down.

"What chutzpah! I have never seen so much nerve in a little girl in all my life. How dare you go against my wishes and publicly mortify me and the whole class? I am too angry now to decide what your punishment will be. You'll be hearing from me in the morning, young lady. Just you wait."

Chavi opened her mouth to speak, but before the words came out Mrs. Golden looked her up and down and declared, "It is a shame that you had to witness this disgraceful behavior, Mrs. Rosenberg. After our phone conversation, I see that the apple doesn't fall far from the tree."

Chavi realized that there was nothing she could say to show the woman how callous and uncaring her attitude was. Answering back would only open Faigy up to more hurt. She said nothing, just looked directly at Mrs. Golden.

The teacher became flustered by the lack of response. She was prepared to fight but didn't know what to do. She looked away from Chavi and left.

Chavi was incensed. Incensed at what Mrs. Golden had done to Faigy's friend. Incensed at how she had belittled and threatened her daughter. Incensed that Mrs. Golden had the nerve to insult the mother of one of her students in front of her daughter. How many indignities had these poor innocent girls suffered over the year? How many students had passed through her classroom over the years? Chavi had no idea what to do now, but she knew she had to do something.

She said to Faigy, "Let's go home now. I'm sorry that you had to go through this, but the *middos* that you exhibited have made me happier than I've ever been."

Faigy smiled, delighted with her mother's approval. "Mommy, do I have to go to school tomorrow?"

"I don't think so, but don't worry. Tatty and I will decide what to do tonight."

Chavi helped Faigy put the rest of the costumes away. She couldn't believe that her daughter was staying to finish her work after Mrs. Golden had been so cruel. Would she have acted the same way in her daughter's situation? Probably not.

Shmuel was still learning with Yitzchak when Chavi and Faigy came home. Faigy asked if she could go say good night to her father.

"No one is allowed to interrupt Tatty when he's learning," Chavi reminded her. "Why don't you get ready for bed and see if Tatty and Yitzchak are finished by then."

Faigy changed into pajamas, brushed her teeth, and washed her face. Then she went into the kitchen to get a drink. As she put the cup in the sink, Shmuel and Yitzchak came out of the back room, both looking happy.

"Come here, little princess," Shmuel called to Faigy. She ran into his arms. "How was your show?"

"It was really nice — I even got to sing a solo." Faigy turned to Chavi to smile at her inside joke.

"Did you really?" Shmuel asked. "I thought you were doing costumes?"

"I did do costumes. But I also helped Esther Lowey sing her solo."

"That's great," he said, kissing her cheek. "Now go to sleep. It's hours past your bedtime."

Chavi marveled at the scene that had just unfolded before her eyes. Although Faigy was barely seven, she had a tremendous strength of character and maturity. Chavi had noticed it before, but her daughter's personality was deeper than she had realized. What else went on in Faigy's life that she didn't feel the need to share? It scared Chavi to think that perhaps she didn't really know what went on in her young daughter's mind.

After the children were soundly asleep, she sat down on the couch to wait for her husband to return from *maariv* and think over the day's events. She had always felt like such an outsider when it came to the children's schools. Everyone seemed to know the system, but she had retained her immigrant status in this area, always unsure of what was required of her and worried that she was doing the wrong thing. The summer before Faigy had started first grade, Chavi had been in such a panic over the proper briefcase to buy, the necessary school supplies, and sundry other details. It was simple enough to find out everything she wanted to know, but she still worried that she was missing some vital piece of information or going about things in a socially unacceptable way. Perhaps Faigy would be hurt or embarrassed along the way from one of her mother's mistakes.

Faigy seemed to be doing all right, despite having been subjected to a horrible teacher in only her first year of real education. Chavi hoped that Mrs. Golden was an exception in the teaching staff and not the rule. She played nervously with the folds of her maternity shirt and wondered if the child she was expecting was a girl who might end up being placed in Mrs. Golden's class. Chavi would never let another child of hers spend a year with that teacher — of that she was certain.

She pulled her thoughts back to the present and wondered what the best course of action was in her current situation. Nothing would come of speaking to Mrs. Golden, and she didn't think the principal would take her complaint seriously. What should she do?

Shmuel entered at last, interrupting her thoughts about her daughter's education. He sat mesmerized as she told him of the night's events, expressing first pity for Faigy's classmate, then pride, then anger. They spoke for a long time, trying to decide how to deal with the situation.

After much deliberation, Shmuel and Chavi decided to take Faigy to school the next morning. They would bring her to the classroom and ask Mrs. Golden directly if she would be penalizing Faigy and, if so, how. With her parents accompanying her, Faigy wouldn't be scared to go to school. Also, she would learn that she didn't have to be afraid when she acted properly. Most important, Mrs. Golden would realize that she was dealing with a family that would be on top of the case if she reacted too strongly.

Chavi wanted Shmuel to come because she knew that a man's presence would have an intimidating effect on the teacher. Afterwards, the two of them would meet with the principal to discuss the situation. Shmuel's presence would help Chavi stay calm and express herself clearly. In addition, he had learned a lot about the Israeli education system over his years of employment in the field, and he knew how to speak appropriately.

27

Faigy awoke very early the next morning and came into Chavi's bed. "Mommy, do I have to go to school today?"

It was half an hour before she had to get up, but Chavi didn't complain, knowing how frightened Faigy must have been of facing her teacher. "Come lie next to me, Faigy." Faigy cuddled up to her, eager for comfort. "Tatty and I are going to bring you to class today and then we're going to your principal."

"Maybe I should stay home," Faigy suggested hopefully.

"You don't want to have to stay home until the end of the year, do you?" Chavi asked.

"That would be perfect," Faigy said, to Chavi's surprise.

"Don't worry, Faigy. Everything will work out fine. You won't have to deal with this alone."

Faigy did not look convinced, but she did not protest when Chavi got out of bed and tucked the covers around her, figuring she could use an extra hour of sleep. Within minutes, the little girl was fast asleep.

At 8:30, the two older boys had left for school and Tzvi was dropped off at a neighbor. Chavi, Shmuel, and Faigy walked the two blocks to Faigy's school. The schoolyard was filled with laughing, talking, and playing girls. That meant class had not yet started. Faigy directed them to her classroom. Shmuel and Chavi entered. Mrs. Golden was sitting at her desk with a cup of coffee, talking to another teacher who was standing nearby. The Rosenbergs approached the desk and asked Mrs. Golden if they could speak with her. Taking the hint, her visitor left the room.

Chavi started the conversation, with Shmuel looking on. "Faigy was nervous about coming to school this morning after you threat...told her that she was going to be castigated for her behavior last night. To make her feel better, we told her that we would accompany her. We wanted to make sure that her fears of being hur...of being strongly disciplined were unfounded. Have you decided how you will react to last night's incident?"

"Um, I decided that since I made it, um, so clear to Faigy last night that her behavior was unacceptable, I would let her off the hook this time," Mrs. Golden answered, adding, "assuming that she will behave herself in the future."

Shmuel rolled his eyes. Not letting her relief show, Chavi said, "That's what I expected. I'll go tell Faigy that there is nothing to worry about, because you decided to forget the incident."

They turned to find Faigy, but heard the teacher say, "As I said, assuming her behavior is acceptable." Shmuel looked back to glare at her, and they went on. Thankfully, there were less than two weeks left to the school year.

After assuring Faigy that everything had been straightened out, Shmuel and Chavi made their way to the principal's office. Mrs. Frisch was in a meeting, but the secretary said that she would probably be free to meet with them in a quarter of an hour. They sat down on two chairs across from the secretaries' desks to wait.

Twenty minutes later, they were invited into Mrs. Frisch's office. Chavi had met her a number of times before, but Shmuel hadn't. Mrs. Frisch was a short woman in her fifties with an old-fashioned, dirty-blond *sheitel.* She was dressed in a conservative dark blue suit with a pink blouse and wore bifocals on a chain around her neck. Her expression was businesslike, but the soft wrinkles on her face indicated the kind heart within.

Chavi introduced her husband, thereby making sure that the principal had placed her face.

"Are you the man involved in setting up the system assisting learning-disabled children in the chedarim?" Mrs. Frisch asked. Shmuel said he was. Mrs. Frisch looked impressed. "I have heard wonderful things about your work. I was told to contact you for suggestions on improving our program. Perhaps we'll set up a meeting before you leave, if that's all right with you."

Chavi was glad he had come. Maybe Mrs. Frisch's respect for Shmuel's work would make her more receptive to their complaint.

"What brings you here today?" Mrs. Frisch asked them.

Chavi repeated the story of the previous night's events and then related a few other incidents when Mrs. Golden had seemed overly strict.

Mrs. Frisch shook her head sadly. "Have you noticed this problem throughout the school year?" she asked Chavi.

Chavi paused for a moment to think. "No, come to think of it, I haven't. I think Faigy's issues started around Chanukah. I didn't realize what a problem it was until last night, I'm ashamed to say. Otherwise, I would have come sooner."

Mrs. Frisch sighed. She looked at a spot on the wall over their heads for a minute and then said, "Before I say anything, I want to tell you how impressed I am with your daughter. The strongest adults would have a hard time acting so selflessly under that amount of pressure. You will undoubtedly merit to see extraordinary things from her in the future. And I'm sure her strength of character comes from what she has witnessed in her home."

Her kind words warmed Chavi's heart. She wondered what was coming next.

"I am not sure what I should say now. As a principal, I know many things about the teachers that they may choose not to share with their students and their students' families, and I am always careful to keep their confidences. In this case, though, I feel that a terrible disservice will be done to Mrs. Golden if I don't tell you something, at least in a general way."

She paused before continuing. "Rivka Golden has been under a tremendous amount of pressure lately. One of her children was diagnosed with a terrible disease over Chanukah, may we never know of such things. For the past five months, Mrs. Golden has been running from doctor to doctor and from hospital to hospital to make sure her son gets the best treatment he can. Nothing has been helping, though.

"Recently, the family heard about a special treatment that offers them their last hope, short of an open miracle. The expenses involved in the treatment are exorbitant, and none of them are covered by insurance. She doesn't know how to proceed. The financial pressures and her son's deteriorating condition allow her no peace. And she still has to take care of her other children, deal with her son's medical treatments, and make it to work.

"I am certainly not condoning her behavior, but I'm afraid that there is nothing I can do right now. I cannot add to her tension. There are only two weeks left to school. I suppose that if you think it's really unbearable, I could say something. But if we can just let things end naturally, it would be an act of kindness to Mrs. Golden."

Chavi and Shmuel sat speechless. Their anger and indignation had been replaced by pity. "I agree with you — we'll let the issue slide," Chavi said at last. She and Shmuel got up to leave.

"My secretary knows my work schedule better than I do," Shmuel told Mrs. Frisch. "You can call her to arrange an official meeting about your remedial program, if you are interested." He opened his wallet for a business card and removed two hundred shekels at the same time. He handed both to Mrs. Frisch. "I know it's not much, but please pass this along to Mrs. Golden."

Chavi followed him out, lost in thought. She was realizing once again that the people she came across were rarely as simple as she assumed them to be. It was time to learn to stop judging other people's characters based on a superficial understanding.

When they reached the outer gate, Shmuel turned to the right, toward his *kollel*. "Have a good day, Chavi."

"Thank you for coming along," she said. "That sure was some lesson in understanding people."

"It certainly was," he agreed.

ꝏ ꝏ

Chavi arrived home feeling exhausted as usual. She would have to go pick up Tzvi in about an hour, but she had a little time to herself until then. Kicking off her shoes near the door, she poured herself a large glass of ice water from the refrigerator and sat down on the couch to review the events of the previous night and that morning. She decided to say a chapter of *Tehillim* for Mrs. Golden's son before tackling her daily chores. When she was done, she surveyed the scene to decide where to begin.

The house was an absolute wreck. Pregnancy always made her less careful about housework, and being out all evening and two hours of the morning only compounded the problem. Crumbs and dishes littered the table, and a milk spill had dripped down to the floor. Tzvi's pajamas lay smack in the middle of the apartment's entranceway. Toys were scattered throughout the living room. The couch pillows were askew and one was on the floor, having not been returned to their places after being played with. The recliner was piled high with unfolded laundry. Both sinks were filled with dishes and emitted a smell that was unpleasant under the best of circumstances and repulsive to Chavi's now more sensitive nose.

Chavi knew that she would have to clean up that day, but she had just enough time to procrastinate for half an hour. She decided to lie down for a bit before beginning her work and went to put on a robe and a snood. The phone rang as she was heading back to the living room to shut the lights.

It was her mother-in-law. She was in the neighborhood and wanted to stop by to drop something off. Chavi tried every excuse she could think of to convince her that it wasn't a good time to visit, but her mother-in-law insisted. She said she was only ten minutes away and wanted to show Chavi something.

Chavi hung up, and panic set in. What should she do first? There was no way, absolutely no way, that her mother-in-law could see her house like this. She started by frantically sweeping the toys into a pile in the corner and dumping the laundry on her bed. Five minutes were used up already. Only five minutes left. What should she do next? She briefly considered running away from home or leaving a note on the door to the effect that an emergency had come up and she had left for the day and would call her mother-in-law when she returned.

Knowing how impractical both those options were, Chavi began to cry. "I can't do it. I just can't do it," she said aloud to no one.

And then, as if a dark cloud had dissipated, her mood changed. Obviously, if you couldn't, you didn't have to. You had to try and do your best, but if you couldn't, you couldn't.

That simple truth was to her an ingenious discovery. Chavi knew that she worried too much and tried to be in control of every part of her life. She would try her best and then a little bit harder and end up dejected when things didn't work out the way she had planned. Shmuel called her very idealistic when he was in a good mood and compulsive when he was upset with her. Chavi was never able to accept things the way they were if they didn't meet her standards. Although this character trait helped her get things done under trying circumstances, it also smacked of arrogance, of forgetting that God was running the world.

She did have to try, but that was it. The results were up to God. What was out of her power wasn't her responsibility.

If the house was a mess, then she should clean it up if she could. But if, for whatever reasons, she couldn't, then she didn't have to. If her mother-in-law saw that sometimes she was a sloppy housekeeper, she would have to swallow the shame and move on.

There were bigger issues in her life where this principle applied, too. She still hadn't really made peace with the fact that Yitzchak was learning disabled. She was still embarrassed of his stutter, although it was much more controlled now. She wanted him to be gifted or at least regular, and she pushed him. It was okay to push him, but her attitude was wrong. She didn't think, *I want to help my son be the best that he can be given the abilities that God has given him*, but rather, *Yitzchak needs to be normal. I will make sure that Yitzchak is normal.*

It was uncomfortable to criticize herself so bluntly, but it was true. Chavi hadn't yet learned how to accept the circumstances that she was given, nor was she able to accept people as they were. She loved Yitzchak completely, but she also wanted to change him. People couldn't be changed, though, and she wasn't supposed to change him. She had to give him the opportunity to be the greatest he could be. And that was it.

What about her relationship with Shmuel? They both knew that Chavi would never accept him until he was who she dreamed he could be. What if he wasn't meant to live up to her ideal? Only God knew his potential. Could she learn to truly appreciate him no matter what?

The real test of her personal success was ultimately her ability to put her trust in God and love Him and the people

He had created. It was His world, not hers. She was just a creation put there to fulfill His will. She had been taught that all her life, but this was the first time that she understood it and realized how far she was from a true faith in God.

Suddenly, she felt free of so much of the worry and dissatisfaction that were her constant companions. Everything was as it should be. She had to do her best to make things good, but that was where her responsibility ended. Yitzchak was okay. Shmuel was okay. Elchanan was allowed to be wild if he needed to be. Even if money seemed too tight, they would always have what they needed. What they didn't have they didn't need.

At that point the doorbell rang, and, without waiting for Chavi to answer, in walked Mrs. Rosenberg. She looked around and almost dropped her bag. "My goodness, what happened? This house looks like a hurricane hit it!"

Chavi laughed to herself. Her mother-in-law's description was very accurate.

"Is everything okay?" Mrs. Rosenberg asked with genuine concern.

"Yes, I was just out last night and this morning and the mess accumulated," Chavi answered simply, without excusing herself.

"Let me call my cleaning lady right now and see if she can come here today. You can't live like this."

Little does she know how often we do lately, thought Chavi. "That's okay. I'll get to it. Things will be back in order by the evening, God willing."

With that, Mrs. Rosenberg dropped the topic. The moment had been much less painful than Chavi had envisioned. They sat down in the living room, and Mrs.

Rosenberg took a gift-wrapped box out of her bag and excitedly handed it to Chavi.

"When we came for Shabbos, I noticed that you light Shabbos candles with the original silver candlesticks I got you and a hodgepodge of junky little candlesticks. I went into a silver store today to buy a wedding gift for a friend's son and I know your birthday is coming up soon, so I decided to get you this."

Chavi unwrapped it with her mother-in-law looking on eagerly. Inside was a gorgeous six-armed candelabrum, delicately ornate. The polished silver shone brightly. "I don't know what to say. It's simply stunning," Chavi said, turning the gift from side to side to admire it. "Thank you. I can't believe you bought this for us."

She got up to give her mother-in-law a kiss. Although Chavi rarely showed any sort of physical affection to anyone but her immediate family, particularly not her mother-in-law, she was so elated over her discovery of that morning and so overwhelmed by the gift that she was moved to demonstrate her appreciation of the gesture.

Chavi's robe had concealed the pregnancy she had not yet mentioned to her mother-in-law, but Mrs. Rosenberg apparently noticed something when she got up. "Uh, Chavi, the crown in the middle is removable so you can add another candle, should the need arise," she said with a smile. Chavi smiled back.

28

Chavi called her mother later that day and invited her over to have dinner and see her new gift. Mrs. Schneider gladly accepted the invitation. She was always looking for something to do and enjoyed spending time in her daughter's house.

At 5:00, half an hour before the children's dinnertime, Mrs. Schneider arrived, bearing a few small toys and a chocolate cake. She never came empty-handed. The children crowded around her, loudly sharing their latest news with their grandmother. Chavi had to referee so that the noise wouldn't be overwhelming. Mrs. Schneider passed out her gifts and listened to each child with real interest. After ten minutes, Chavi sent the children to play so she and her mother could talk while she made dinner.

Mrs. Schneider sat at the kitchen table while Chavi stirred her spaghetti sauce and removed some vegetables from the refrigerator for a salad. "How are things going, Ima?" She knew that Mrs. Schneider wasn't as happy lately. She missed Max's companionship, and her days were much emptier than they had been before she met Max. When they married, Max had requested that she cut down on her charitable activities so she could spend more time at home with him. She complied with his request. But now, a year and a half after his passing, she had yet to fill up her schedule again. Still, she filled Chavi in on the news at her job and at the library, where she had continued to volunteer.

"How are your boarders doing?" Chavi asked.

"Funny you should ask that today," Mrs. Schneider said. "Right before I came, I told them both that they need to leave at the end of the month."

"Why?" Chavi asked.

"I'm finding it too much to live with such young women. They come home very late, and I don't like to go to sleep when not everyone is home yet and the door is unlocked. I know they're not my responsibility, but I end up lying in bed waiting to hear them come in and then my night of sleep is ruined. I can't ask them to come home earlier. I'm not their mother, just their landlady. I also don't like the mess and the noise and the lights left on all the time. At this point in my life, I've had enough of living with young people."

"Would you consider living here, then?" Chavi asked.

"Thank you, dear, but no. I need to live in my own house and be able to do things the way I want. I know you'll do everything you can to make me comfortable, but it's still not the same. I've gotten used to the quiet."

As if to underscore the unfeasibility of Chavi's suggestion, Elchanan and Tzvi began to fight in the other room. Chavi listened to their yells for a minute and decided they could work the squabble out on their own. "Aren't you scared to live alone?" she asked her mother.

"Sure I am. I've thought of all my options, and I've decided what I want to do. Do you remember Lily from the library? Well, she moved into a retirement complex in Katamon last year. She's thrilled there, and she invited me to come see it one day. I was very impressed with what I saw. The whole project is only two years old. After you buy a condominium in this complex, you pay a monthly assessment fee for the services they offer. The condominiums are small studio apartments with a bedroom, a living room, and a kitchenette. If I sell my apartment, I'll make enough money to buy a condominium with plenty left over.

"The assessment fee is high, but it includes security for the whole complex, a nurse on staff twenty-four hours a day, a daily cleaning service, and medical insurance. There is also a *glatt*-kosher restaurant on premises, so you can order meals if you don't want to cook. They have a shul, too, plus all kinds of entertaining activities. Everything is new and pretty, and most of the people are religious.

"There is a waiting list for condominiums, but when I visited Lily a while ago, I put my name on the list. A few days ago, I got a call that there would be a condo opening up in three months, enough time, I hope, to sell my apartment. I went to talk to our lawyer yesterday to make sure that the financial details were favorable. He called me this morning and said that everything checked out okay. What do you think?"

Retrieving the plates and silverware that she needed to set the table gave Chavi a minute to think before she answered. The fact that her mother had done all this planning and inquiry without including her made Chavi feel very left out. That was one of the changes that Mrs. Schneider's marriage to Max had brought about. She had once shared everything with Chavi; they were close confidantes. But when Max entered the picture, appropriately he took over Chavi's role. It had hurt Chavi then, too, but at least she understood. Now she just felt left out.

Her mother was considering a retirement home? That was for old people. She put the silverware down on the table and paused to look at her mother with a fresh eye. Mrs. Schneider's face was adorned with smile lines and creases. Her chin drooped. Her soft hands were worn and sun spotted. She would be seventy on her next birthday, past every civilized country's retirement age. Was she really old? Chavi chose not to think about it, as it saddened her too much to continue along this vein.

Pushing aside all emotion, she told her mother, "It sounds like the place might be nice. We'll be glad to help you out with the move if you decide to go through with it."

Chavi called the children in to dinner. Her mother, who liked to eat early, ate with them. Afterwards, Mrs. Schneider helped Chavi clean up while the kids played a bit and finished their homework. Then Faigy, Elchanan, and Tzvi started getting ready for bed.

Mrs. Schneider enjoyed the domestic tranquility and homey feeling of her daughter's home. It was a warm and comfortable place to be. Thinking back to Chavi's dating years when she had wondered if she would ever be lucky enough to see her daughter's house alive with the laughter of children, she felt doubly blessed.

As she was getting ready to leave, Shmuel came home in an excited, happy mood. He exchanged greetings with his wife and mother-in-law and then went to say good night to the children. When he came out, he saw that his mother-in-law had her coat on. "So soon?" he asked.

She laughed. "I've already been here a while."

"Well, before you go, listen to my good news," Shmuel said. Both she and Chavi gave him their attention. "The *rosh kollel* called me into his office this morning. He told me that I learn well — that I think clearly and have a good memory." Shmuel blushed. "He also said — get a load of this — that he was impressed with my *hasmadah*. Someone called him last night looking for a suitable candidate to give a *shiur* to boys in an American yeshivah here, and he highly recommended me. He thought my learning was good enough and with my personality I could connect to the boys."

"*Mazal tov!* When are you going to start?" Mrs. Schneider asked.

"Oh, I'm not going to take the position."

"You're not?" Chavi asked.

"Oh, no," he answered matter-of-factly. "I'm already working one *seder*. I'm not ready to leave *kollel* yet. I haven't even gone through *Shas* once yet."

He took the drink that Chavi was holding out to him and thanked her. "Isn't that nice news?" he asked and left the two ladies standing there to go find Yitzchak.

ꙮ ꙮ

Mrs. Schneider signed a contract for the apartment in the retirement complex which was to be ready in three months. She found an agent to sell her home and began packing. Although the packing tired her out, she knew better than to leave it all for the last minute. Chavi and Shmuel took turns going over in the evenings to help her. One Friday, Chavi sent

Yitzchak and Faigy to Bayit Vegan to assist their grandmother. Mrs. Schneider was worried at first that they would be careless and ruin her organization or her belongings, but the children were so excited about the prospect of helping her that she decided to risk it once. It turned out that there were many jobs they could do. She marveled at how mature and capable they were.

Mrs. Schneider's apartment was sold in less than three weeks. She was delighted that the sale went so smoothly, but the knowledge that there was no turning back was a little difficult for her. She had never been one to enjoy change, and the older she got the harder transitions became. The new owners were interested in moving in as soon as possible. Mrs. Schneider decided to make a month-long trip to America to visit her children and grandchildren there and return a week before the scheduled move into the retirement complex. The retirement home had plenty of storage space to house her belongings for the month prior to the move, so that was no problem.

The month passed quickly, and soon Mrs. Schneider was moved in and settled. Although Chavi's pregnancy tired her out, she tried to make sure that either she or Shmuel went to Katamon every day for the first few weeks to make sure that her mother was comfortable and to help dissipate the loneliness that usually accompanies the first few weeks in a new locale. When Chavi saw that her mother had adapted to her new home and made a few friends, the Rosenbergs cut down on their visits somewhat. The nightly visits were a big strain on their schedules.

Mrs. Schneider made sure to visit the Rosenberg home at least once a week. Chavi tried to go to her once a week, too, and Shmuel often took the kids on Friday. Before the move, they had popped in on each other more often, but the complex was much farther away than the old apartment had been and the journey now involved two long bus rides or an expensive taxi fare.

On Mrs. Schneider's seventieth birthday, two months after her move into the retirement home, Chavi packed up a cake, drinks, some paper goods, and a bouquet of flowers and took the children to visit Bubby for an impromptu birthday party. Birthdays had never been elaborately celebrated in the Baumel home, so this was considered a good way to mark the auspicious occasion.

When they arrived, Chavi sensed immediately that something was wrong. Mrs. Schneider barely smiled at the children and let them in without a word. It was rare to find her in such a state — although Mrs. Schneider had always been an emotional woman, she was generally very upbeat and positive.

Chavi pretended not to notice her mother's melancholy and roused the children into an energetic rendition of "Happy Birthday" while she presented the cake and flowers. Her mother smiled and did her best to mask her feelings, but, after a while, Chavi asked her what was the matter.

Mrs. Schneider said bitterly, "I got a birthday present from my office today." She handed Chavi an envelope that had been sitting on the window ledge. Chavi pulled out the letter inside and read it quickly. Her mother's employer congratulated her on reaching the organization's retirement age and reminded her of their mandatory retirement policy. He went on to say that she was eligible for a significant bonus in recognition of her years of devotion to the organization and wish her well.

Chavi well understood the bad mood now. Mrs. Schneider's main daily occupation was being taken away from her. Besides the lost income, she was surely feeling bereft. What was going to fill her days now? She had always been an active woman. She had had too much time on her hands as it was since Max's death. Rejection from her workplace undoubtedly made her feel useless and abandoned.

ꝏ ꝏ

The arrival of a new baby girl in the Rosenberg home, Chaya, lifted Mrs. Schneider's depression for a brief period. She came to help with the children and cooked supper for the family every day for the first couple of weeks. But with Chavi's return to regular activities, she saw her mother sinking back into depression. Mrs. Schneider cut back on her visits to the Rosenbergs, saying she was getting in the way, so Chavi and Shmuel resumed the visiting schedule they had dropped. Chavi also spent time on the phone with her mother in the morning, in the afternoon, and at night before Mrs. Schneider went to sleep. She pushed her mother to go back to the volunteering activities that she had been involved in before her second marriage.

Mrs. Schneider refused, saying she was too old and tired to run around the city all day. As time passed, she started to complain of aches and pains. She complained about the competence of the nurses at the retirement home. She lost interest in cooking her own meals and soon began complaining about the meals in the restaurant and then about her neighbors.

When Chaya was six months old, Chavi could no longer ignore the situation. Her mother was becoming a snarly, bitter woman, nothing like the person that Chavi had known all her life. In desperation, Chavi made her way to the Kosel and poured out her heart to Hashem, asking Him to have mercy on her mother.

That night, after several sleepless hours, Chavi got out of bed in frustration. She put on a robe and slippers and went to sit on the porch to enjoy the peaceful stillness of the night. She couldn't take her mind off her mother's slow self-destruction. Something had to be done.

At last, an idea popped into her mind. Chavi seized it eagerly and began to plan out the details. An hour later, she made her way contentedly to bed.

29

The next morning, before her usual visit with her mother, Chavi went to meet with the director of the retirement home. She described the decline that her mother's idleness was causing and shared her distress over the situation and the difficulty of bearing the burden of occupying her mother.

The director listened sympathetically, nodding throughout her story. "This is a common problem among the elderly who suddenly find themselves with too much time on their hands," he commented.

"Both my mother and I were impressed with the variety of activities that your home provides," Chavi told him. "My mother is a very talented baker and she knows how to make many decorative and delicious desserts. Would you be willing to ask her to give a baking class for the residents of the complex?"

The director looked at her in surprise. He had obviously not expected her to come up with a solution to the problem that he faced daily.

Chavi went on, "I'll pay for the supplies needed and for a small salary for my mother if you just provide the appropriate facilities. The baking class should benefit many of your residents. Perhaps their creations can be served in the restaurant or put out in the coffee room for other residents to enjoy."

"That's a wonderful idea, Mrs. Rosenberg," the director said warmly. "I don't mind having you pay for your mother's salary, but the home will gladly pay for the ingredients and supplies, since it will certainly be a benefit to us. Give me a few days to work out the technicalities and then I'll talk to your mother."

Chavi spent the next few days waiting for an excited call from her mother about her job offer. Five days later, unable to wait anymore, she brought up the topic during one of her visits, saying that the director had told her of his plans to hire her mother.

"Oh, yes, he did ask me to give a class," Mrs. Schneider said. "I told him I wasn't interested."

Chavi felt like screaming, "Why?!" She stopped herself just in time and managed to ask the question in a conversational tone of voice.

"I don't know. I just don't feel like it."

"But, Ima, he told me he was going to pay you. I'm sure the extra money would come in handy. It sounds like fun to me," Chavi tried.

"Maybe it sounds like fun to you, but not to me. The money would be nice, I guess, but it's really not much. I don't know. I'll think about it, but, so far, my answer is no."

Chavi tried to stay calm, reminding herself that progress had been made. It seemed to her that her mother's life depended on her plan working, but she stopped this train of thought before she became too upset. Nothing was contingent upon her actions. She had to try, but ultimately her mother's life was in God's hands, not hers. She had repeated that mantra so many times to herself over the last few years. Slowly, it was sinking in.

On her way out, she stopped by the director's office and asked him to try again.

With a few more attempts by the director and Chavi's carefully applied pressure, Mrs. Schneider acquiesced. Chavi helped her choose a recipe to start off the course and give the restaurant kitchen the list of ingredients that she needed. The director did his part by making the restaurant kitchen available for a few hours in the early afternoon and doing some heavy PR work to get the class get off the ground.

Within a few weeks, Mrs. Schneider's class became extremely popular, and the group had to be divided into two separate classes. She spent hours choosing recipes and perfecting them to make sure that her students wouldn't be disappointed. Many of the women in the baking club, as it came to be called, had plenty of culinary experience themselves. Soon the women were swapping ideas and learning from each other.

Mrs. Schneider enjoyed the new friends she was making and found she had a lot more in common with many of them than she had realized. As they perfected their products and became more involved in the club, the women decided to branch out. With the permission of the director and a detailed business contract with him, The Grandmothers' Sweets was opened. It was a small old-fashioned shop on the premises of the complex that sold the women's baked goods.

Many of the residents and their visitors became regular

customers. Within two months of the store's opening, the women were called with their first outside order. The son of one of the residents explained that he loved the cookies that he bought every time he came by. He owned a factory and asked if The Grandmothers' Sweets could deliver twenty dozen of his favorite cookies to his factory each day for his employees to enjoy.

Mrs. Schneider and the other two women in charge discussed the feasibility of this undertaking and decided to try to meet the challenge.

Soon afterwards, a second, similar order came. Mrs. Schneider and her friends recruited as many women as they could from the complex, bought two commercial ovens, and got to work. The director supported their efforts and helped with what he could, realizing that many wonderful things could come out of this start-up enterprise. The women hired a van to deliver the cookies early each morning, and they were off!

Although it seemed simple enough, the amount of work invested in the bakery was tremendous. The women learned about obtaining kosher certification, about packaging, about accounting. Soon, almost everyone in the complex was involved. Men were hired for the bookkeeping and cleaning. They consulted with the director and his employees and gained from their connections and experience.

Word of the delicious and friendly bakery continued to spread. Mrs. Schneider was exhausted by the effort involved in running her new business, but very satisfied. She also turned the business into a charitable endeavor. Whatever cookies were left unsold at the end of the day were delivered to an orphanage and a soup kitchen.

Chavi was absolutely astounded by the project's growth from a small class to a full-fledged, lucrative business. Now she had a new worry — her mother was running herself ragged. But Mrs. Schneider's enthusiasm for the project whenever they discussed it put her mind at ease.

ꟼ ꟼ

With her mother more self-sufficient, Chavi found herself with more time, but exhausted from the whole ordeal. She went through her days mechanically, trying to be responsible. But she found herself too easily distracted at work and bored with her household chores. Shmuel noticed her discontent, too.

One day he announced that he had received a bonus for "rest and relaxation" from work. It was a common bonus in Israeli workplaces, but this year he had been given more than usual. He told Chavi that he thought it was time they went on a family vacation.

A vacation? The idea hit Chavi unexpectedly, but it sounded very appealing. A vacation would mean a lot of planning. She would have to get permission to take off from work. There was a lot to be done, but it was certainly manageable. She felt herself becoming energized with the thought of a change of pace.

They planned their vacation for the second week after Tishah B'Av, when all the children would be home from school. Chavi could not take her mind off of it. Most of her conversations with her husband and children related to their upcoming trip. For over a decade, she had watched her neighbors pack up during the summer break and leave for a family vacation, but the Rosenbergs had never allowed themselves this luxury before. She was excited to be joining the club.

After some deliberation, they decided to go to a moshav with air-conditioned guest caravans for families. Two of the moshav's main attractions were a large children's park and a petting zoo, and there were many tourist sites in the vicinity.

On the first day of their vacation, the Rosenberg family traveled to the moshav, settled into their rooms, and had a picnic dinner on a nature reserve a short distance from the moshav. The next day they went to the petting zoo and then went swimming in separate men and ladies' pools. Before bedtime, they went out to the park, an aberration from Chavi's generally tight schedule for the children. The children ran to play and Chavi and Shmuel sat down on a bench.

"Thank you for coming up with this idea," she said.

"It's nice here," he answered. "I think we picked a good spot."

"Yes," Chavi agreed. "And truthfully I was getting so very tired of my routine. I fell into a rut, and I didn't know how to get out of it. I needed a change of pace. I even considered quitting my computer job and asking my mother to hire me to manage her bake shop, just for a change."

"Would you like that?"

"Actually, I think I would, but it's just a fantasy. It would mean taking a significant cut in salary, at least initially, and that's something I don't think it would be wise to do at this point in our lives."

One-and-a-half-year-old Chaya's screams interrupted their conversation. She was stuck, scared, on top of a slide and did not know how to proceed. Shmuel got up to help her make her way down.

Chavi remained on the bench, relaxing and watching

the scene before her. She loved watching Shmuel play with the children. It made her feel serenely at peace, as if everything in the world was right, and gave her a rare chance to observe her family from afar.

Shmuel's temples were beginning to gray, another sign that time was passing. They had come a long way together. Although they still disagreed on many things, their arguments were no longer threatening. When they had to discuss a corollary of some common area of disagreement, they would each take their defined and comfortable positions, no longer racked with guilt or worried that their relationship was in trouble. It was quite a change from the emotional drama that they had each lived through after every disagreement in their early years together.

She had gained a real respect for her husband over the years. In the first years of their marriage, she had sometimes felt superior and looked down on Shmuel for what she viewed as his lack of spiritual yearning. As the years passed she learned to see that his patience, compassion, and foresight were in many ways more real than her undefined desire for perfection. They had both learned to share each other's positive characteristics and had become much enriched.

Shmuel noticed her eyes on him and sent her a questioning look, asking if she wanted anything. She just smiled at him. He shrugged his shoulders, oblivious to her thoughts, and went back to pushing Faigy on the swing.

Elchanan and Tzvi were building a sand castle together in a sand pit a few feet away. Chavi delighted in their camaraderie. They were so different, those two boys. Elchanan was still energetic and free-spirited, although at seven he was learning to tame himself when necessary. Nothing was too hard for him to try. Tzvi, on the other hand, was reticent and quiet. He preferred to play quietly, surrounded by familiar things. Chavi always marveled at the bond between them. She couldn't figure out how they played so much together.

Tzvi himself was a bit of an enigma to her. He was a shy, scared boy, but he was also disobedient. If he were only timid, she would love him and protect him to give him security and encouragement him to step out on his own. If he were only defiant, she would discipline him with a heavy hand to make him toe the line. But he was both and she was at a loss. She hoped that with time God would teach her how to proceed.

Just then, she saw Chaya approaching them, curious, and then carelessly smashing part of their castle.

"No," Tzvi scolded her.

Elchanan showed her where to sit down and build her own castle. Then the boys went back to redesigning their ruined work. That was it. No yelling. No hitting. There were, of course, plenty of both in their house at times, as she supposed there were in most houses with a bunch of children. But she was happy to see that rather than being aggravated, they had learned how to be kind and giving.

Where was Faigy? Chavi asked herself, scanning the park. She wasn't swinging anymore and Chavi didn't see her. Her heart skipped a beat and she called out, "Has anyone seen Faigy?"

"I'm right here, Mommy," Faigy said, laughing, right beside her on the bench.

Chavi had been so lost in her thoughts that she hadn't noticed her sitting down. She gave Faigy a squeeze. At nine years old, Faigy had grown into a girl wise beyond her years. Sometimes Chavi had to stop herself for sharing problems that weren't age appropriate with her daughter, since Faigy's sophistication made Chavi forget that she was just a little girl. At other times, though, Chavi was exasperated by her childish ways and had to remind herself that Faigy was only acting like the young girl she was.

She noticed her own hand, hanging over Faigy's shoulder. It was older, a bit rough and worn, reminding her of what she had become. There was so much about her life that she was happy with. She was proud of the person she was becoming. She wasn't yet satisfied with herself, but she knew that she was a more mature, kind, and noble person than she had started out.

She knew that on the outside she looked like that stereotypical *kollel* wife she had met so many times during her seminary year. Her clothes weren't as stylish as they had once been. Her tastes were simple, but she wasn't dissatisfied with her appearance. She was comfortable with it; it was the way she wanted to be.

She looked for Yitzchak and found him trying to do chin-ups on the monkey bars. He had grown so tall lately. He was certainly nowhere near being an adolescent, but he was also no longer a small boy. Chavi could hardly believe that in less than a year he would celebrate his bar mitzvah and enter Jewish adulthood.

She knew it was time to start thinking about the bar mitzvah and decided that she would begin planning when they got home. As for now, there was no planning, only relaxing.

30

Reenergized by her vacation, Chavi resumed her regular schedule and prepared the children for the new school year. She used her free time to think about the bar mitzvah. Shmuel had already ordered tefillin. In their shul, the bar-mitzvah boy only *lein*ed *maftir* and the Haftarah, and Shmuel hired the *baal korei* from their shul to teach them to Yitzchak. Chavi decided they would host a *kiddush* in shul after the Shabbos morning services and a family meal for close relatives and then make a drop-in reception during the week at a local catering hall. She would bake for the *kiddush* and either hire a caterer or cook the Shabbos meal, depending on how many people would be involved. At the reception, which would be completely catered, they would serve salads, kugel, and cakes.

Several months after this had all been settled in Chavi's mind, with six months to the bar mitzvah, her mother-in-law dropped by one morning to discuss the upcoming bar mitzvah. Chavi outlined her plans.

Mrs. Rosenberg pursed her lips and shook her head. "I don't like to step on your toes, dear, but that simply won't do. My whole family will be in for this bar mitzvah. There will have to be a plan for all the guests for the entire Shabbos. Also, I'll be having many guests attend the reception, and both the hall and the menu don't seem appropriate. Why don't you plan a Shabbos for family in one of the hotels and make a party there after Shabbos for everyone else?"

Chavi didn't like the idea for many reasons, but she only mentioned the one that her mother-in-law was most likely to understand. "I can't afford such an extravagance."

"We've helped each of our children with the financial expenditures for their sons' bar mitzvahs and your *simchah* will be no exception," Mrs. Rosenberg told her. "There's nothing to worry about. If you find yourselves a nice hotel, we will gladly pay for the whole thing."

"I really don't think that Shabbos in a hotel is necessary," Chavi said, seeing that she'd have to be honest. "Even the party doesn't have to be in a hotel. I'm worried that it will make our friends and neighbors feel uncomfortable. Most of them don't have such generous parents, and it would be doing the community a disservice if we introduced a new standard for *simchahs*. Some people might want to imitate us and feel bad because they aren't able to. Others might try to copy our idea without the financial resources to do so and hurt themselves by falling into debt. I just don't think we can do it, even though I truly appreciate the offer."

Mrs. Rosenberg thought frankly that her daughter-in-law was crazy. She had a chance for a beautiful, all-expenses-paid affair that would make her husband's parents happy, and she was turning it down! She thought of telling Chavi that they would be fulfilling the mitzvah of honoring their parents if they took her up on her suggestions, but the years had taught her that there was no arguing with Chavi on matters of principle. She thought she was wrong but respected her conviction.

The silence gave Chavi a chance to think a little. She said, "You have a real point about all the relatives coming for Shabbos, and I want you to be comfortable hosting your friends. I'm glad you brought up those points. You know, our building has a room downstairs which can seat up to sixty people. I'll serve all the Shabbos meals there. I'll find housing for anyone who wants it, and there is a hotel a twenty-minute walk from here that people can stay at if they prefer nicer accommodations. Does that sound good? I don't know why I didn't think of it before. It would have been selfish of me not to consider everyone's needs. Thanks for saving me!"

She grinned at Mrs. Rosenberg, who couldn't help but be charmed by this woman who had married her son. She was so easygoing and natural. Their relationship had been a little rocky in the beginning, she remembered, but now that they were used to each other, everything was fine. Mrs. Rosenberg even felt herself loosening up around Chavi.

"What should we do to make the reception nicer for you?" Chavi asked. "I really would like to hold it at the catering hall I mentioned before. It's conveniently located and doesn't look so bad inside. I was planning on using the smaller room in the hall, but maybe we could rent the larger, more decorative one, since you offered to help with the bills. We can also spice up the menu a bit. What do you think?"

Glad that Chavi wasn't being rigid, Mrs. Rosenberg suggested, "How about a small band for background music or dancing?"

Chavi's look said it all. She was trying to be accommodating, but wasn't looking for suggestions of that sort.

"All right, all right. Let's work on what you're going to serve...."

They spent the next hour leisurely discussing the menu, the invitations, and the children's outfits. When Mrs. Rosenberg got up to leave, they were both pleasantly surprised at how well the conversation had gone. Chavi had listened to and considered Mrs. Rosenberg's opinions, and Mrs. Rosenberg had restrained herself from pushing ideas that didn't fit with Chavi's style. After fourteen years, their relationship had actually become quite comfortable.

ଌ ଌ

The invitations went out and to her delight Chavi soon heard that both of her siblings and all of Shmuel's would be coming with their spouses, some with all of their children and some alone. It was going to be a real family reunion. Her biggest surprise came when Gitty called to announce that she coming in with her husband and children. She said that she owed Chavi her life and couldn't imagine not being there to share such a momentous occasion.

When her son tried on the hat he had purchased with his father and his tailored new bar-mitzvah suit, Chavi's heart swelled with pride. Yitzchak was growing up and was nearly ready to accept upon himself the full obligations of a Torah life. She had reached a landmark occasion that assured her that her child would follow in the traditions of his forefathers.

With the arrival of the week of the bar mitzvah, Chavi reveled in welcoming each family that came from abroad, making sure someone greeted them at the airport, setting up comfortable accommodations, and spending time with them. It had been so long since she had had so much family close by. Mrs. Schneider moved into her house for the week, leaving her business in the capable hands of her partners, so that she could be a part of the festivities.

Friday was a rushed day. Chavi had an endless list of things to take care of for the bar mitzvah and at the same time had to make sure that the needs of her visitors were met. She felt herself drowning in her responsibilities.

Just as she felt that she could handle no more, there was a knock at the door. "Now what?" she muttered under her breath, sending Faigy to see who was there.

Faigy returned carrying a large white box. "A man dropped this off. He said I should give it to my mother."

Chavi pulled off the card, wondering who had sent her a package. Inside, she found a note written in Shmuel's familiar handwriting. It read, "To the woman who has always been an inspiration and the power behind us. We love you. Shmuel, Yitzchak, Faigy, Elchanan, Tzvi, and Chaya."

Chavi opened the box slowly, savoring the moment. Inside were a dozen beautiful white roses. She sat for a long moment holding the flowers and gently touching their soft petals before she put them in a vase and went back to her work, which suddenly didn't seem overwhelming anymore.

ജ ജ

The Friday night meal was filled with song and laughter and *divrei Torah* skillfully connected to the parashah, the bar mitzvah, and Yitzchak all at the same time. It was attended only by close family. Chavi had invited Gitty and Aryeh and Yair and Nava, who were as close as immediate family, for Shabbos, but Gitty said that since they were only in Israel for less than a week they had to go to Aryeh's relatives. Nava was under the weather and canceled at the last minute.

After the meal, Chavi stayed up late cleaning up and talking to her loved ones. She went to sleep content and at peace, feeling secure in the bosom of her family's love.

She was still worried about how Yitzchak was going to manage the *lein*ing. He knew it well, that was for sure, but what if the public reading made him nervous and he started to stutter? Chavi hoped and prayed that he wouldn't be humiliated.

When the time came for Yitzchak to *lein*, she moved closer to the *mechitzah* to be able to hear every word clearly. He read beautifully. Once or twice he did start to stutter, but he stopped, composed himself, and continued. It was a monumental accomplishment which left Chavi delightedly satisfied.

The lunch meal was also warm and happy. All in all, the Shabbos was a wonderful success.

As Shabbos came to a close, Chavi was saddened knowing that the event that she had looked forward to and planned for so long was halfway over. She was glad that the reception was still a few days away, so she could savor the affair a little longer.

The night of the reception was a busy one. The children had to be fed, bathed, and dressed; Chavi had to dress herself; and everyone had to get to the hall early enough for the photo session that Mrs. Rosenberg had insisted on. As Chavi rushed about, she wondered where Shmuel and Yitzchak were. She was a little annoyed that Shmuel had chosen this moment when she very much needed his assistance to cloister himself with the bar-mitzvah boy, but she assumed that he was helping Yitzchak with last-minute preparations for his speech.

At the hall, the family posed for picture after picture until it was time for the guests to arrive. Then the men and women separated to their respective sides of the *mechitzah*. The hall began filling up. Chavi did her best to let each and every guest know how much she appreciated her attendance and to make sure she found a place to sit near someone she knew or at least to introduce her to the other people at her table.

As she was engaged in small talk with one of her neighbors, she noticed Gitty entering. Chavi finished the conversation with the woman and, when it was polite, she practically flew across the room to embrace her dear friend, whom she hadn't seen in so long.

In her tailored suit and modern *sheitel*, Gitty looked both happy and well cared for. "Oh, I'm so glad to see you," Chavi said, releasing her from the hug. "You look wonderful. It really means a lot to me that you are here."

Then she noticed two little girls in white dresses with large black sashes standing shyly next to Gitty. The older one had a cute pixie haircut and the younger one wore a ponytail. "You must be Chani. And you must be Sara Leah. I am your mother's friend from a long time ago, even before you were born."

She touched the older girl's cheek tenderly and picked up the younger girl to kiss her cheek.

Sara Leah seemed uncomfortable at the stranger's affection, so Chavi put her down. She found Gitty and her daughters a seat at the head table and sat down to talk. After three interruptions from well-wishers, though, Gitty encouraged Chavi to get up and mingle. Chavi agreed to go only after Gitty gave her word that she would meet her for lunch the next day, Gitty's last day in Israel.

Chavi noticed a pregnant woman wearing a black *sheitel* walk in. She could only see the side of the woman's face and didn't know who it was, but she was embarrassed to note that the woman was wearing the same exact maternity outfit that Chavi herself was.

Her momentary discomfort was soon replaced with delight when she saw the woman's face. It was Nava, in a *sheitel* and in maternity! Chavi ran over to greet her.

When Nava saw her and their matching outfits, she started to laugh. "Oh, I'm so sorry. But at least it means I have good taste."

"Nava, you look marvelous, simply and absolutely marvelous. Why didn't you tell me about this?" Chavi responded.

"I wanted to surprise you. It looks like I did!"

As soon as Chavi got Nava settled, she heard her mother calling her to sit down. Yitzchak was about to speak. Chavi seated herself near the front of the *mechitzah* to be able to listen.

Yitzchak gave a short but clear speech on a relevant topic in Gemara and ended by thanking his parents and grandparents for their constant support. Chavi beamed with pride as he finished. To her surprise he didn't sit down immediately, but waited for Shmuel to join him at the lectern.

Standing next to Yitzchak, Shmuel began to speak. "Both Yitzchak and I have reached major milestones in our lives this week. Yitzchak has reached adulthood and now has the maturity necessary to follow in the path of his ancestors and develop into a true servant of God. It is a moving time for him and a time for introspection, a time to determine the direction that his life will take.

"I have also reached a milestone in my life, although a different one. I now have a son who is a man. I feel a tremendous gratitude to the Almighty for allowing me to reach this stage. Parenting is a complex and full-time job. Before Yitzchak was born, I thought that raising children was going to be a piece of cake. Both my wife and I are fortunate enough to have devoted parents who always made child raising seem easy. But from the first time I held Yitzchak in my arms thirteen years ago, the magnitude of the responsibility overwhelmed me. I still remember that first time I held him, afraid that I might break him and wondering where life was going to take us both.

"As I prepared for this bar mitzvah, I looked at where we are today and thought back over our years together. Each event of our lives has added to who Yitzchak has become. Yitzchak, I am very proud of who you are, and I know how hard we both worked to reach this point. I learned from you that things don't always just fall into place. Sometimes you have to work to try to reach your goals. Sometimes you'll try and things won't go your way, but you can't give up. You just have to look for a different way, a better way. And if you really believe in what you want, you'll get there no matter what obstacles stand in your way. What I've learned from the fatherhood that you, Yitzchak, initiated, is that just as a house can only be built brick by brick, a person can only be built one step at a time, each person in his own way.

"As many of you know, Yitzchak and I became *chavrusa*s four years ago, at the behest of my wife. We managed to stick it out over the years, no matter what the circumstances, and we've helped each other grow in our learning. Generally, we study whatever *masechta* Yitzchak is learning in school, but years ago, we set for ourselves another goal that was a secret between the two of us. We decided that by the time Yitzchak would reach bar mitzvah, we would both make a *siyum* on *Shas*, he on the Mishnah and I on the Gemara. It was a struggle and we often thought that we had bitten off more than we could chew, but we encouraged each other along the way.

"I am very proud to say that this afternoon we both met our goals.

"Besides giving thanks to the Eibeshter, I also want to thank my wife, who is always the force behind anything that any member of our family accomplishes. We recognize that without her, we never would have even dared to dream of reaching this point. So to her I say, 'Thank you.'

"I will now ask Yitzchak to make his *siyum* and read the *hadran*."

Chavi listened as Yitzchak proudly finished. She let the tears roll unabashedly down her cheeks, too involved in the moment to notice anything else around her. She saw the firm foundation her house stood on and caught a momentary glimpse of each brick that comprised it. The joys, the trials, the mundane — she was grateful for each and every one.

#2

DATE DUE	BORROWER'S NAME	ROOM NUMBER

Silent Dreams

JAN 06

OCT 28

MAY 11 '05

NOV 15 '05

DEC 14

J

Bought in bookfair